BELONGING

A Tale of Downieville and California's Modern Gold Country

by

Bill Pieper

Comstock Bonanza Press
2006

BELONGING

Despite the frequent use of geographical names and historical facts, this book is fiction and everything in it must be read as such.

Cover art by **Robert Else**
  Downieville Bridges, 1993 (front)
  Creekside, 1993 (back)
Cover design by **Gail Segerstrom**

US Edition
Published by **Comstock Bonanza Press**
       18919 William Quirk Drive
       Grass Valley, CA 95945-8611
       Phone (530) 263-2906

Printed by   LightningSource Inc.
               LaVergne, TN, USA

Pieper, Bill
    Belonging / Bill Pieper.
ISBN 0-933994-33-8
       1. Title
Library of Congress Control Number: 2006901132

Trade distribution is direct through the publisher or via Ingram Book Company

Retail copies available at http://stores.ebay.com/bpbooks, in bookstores or with a shopping cart at www.amazon.com or www.bn.com

For information, or to arrange author interviews and appearances at stores, events or book clubs contact:
Holden Research & Marketing
P.O. Box 254733, Sacramento, CA 95865-4733

BELONGING

To Charles G. "Mac" McDermid, the best guy I know,
and to the abiding spirit of the North Yuba River.

Other Titles by This Author

So Trust Me (novellas)
Fool Me Once (novel)
Gomez (novel)

BELONGING

Acknowledgements

As with all my work, *Belonging* has benefited immeasurably from the generous support of family, friends and fellow writers.

Here, in alphabetical order within groups intended to recognize the quantity of time and effort I exacted from them, is what I hope makes up a full list. Sincere thanks for their patience, perseverance and good cheer on this project go to:

My very dear wife Cathy Holden; my son Nick Pieper; the writers Sands Hall, Tim Holt, Ronn Kaiser, Nan Mahon, Harvey Schwartz, Beth Volz and Naida West; other writers Bill Breault, Randy Haynes, and Persia Woolley; cover artist Robert Else; reader/commentators Doug Bothun, Henry Brodkin, Steve Cagle, Joann Cochran, Dave Dawson, Glenn Durfee, Diane Durrett, Claire McDermid, Scott McDermid, Paul Samuelson, Tom Taylor, Gene Volz, Earl Withycombe and Lynn Young; plus fly fisherman extraordinaire Ed Klingelhofer.

Nor could I have done without four institutions that foster creative endeavors of many kinds: the California State Library, the Sacramento Public Library, Nevada County's Literature Alive! and the Sierra County Arts Council. Finally, my thanks along with a *mea maxima culpa* to anyone forgotten above.

Foreword

Belonging describes two months of life in a tiny mountain community and the tragedy-born change in dynamic between natives and newcomers during that time. Since no one is anonymous in such places, the reality that everyone knows everyone else, though often quite superficially, is integral to the story.

Of the many characters, the major ones, including the two narrators, are easy to follow. For readers who wish to track the rest, anybody mentioned more than once is shown in the alphabetic glossaries on the book's final pages. Employing this device lends verisimilitude and more faithfully conveys the small-town experience, but *Belonging* is entirely a work of fiction. All events and details are products of the author's imagination, and no character represents any real person who may have lived in the locations stated or anywhere else.

Also, as a point of information, June election results in California's nonpartisan local races are final for any candidate who polls a simple majority—at least one vote more than fifty percent of those cast. This happens automatically when there are two candidates. Only if the field is three or greater and no one polls a simple majority is there a runoff between the top two in November.

PROLOGUE

A hiker on just the right trail up from the river to Highway 49 that April Sunday would, at just the right moment, have seen the lemony tangerine hues of some early-blooming sticky monkey brush form a momentary halo around the dark-green and cream paint of a passing patrol car.

Alone in his none-too-new cruiser Acting Sheriff Buck Thompson was eastbound toward Downieville and home, looking worried, or at least preoccupied. The vividly flowering brush, having spread year by year into a broad patch, flourished in a south-facing road-cut across the pavement from where the hiker's trail would end. Wisps of cloud drifted in a brilliant blue sky and the sun hung slightly above the forested canyon rim to the southwest.

At the moment, however, Buck was so lost in layers of thought that all he saw, instinctively, was the road. Everything from his election campaign to his daughter Ginny and to the long-dead Frank Pezzola had his conscious attention directed inward. A mile farther along, as he climbed away from the water in the stretch before Ramshorn Campground and the turnoff to the dump, the cruiser's radio gave a shot of static and the dispatcher came on.

"Buck, you copy?" Sam Beals said tersely. "We got a situ..."

"God damn it, Sam! Start with the clock reading. Why do I have to keep tellin' ya'? None of us can drive these mountain roads and have eyes left over to check our watch."

"Yeah, sorry...4:42 p.m. Guess I'm shook up. Looks like we got a situation here."

"What's it this time?"

"Phone's are ringin' and somebody yanked the town call box for Search and Rescue. Alarm is still going off. People say a boy's lost in the river, maybe more than one."

"Jesus Christ! The Yuba?"

"Best we know." The signal crackled and wavered.

"OK, speak clear now and give me all you have. Any names yet?"

"No...and that *is* all. Soon as there's more, I'll be back." Another spate of crackling broke in.

"If it's real, have 'em stake out the streambed down to the bridge at Goodyear Bar fast as they can," Buck ordered. "I'll head for Goodyear myself."

"Will do. Over and out." Sam signed off with a pop and fading buzz.

Jamming down the accelerator, Buck flipped on his bubble-gum light and siren as the car lunged forward. Damn, he grumbled to himself. How did things like this happen? Probably some fool tourist. Locals knew to stay out of the water at this season.

Of course he'd had no idea then where the event just reported would lead, nor had he or any of the others involved sensed it coming. But all of them would remember with great clarity exactly what they were doing, who they were with and what they were thinking in the hours beforehand.

CHAPTER 1

WANTED
For Sierra County Sheriff
HAROLD "BUCK" THOMPSON

A Tradition of Justice
Vote Buck Thompson
June 4, 1974

Elect HBT Committee

Well, there Buck was, a picture of him anyway, fortyish and porky in his tight-fitting deputy's uniform, with one cowboy-booted foot resting on the front bumper of his patrol car in a classic good-old-boy stance. Stetson tipped back, he held his arms away from his body, and the shiny leather of his belt and holster set off the curved handle of his service revolver. The photographer, working in black-and-white, like the rest of the poster, had even managed to coax a relaxation of the lips and a partial show of teeth onto Buck's jowly and typically sullen face.

Greg Fulton stood smiling in front of the bulletin board at the edge of the graveled community center parking lot. His watch said 3:05 and this hadn't been here ninety minutes ago when he, his wife Molly, and the two couples they were with had arrived for a County

Historical Society meeting. They would certainly have seen it in the afternoon light, and commented on the intended humor of the headline juxtaposed against the unintended, but far funnier, humor of the photo.

If that was the Elect HBT Committee's best pitch, Buck had less chance of beating Kenny Pritchard than Nixon did of staving off Watergate to remain in the White House. Not that Greg would shed a tear for Nixon or Buck. All his friends had been disgusted with Tricky Dick for years, and locally they were supporting Pritchard.

Buck's challenger, like Greg, was a Sierra County immigrant, a term usually — and pejoratively — expressed as *newcomer*, and was applied to anyone who had moved here from anywhere else, near or far, at any time in living memory. Greg and Molly Fulton lived with their son Ned in Downieville, the county seat, and had for the last three years. Greg was a social studies teacher at the town's sixty-five student Jr./Sr. High School, the second smallest in the state. Sierra County, for its part, was California's second smallest county, claiming fewer than 2,500 inhabitants.

In the sheriff's race, though, the political calculus favored the newcomers. They might be an afterthought to the natives, but they were numerous enough to ally with the east-county ranchers and millworkers, always jealous of Downieville's hold on local politics, in dumping good old Buck — who everybody knew was neither good nor old. Nor bright, apparently.

Even with popular incumbent Curt Foley dead in a plane crash, and Buck's having replaced him on an acting basis two months ago, the guy should realize he couldn't win. Led by Greg's faculty friend and mentor, Seth Holmes, former Democratic Party Chair, the newcomers had already shown swing-vote power in 1972. Their ad hoc alliance with the west county's struggling miners and loggers had made Sierra County the only jurisdiction in California except San Francisco to give George McGovern a majority for President. This time they'd tip the balance again.

Then, with a too familiar stab of anguish, Greg reminded himself that Seth was his *former* mentor, as well as being former party chair. And *former* friend, if not outright enemy, might soon follow. Like his frustration with the closed-rank treatment he and Molly typically got from the county's natives, Seth Holmes was something Greg tried not to think about. The problem was, a Buck Thompson poster or who-knew-what would always show up to trigger mental reruns. He hoped no one, and especially Molly, would mar the day with yet another review of the Holmes mess during the drive back. To his relief, she hadn't on the way over.

Her happy-sounding voice and those of their four Downieville companions came from behind Greg's right shoulder as he began turning his six-foot frame in that direction. A minute before, he had buttoned his plaid wool overshirt in response to the breeze and lowering sun. They were beyond Yuba Pass, forty miles from home in the Sierra Valley, at an elevation of 5,000 feet where daytime temperatures in April seemed to fluctuate by ten degrees any time a cloud moved. Other figures departing from the meeting crunched across the gravel around him, retrieved their vehicles and drove off. Greg had been first out of the building because he'd finished a restroom visit while everyone else was jostling for an extra piece of Francine Cooper's famous cheesecake.

Calling to Molly, "Hey, check this out. It's a hoot!" Greg stepped backwards into a puddle that slurped over his right shoe and soaked his sock before he could yank himself clear. A cold jolt ran up his leg.

"Damn," he said under his breath, and was thankful that he was driving today so he'd be the one controlling the heater. Molly had warned him not to wear desert boots this early in the season, and she'd been right.

From ten yards away, Hal Voorden, a stoop-shouldered, round-bellied old Paiute who was a school district maintenance supervisor, had seen what happened. He gave Greg a stony smile and commiserating wave. By common acknowledgment, Hal was the county's best stream fisherman, an honor for which there was strong competition. He was said to be a genius with wet flies and nymphs in the Little Truckee, and could handle worms, grasshoppers or dry flies as well. Greg had hinted any number of times at school district meetings that he'd love to go out with Hal sometime, but an invitation never came.

Hal lived next door to the community center and functioned as caretaker. He was on his way up the front walk to re-lock the door after straightening the room that the Historical Society had just vacated. Their bimonthly meetings, followed by a dessert table, were held on the third Sunday, at a fixed series of locations, which had made the east-county town of Sierraville today's destination.

The meetings were fun. Greg liked learning about local history, made a point of trimming his reddish beard for the occasion, and was glad to find one forum where he and Molly, as eager listeners to the old-timers, were appreciated and treated as equals. Or almost as equals. The Fultons had become Society members a year ago at the urging of Pat and Jim Crandall, who had business reasons for joining and wanted other newcomers for company.

Molly crossed a corner of the parking lot to take Greg's arm. Pat, Jim, and Ian Dudley, along with Ian's wife Sandra Torkin, passed by to stand laughing and talking in front of the poster. Having arrived in the county only last fall, Ian and Sandra were fresh from their first encounter with the Historical Society, and seemed to be enjoying themselves. Tonight, when they all got home, would likely turn into another informal potluck at Pat and Jim's, though an early one, with tomorrow being Monday.

"What's so funny?" Molly asked, looking up at Greg. She was 5'7", slender and pretty, with bright hazel eyes, clear skin, and short dark hair. Little or no makeup had always been Molly's norm, but now, at 32, she was fretting about tiny wrinkles that Greg, a year older, claimed he couldn't see, but could. Like a model in an L.L. Bean catalogue, she wore a down vest and turtleneck to go with her navy cord slacks and rubberized boots.

"Buck's poster," Greg answered. "Take a look."

"I saw one yesterday…in Goodyear Bar, when I was dropping something off for Om. Seemed more upsetting than funny." She glanced down at Greg's wet foot and made an *I-told-you-so* face.

"Upsetting?" Greg asked. "Why? He looks like a rube who'd be the foil on a TV cop show. Think of him up against *Kojack*."

"That's what I mean…and he could win."

"Not a chance. Buck's got too much baggage, and Pritchard's a pro. He'll know we helped him win, too. It'll be nice not to feel paranoid when a patrol car goes by."

"Especially after Buck sicced the FBI on Jared. Om's been on pins and needles for a month. If they bust her boyfriend over a bounced check, who's next?"

"Good question," Greg replied. "It doesn't help that Jared and Om are hippies, but getting the FBI involved was nuts. If Curt Foley was still alive, he'd at least have done the collar himself."

Sandra led Ian and the Crandalls away from the poster toward Greg and Molly. A lawyer, Sandra—she never let anyone use

Sandy—was opinionated and loved to argue, though her softly feminine features and rimless glasses belied those traits. "How come it doesn't say *Dead or Alive* after the *Wanted* part?" she joked.

"Waste of ink," Jim Crandall countered. "The way Buck looks most days, you couldn't tell."

Known for quips and puns, he let his laugh echo the laughs and groans of the others. Kennedy-esque was how people described him, which Jim dismissed, though it made sense to Greg. At 41 Jim had a hint of JFK in his mouth and jaw, along with RFK's bouncy energy, wiry build and tousled head of chestnut hair. Jim's standard wardrobe of jeans or khakis topped with T-shirts and sweaters could even pass for Hyannisport chic. His family, a teenage daughter and two younger sons, might meet the Kennedys' minimum size standard as well. Trained as a scientist, Jim had worked at RAND and co-authored a top-selling futurist book before realizing his dream of owning a country newspaper.

Greg felt a light punch land on his shoulder and heard passing footsteps followed by a voice saying, "Vote Pritchard."

Greg turned and waved. "Don't worry," he said to the retreating form of Matt Gagliardi, that day's speaker, headed for his pickup carrying a slide projector. Matt was one of Greg's social studies counterparts in Loyalton, at the district's other high school, much larger than Downieville's, but still small.

His topic had been Loyalton itself, starting with the derivation of the name. Originally known as Smithneck after a founding family, the town had renamed itself in 1862 to prove its loyalty to the Union. Apparently there were a number of Confederate sympathizers about in those days, and California's gold rush counties were such a monetary prize that measures to thwart the South had been imperative even here. Greg was already planning ways to use this information with his own students when they got to the Civil War at the end of the semester.

Soon the three couples were in the Fultons' roomy red and beige Travelall, with Greg at the wheel and Molly beside him. He pulled away from the steep-roofed community center and adjacent rodeo grounds toward Sierraville's minuscule main drag and the highway west. Sunshine beamed down, and round, puffy, cotton-ball clouds blew rapidly across a huge blue sky. The white-trunked aspens dotted along the road hadn't put on leaves yet, but the alders and willows lining every ditch and stream were pushing succulent, immature foliage of the palest jade, making the darker color of the pines look black. And grass—burstingly, vividly green, and getting long enough to billow erratically in the spring wind—thrust up everywhere.

Yikes, Greg thought. Whenever he came here it hit him, yet day-to-day, he'd forget. The vast Sierra Valley, in which Sierraville, Loyalton, and their scattering of satellite communities all nestled, was a slice of Wyoming geologically smuggled into Northern California. It would be no surprise to have John Wayne or Clint Eastwood, in a full set of chaps, standing in one of the driveways, tipping his hat as they went by.

Ahead, to the north, Greg could see thirty miles—eighteen or twenty to the valley's perimeter, and farther over layered ridgelines of rock and snow. To his right and left, visibility was curtailed to ten miles by closer, taller ranges still showing snowfields, but with gray-brown desert slopes breaking through in the east and vast stands of white fir in the west, marking the ascent to the pass on their route home.

Moreover, the panorama outside his windshield explained all of the century-old political conflict between the east and west county. Physically, the two could be separate planets. The east was cattle country—big ranches, open grassland, and straight, flat roads favoring enterprises like lumber mills, gravel pits and cement plants. The population had barely changed in fifty years, but by default, with the cessation of gold mining in the west, the east had become numerically superior.

The west, by contrast, was a precipitous, densely forested bas-relief of high ridges, deep canyons, and rocky peaks drained by two winding forks of the Yuba River and their countless tributaries. Roads were few, paved roads fewer, and straight roads nonexistent. Studded with gold mines, nearly all abandoned but for a handful maintaining token operations, western Sierra County had once produced unimaginable wealth and supported a large population.

It now relied on tourism, primarily hunting and fishing, plus haphazard cycles of logging, to generate a tenuous livelihood for many fewer people. Whatever middle class there was drew on inherited money, or earned it in jobs with the Forest Service, the State Highway Department or the county itself. But by tradition, luck, guile, perseverance, and the fact that it contained the courthouse and virtually all other government infrastructure, the west had been

politically dominant since day one and put a high premium on remaining so.

Of course, the newcomers couldn't care less about who won a
particular office in terms of which part of the county the candidate
was from. They thought the east/west rivalry was stupid given the
social and economic problems both areas were facing. They wanted
government jobs awarded on merit to the maximum extent, felt that
education and experience in the outside world were the best indi-
cators of merit, and thought the whole Downieville establishment
needed shaking up. To top it off, no one embodied that inbred establishment more than Buck Thompson. If the newcomers' attitude
toward local politics made the natives, who were guardedly polite
face to face yet wouldn't want you to marry their daughters,
squirm, so much the better.

But outsiders or not, Greg and his fellow transplants were always amazed at how many people they had come to know—by
name, if nothing else—through living in a place like this, and it
seemed to happen overnight. There were even dead people you'd
never laid eyes on in life whose names you found yourself learning.
He and Molly had wanted an antidote to urban anomie, and this
was how it worked in practice, amounting to the best and the worst
of being part of an isolated, rural community. "It's what puts the
small in small town," Jim Crandall liked to joke.

Nobody was ever just a face or a passer-by, and you lost the
ability to think of them that way. Without any special effort you
could often also attach their names to how they made a living and
which houses they lived in, who they were married to and who
their kids were, and if they were natives, who they *had* been married
to, the names of their parents, as well as of their cousins and in-
laws, and their reputations, savory or unsavory. They, in turn,
automatically knew many of these things about you.

Some of this information was dispensed in-person when you
interacted with each other, but typically it was second- or third-
hand on the grapevine that never slept. Yet only a few among those
names, and invariably newcomers, could Greg count as friends, no
more in total than anywhere else he'd lived, really.

The standard mode of relating, personal but highly superficial,
was like the pseudo-intimacy of a movie magazine. He and the
town postmaster or garbage collector, and dozens of the other locals, though they were virtually neighbors, knew one another to ex-

change waves with and talk about by name only in the sense of fans imagining they knew Barbra Streisand or Robert Redford. Occasionally Greg felt a potential for real connection with one native or another, but some last separation always remained and the moment evaporated.

Oh, stop, he thought, catching himself. In such jolly company, with the weather so perfect, and with everything to be seen from his moving vehicle so indisputably, oh-my-god gorgeous, why dwell on minor discontents?

CHAPTER 2

At the opposite end of the county about the time the Historical Society was serving dessert, Buck Thompson scratched his ear just below his hat brim and put the pedal to the metal along Alleghany Road. It was great, he thought, how Dan Hogan had asked to help with posters. Buck didn't even have to drop a hint. That's when a man learned who his friends were. And Dan wasn't just anybody. Hell no. He ran Hogan's Joint, the only bar in the area, and was the closest thing to a mayor this part of the world had.

Yeah, there Buck was, spending a gorgeous April Sunday in uniform, in his Plymouth Fury cruiser, making the rounds of Alleghany, Forest City and Pike, each town smaller than the last, trying to be sure folks saw his face and remembered who to vote for. Of course, it had to look like a regular patrol. Buck had given the Garland kid, one of his newest deputies, the day off, and taken the kid's shift. That meant young Garland would be grateful and talk Buck up to his buddies, and it gave Buck a chance to see and be seen out where it counted. He'd heard Sheriff Huey, his daddy, talk about this kind of campaigning a hundred times, and seen the old man practice it, too. Next weekend Buck'd be over in Sierra Valley doing the same thing, Saturday and Sunday both.

One thing for sure, though, you couldn't be stopping the cruiser, climbing out and tacking up posters yourself. Even on the dirt roads, where you might see only one vehicle an hour, you couldn't take the chance. Especially if they were election posters and had your own picture on 'em. Pritchard'd find out and cry foul play before you knew what hit you. "The bushes in this county have eyes, boy, and don't forget it," Huey used to say, talking more to Cal, Buck's brother, than to Buck. But that didn't matter. Buck remembered.

Buck's MO was to keep a hefty stack of posters in the trunk, wrapped in butcher paper, five to a pack. Then, if somebody just happened to ask, like Dan Hogan, or could be nursed into asking, long as it was somebody Buck trusted, Buck would find a way to let the person help themself to however many packs that person could use. "Now don't be hangin' any of those till I'm down the road a piece," Buck would say, forcing a smile and adding, "We understand each other?" followed by a handshake or nod. He'd already driven by a couple of his posters today that the Elect HBT Committee had got up, but you couldn't have too many. That's one thing about their being black and white. You could afford a lot of 'em.

Back in 1970 when Buck had first returned to the county, he'd put out posters this way for his dead boss Curt Foley and nothing ever backfired. Seemed like he ought to be able to do it for himself. And sure was strange how things turned out. Curt would never have been Sheriff and running for re-election if old Huey hadn't set Curt up for it, and Buck wouldn't be running this year if Curt hadn't set him up. Some of that went back to Huey, too, but Curt had a lot to do with it.

A damn good man, Curt Foley. Hell of a shame, that plane crash in January. No one even knew why it happened. Weather had been good, pilot was experienced, a friend of Curt's from Susanville flying the two of them back from a Sheriff's Association conference in San Diego, and down they go, east of Sonora Pass, crossing the Sierra to come home via Reno.

They'd radioed Carson City for an emergency landing, but never made it. Both dead and tore up real terrible from what Buck had heard. The funeral was closed-casket, which told more than you wanted to know. Sure, Buck had hoped to be Sheriff someday, but would never wish for anything like that. Curt had been talking retirement in 1980 or so. Buck was young enough to've waited. Being Undersheriff was the best thing that had happened to him till then, anyway. But suddenly he was Acting Sheriff, as well as Acting Coroner, since those duties went with the job. If Curt's plane had gone down in Sierra County, Buck would've had to sort through the gore no matter how he felt. That Curt crashed in Nevada was the only good thing about it.

Christ, you could see forever from Alleghany Ridge on a day like this! All the way out to Saddleback, Gibraltar and the Buttes in the northeast as the road swung to Buck's right, and up the Middle Yuba canyon to English Mountain and Mount Lola when it swung back the other way. Always a thrill, those high-country peaks, as many times as he'd seen 'em. They're never the same twice if you look close enough.

Buck had the windows down and right now was feeling so good he'd as soon spend the afternoon doing what he was doing as anything else. A warm spring, but still plenty of snow out there. They wouldn't be able to plant old man Flynn in Poker Flat till way into June. That's just how it was. The body'd have to stay froze for months yet in the morgue in the Courthouse basement downstairs from Buck's office.

At the field near the Plum Valley crossroads Buck got out to watch a softball game and cleverly—very cleverly, if he did say so himself—led Rob Casey's wife and a couple of the Kenton clan to *ask* for posters. His ex-wife Luann's long-time girlfriend Jesse Foster was there, but kept her distance and just gave Buck dirty looks, so he pretty much had the run of the place shaking hands and talking about next week's fishing prospects and how nice the weather was.

He also fooled around with some of the little ones, shining the cruiser's big chrome searchlight at them and giving the siren a few pops. Best of all, though, somebody'd offered him a beer, which he refused not just on account of being on duty, but because he'd quit drinking for years now. People needed to hear that. Over and over. It was good that you knew your neighbors so well in a county like this. Nobody was ever just a face or a name, but it made living down your past a tough go. One slip and the word'd be out faster'n a turkey on a June bug.

Buck had rolled by Jesse Foster's house in Alleghany earlier on, and hadn't been surprised to see a Pritchard sign. He'd seen one of the guy's posters at the store, too, but somebody'd inked in big ears and a beard on him, so it hadn't bothered Buck much. And at Jesse's, what would you expect? She'd been Luann's best buddy in high school, had managed to run her own husband off by fucking half the men in Hogan's Joint, and still hated Buck because Luann told her to. If that's the best Pritchard could do over here in hard-rock mining country, Buck could breathe a little easier.

Of course he hadn't driven down to the river, where those new people, the Wetzels, had gussied up a gone-to-seed mining camp and called it the Middle Fork Inn. Some kind of dude ranch they advertised in that pussy-ass *Sunset Magazine*. Buck knew damn well there'd be a Pritchard sign out front. Seemed like the new people couldn't wait to line up against him. Luckily next to nobody drove into the canyon to use that one-lane bridge till summer, and by then the election would be over. Still, it was bad enough the county elections had become such east-west pissing matches every four years without the new people playing spoiler.

Huey hadn't cared that Curt Foley was originally from Loyalton, and Huey'd been Downieville through-and-through. The east-west thing didn't mean shit when it came to law enforcement. It was a matter of paying your dues, knowing the whole county, and knowing how to work it so everybody got along as best they could, nobody took advantage, and nobody got screwed. That's what being Sheriff was about. Using the law to bring out the good in people, hold back the bad, and just as important, knowing when to ignore what didn't matter. That'd been Huey's approach, was more-or-less Curt's, was Buck's for sure, and people in the east and the west had always bought into it.

Where did damned Kenny Pritchard get off with this professionalism bullshit? What that meant was snooping and nit-picking, if people would stop and think. Pritchard's whole game since he moved here from Reno had been to run for DA, but after that Sierraville shyster Troy Bartlesman lined up enough Loyalton folks in 1970 and beat Pritchard to the punch, Pritchard and his fat-cat uncle set their sights on Sheriff.

Curt Foley had half expected Pritchard to run against him this time, and was planning to paint Pritchard as an out-of-state carpetbagger even though Pritchard had actually been in the county a pretty respectable time. Probably would've worked, too. Curt could have split the Loyalton vote and Buck would've pulled most of the west county for him by trading on Huey. But then, with no Curt to worry about, Pritchard had declared the day after the funeral. It was going to be a tough race, and a close one.

Buck's big asset was the Thompson name, he didn't kid himself. Buck also had baggage. He didn't kid himself about that, either.

With or without Pritchard stoking them, there were always rumors about his drinking and about Luann. And he *had* been an asshole in high school and for a good many years after. There was no way around it. But the Luann thing was a locked box only Curt'd ever had the keys to, and Buck had learned never to duck the drinking issue.

He admitted to it, and people who knew him respected that he'd quit. Also, with Pritchard trying to blunt the carpetbagger charge by touting his own east-county roots, he'd actually solidified Buck in the west. Even the people on this side of the pass who remembered Buck as an asshole were supporting him because he was *their* asshole.

And Buck had some traction in the Valley. Not much in Loyalton, except for the Indians working at the mill, and the two or three blacks, plus Curt's family and people close to them. But outside town, he had quite a few ranchers and the rest of the Indians. He estimated fifteen to twenty percent Valley-wide, again tracing back to Huey. People didn't forget how the old man had done 'em right over the years.

If Buck held upwards of that fifteen percent and kept the west wrapped up, it came down to the new people. They had no ties to Huey, probably liked that Pritchard himself was new, in a way, and were real impressed by Pritchard's law degree and experience as a Reno cop. What horse pucky. Not only was there nothing about being a big-city cop that meant squat in terms of Sierra County, lawyers were overtaking tourists as a curse on the land.

Anybody who knows anything knows old Bill Robbins, rest his soul, was the best judge this county ever had, that he'd held office even longer than Heuy had as sheriff, and the only diploma on his wall was from barber college. California was jammed with twice too many lawyers already. If they owned the secret to stopping crime, crime would be dead enough by now people'd miss it.

And to top that off, shyster Bartlesman, who's a piss-poor excuse for a DA if there ever was one, is so devoted to sitting on his ass that he's hired an assistant to cover the County Counsel duties. In what lifetime would Buck have the budget to shift being Coroner off on some assistant? It was all he could do to keep his department's cars and gear in basic repair. Going back to when the county had double the population it did today, one lawyer was all it took to be DA and County Counsel both, whatever the hell County Counsel is, exactly.

And naturally Bartlesman brings in an outsider. That way there's no chance he'd be priming some local attorney to run against him in '78. Which is also why Bartlesman is supporting Pritchard this year. If Pritchard is Sheriff, he won't covet being DA. But who'd imagine Bartlesman would find a self-important twit like that Ian — Jesus, what a name — Dudley, to be his flunky, or that Dudley would have another lawyer for his so-called wife? Sandra something — not even Dudley — a cute little bitch who'll be whining to Buck about due process every time Judge Sturdevant taps her as Public Defender. The joke among the deputies is they only want to be cross-examined in court when she's wearing a tight skirt.

Buck was three miles west of Plum Valley now, turning off the paved Ridge Road to take the red-dirt cutoff through the manzanita flats into Pike City. Almost as many hippies up there as in Goodyear Bar these days, and Buck had to figure out how to bring 'em his way politically before June.

Freaky-looking specimens, but a lot had registered in '72 when that pervert Seth Holmes ran the county McGovern campaign. Had to give the bastard credit. He pulled the new people together, hippies or not, signed 'em up and made sure they voted. If Buck could swing some of the Pike long-hairs, word'd get around to the other hippies quick enough, and some of 'em were close to Jim Crandall, the *Mountain Mercury* owner, and the clique he runs with. Buck had to start somewhere with the new people, and the hippies might be easier than the straights.

"Base to Patrol 41," the radio crackled. "Base to 41. Buck, you copy?"

"Got you loud and clear. I'm up on the ridge." And a good thing, because these old radios didn't work for shit anymore down in the canyon. The dashboard clocks in half his fleet didn't keep time either.

"3:05 p.m.," said Sam Beals, the weekend dispatcher. "Another lady thinks she's seen Patty Hearst. Indian Valley campground this time."

"Fat chance," Buck snorted. "Patty and that bunch of terrorists know they'd stick out more up here than in the lobby of her family's newspaper building."

"Tried to tell the lady that. But she says no, she saw a red-head gal and a black man in the same car heading south on 49. You're over that way, so thought I'd call."

"I'm headed into Pike right now. South, you say? They'll be up Depot Hill and across the county line in ten minutes. How about you radio our good neighbors at the Yuba County substation to check it out. Tell 'em Buck wanted to share the glory."

Sam laughed. "Will do. I can hear those thank-yous already."

"Who's the lady that phoned?" Buck asked.

"Some tourist buying film at the Outpost. I logged her name."

"Least it wasn't Thelma Zerloff. She sees Patty three times a week in Sierra City."

"Thelma we know needs glasses," Sam said. "When you comin' in?"

"By 5:00 or so," Buck answered. "Enjoy the quiet. We'll have fishin' season and a whole army of yahoos to deal with next week."

"Don't remind me," Sam acknowledged. "Take 'er easy, boss. Over and out."

Back in February, when the Hearst girl was kidnapped from her Berkeley apartment, Buck had gone over the *Wanted* fliers for all those Symbionese Liberation Army kooks with his deputies, and they'd kept an eye out. But once the group had successfully disappeared, Buck knew they were smart enough to stay where they'd blend in—LA, he'd bet, the Bay Area, or maybe Sacramento. Eventually Thelma got tired of looking for the SLA and stopped calling until last week, when Patty resurfaced as "Tania" and helped rob a San Francisco bank. That proved Buck's point about where their hideouts were, but it got Thelma stirred up again. Now tourists were getting into the act.

Patty and them'd never be on Highway 49 unless they were in heavy disguise, and the black guy'd still have to hide under a blanket in the back seat. Black faces were an event in Sierra County, and Buck and everybody he knew would rather it stayed that way. Hard enough to keep the peace among the tourists, Indians and all the flavors of local whites his deputies had to keep up with. What they ought to do was yank Thelma Zerloff's subscription to the Sacramento newspaper and make sure her TV didn't work.

County Sheriff is a non-partisan office, so with only two candidates, there'd be a clear winner in June. But Buck was a Democrat himself, meaning he had choices to make in the party primary, and

17

for Governor he was leaning toward Pat Brown's son, Jerry. Young Brown was an oddball, yet it had appeal that he was born to a political father, and was unmarried, also like Buck. And jeez, wives could be such wild cards during campaigns, Buck was glad he didn't have that to worry about.

He had some of Luann's freight to carry regardless, but at least she was in the past and those problems looked to be contained. Buck wondered how Mrs. Pritchard was holding up. Poorly enough, he hoped, to give her husband jitters. Politics was hard on the wives. Buck's mama had always liked the status she got out of it, but she sure hated the process. It occurred to Buck, though, that it might help with the new people if they knew Pritchard was a Republican, like old Tricky Dick, and Buck wasn't. Tough as this race was shaping up, Buck wouldn't trade places with Nixon, no sir.

CHAPTER 3

"**W**ow!" Ian cried from the Travelall's farthest rear seats, as though he'd been reading Greg's mind. "What a day!"

Ian Dudley, as Scots-looking as his name would suggest, was ruddy and strawberry blonde, but already, at 29, well on his way to bald. He was a phenom as a hiker, though, and kept himself in terrific shape. Shy compared to his wife Sandra, he was also a lawyer, and by all accounts at least her equal in ability. "If Aaron Copeland had seen this," he continued, "that ballet would be named *Sierra Spring*."

"God, I guess," agreed Pat Crandall, sitting with Jim in the middle row.

Greg swung his glance to find Pat's teeth and lips in the rearview mirror, below her keen blue eyes. Her ash-blonde hair, straight and parted in the middle, swung at her shoulders as she spoke. Despite her husband's appearance, she would not be taken for a Kennedy wife. At 37, she was more an earth mother, or the grownup version of a surfer girl. She was also beginning to look her age, with her years in the Southern California sun having taken a toll on her skin, and some of the ash in her hair now actually gray. "Where do you suppose the Buck Thompson poster came from?" she asked. "This is Pritchard country, and it wasn't there when we went in."

"No big mystery," Jim replied, unthinkingly making a Kennedy-like hand gesture with his palm up. "Any number of folks could have brought it from Sierra City or Downieville, but more likely it was Hal Voorden, the janitor guy."

Greg was puzzled. "Him?" he asked. "Why?"

"Hal's a Paiute," Jim answered. "The valley Indians always supported Huey, Buck's father, when he was sheriff. There was some favor Huey did. Goes way back."

"How do you know that?" Sandra asked, seated in back with Ian, behind the Crandalls.

"I'm in the newspaper business," Jim Crandall laughed. "That's what the *Mountain Mercury* supposedly is. People tell me all kinds of stuff. If I'm lucky, I remember half."

"We're almost at the highway junction," Molly stated from the front next to Greg. "A prime spot. Want to bet whose poster's the closest to the corner?"

"Bet you a beer it's Pritchard," Ian said.

"Sorry, no deal," Molly answered. "I think the same."

"OK, I'll bet on Buck," Jim offered. "Just for the hell of it."

Although Greg slowed to a crawl so the disputants could settle their bet, they'd have had to stop and use a tape measure to pick a winner. To their right, on the well-kept clapboard wall of the Sierra Cafe, was a Pritchard poster. The standard sort of thing—his name, the office in question, the election date, an exhortation, a photo, a slogan—except Pritchard's was a tasteful teal-blue ink on beige paper, and the photo, actually a split-frame, was in color.

One frame showed the vigorous-looking candidate, dressed in a suit, standing outside the County Courthouse with a Stetson in his hand, and the second was of him in slacks and a western-cut shirt, accompanied by his wife and kids, on the couch at home, with a glass-enclosed gun rack in the background. Greg had already seen identical posters around the county. The slogan read **Time For Professionalism**.

Directly opposite, however, on Greg's left, the paint-peeled wall of the sagging Globe Hotel held one of Buck's no-frills, black-and-white efforts. In addition, along both sides of the street were posters for other state and local races, including a Supervisor seat and the hot contest for County Treasurer.

But the Sheriff's race was by far the most interesting, since technically there was no incumbent, and it pitted the black-sheep scion of the Thompson dynasty against a well-connected newcomer of proven competence. Ken Pritchard had grown up in Reno, been a cop and was now a lawyer there, yet had moved to Loyalton over a decade ago despite the long commute. His uncle, in fact, was the long-time superintendent of the Feather/Yuba sawmill, Loyalton's biggest employer.

The Travelall's back seats had meanwhile erupted in hilarity, as Ian and Jim whacked at one another, each claiming the poster he'd bet on had been first by this or that increment. Laughing, Sandra and Pat egged on their men until Molly yelled smilingly at them to shut up. "You're worse than the kids!" she accused.

"I'm driving, I rule," Greg said, speeding up after swinging onto the highway for the run up the pass. The other direction led toward the newly reopened hot springs, reputedly the locus of strange doings, which they had joked on the way over about visiting some time. "It was a tie. But if one of you buys *me* a beer, the ruling could change."

"Don't encourage bad behavior," Molly teased. Then, turning to face behind her, she asked, "Well, first-timers, what did you think?"

"The meeting?" Sandra replied. "It was pretty cool. I had no idea about that Civil War stuff."

In Greg's mirror she was leaning forward between the profiles of Pat and Jim, eyes slightly magnified by her glasses, pushing her brunette pageboy away from her cheekbones. No getting around it, she was cute, a youthful munchkin in her late twenties, with a button nose and thin, mobile lips. Nothing below her collar was visible to him at the moment, but Sandra's body had always struck Greg as cute, too. In a few months the group would be skinny-dipping at picnics in secluded spots outside town, and he hoped she would participate.

"And, my god, that cheesecake," Ian chimed in from next to her. "I thought you'd been over-hyping, but no." He adjusted himself to rest a husbandly arm over Sandra's shoulders.

"Everybody was sweet as can be," she went on. "Teresa Powell snubbed me in the post office last week, but she talked my ear off at the meeting. Of course it was 'Mrs. *Dudley*, how nice to see you.' God forbid the words *Ms. Torkin* would cross her lips."

"One step at a time," Ian said dryly. "But listen to this," he gloated, "I got the famous recipe."

"Yeah, right," Pat Crandall laughed. "Where is it? Show me."

"She's mailing it to Downieville," Ian protested. "You know…Mrs. what's-her-name…the cheesecake lady. She took my address."

Now Molly and Jim laughed, too. "Good luck," Molly said. "Let me know right away when it comes."

"What do you mean?" By now Ian knew something was up.

"Francine Cooper never gives out that recipe," Greg said. "Easier to get the keys to Fort Knox, but she always promises to send it to you."

"Typical," Sandra said with disdain. "Welcome to Sierra County."

"I asked her three times before I caught on," Pat said.

"And *I* asked her twice," Molly concurred.

Maybe it'll help that I'm a guy," Ian shrugged.

"Don't hold your breath," Jim answered. "But I know the reddish layer on the bottom is made from choke cherries, the sour little ones that grow wild along the edges of the valley. She told me that much when I said I'd like to run the recipe with her name on it in the paper. We have choke cherries in the west county, too. Of course, if you eat 'em off the branch, they won't taste like hers. You'll be puckered for a week…at both ends."

"Fact is," Greg added, "guys don't really count in the food-prep department. I make the oatmeal cookies Molly and I always bring, and the ladies queue up afterward to congratulate Molly on how good they are."

"And I'm honest," Molly laughed. "Every meeting I tell them Greg did the baking, but it never sinks in."

Now, at the eastern base of the Sierra escarpment, the sun was temporarily gone and they were in deep shadow. Greg eased through the hamlet of Sattley and could smell the fumes of the sawdust burner at the pint-sized lumber mill that was Sattley's reason for being. Ahead, where the road made a ninety-degree turn, a weathered fence of rough-cut boards guarded a decrepit, one-story house with four or five junked cars upside-down in the muddy yard. Immediately past the turn, Greg knew the Travelall would have to pull miles of steep switchbacks before gaining the summit.

"That's the Chilcutt place," Jim pointed. "Indians who I doubt will be voting for Buck. He nailed the two younger brothers on Friday. Most of the family's been in the slammer for one thing or another over the years, and now these two, surrounded by the inventory of a burgled Radio Shack, are drunk on the living room floor when the deputies walk in. Talk about brains."

"Well, they won't be on the street to vote for Pritchard, either," Pat joked. "Maybe that's Buck's plan."

"Felons can't vote, period," Ian put in from the back, sounding authoritative. "And I'm happy when they're off the street. But Buck better've had a search warrant. The last thing he needs is for those guys to walk on a technicality before the election. He already looks bad having the FBI bust Jared."

"He had a warrant," Jim affirmed. "I checked. And he denies any knowledge of the Jared Smith thing."

"Really, where *do* you get all this?" Molly said.

"Routine," Jim answered. "I've got a reporter hat to wear, too. That story'll make this week's front page unless something bumps it inside."

"Front page, front page," Greg joked. "I can hear Buck praying for it from miles away. But now I won't have to buy a paper. I've already got the scoop."

"Buy one anyway," Pat Crandall said. "We need the money."

"Sounds like the Chilcutt boys could be my next clients," Sandra put in. "Wearing my Public Defender hat, I mean, by the looks of the house."

"Tell them to cop a plea," Jim replied. "It's a sure loser in court."

The Travelall, a truck-sized station wagon four years old, began laboring mightily and Greg downshifted to relieve the engine. He had convinced Molly to buy it during their Berkeley days as a statement of their back-to-the-land ideals.

"This thing's four-wheel-drive, isn't it?" Ian asked.

"I don't have it in four-wheel now," Greg replied, "but yeah. A big plus in winter."

"What sort of mileage do you get?"

"That's the down side. Probably only eight, pulling this grade. I'll be lucky to average twelve for the trip."

"Ouch!" said Ian. "Our Pinto wagon gets twenty-five."

"So does our VW hatchback," Molly said. "With gas up to sixty-five cents now, we drive that whenever we can. This one is Greg's toy…you know, for camping and fishing."

"And weather emergencies," Greg quickly defended, "or carrying extra folks, like today. Remember, before Henry came, when there was no doctor in town we drove it fifty miles in a snowstorm taking Ned to Grass Valley because of an ear infection."

"I remember," Molly acknowledged, touching his arm. "It's just that gas was thirty cents a gallon then. The VW does pretty well in winter, too, with the motor in back."

A subtext to Greg's memory of his son's ear infection and the snowstorm was how fond Molly had become of Henry Segal, and how much happier she'd been since she started working part-time as his receptionist at the health clinic. An unintended career turn for a trained and experienced librarian, but that's how things had gone. Grinding uphill, the Travelall overtook and passed a long, squat snowbank caked with road grime and dead pine needles. It would be there, at the approach to the summit, well into July.

"Thank god Downieville doesn't have big lines waiting to gas up," Sandra said. This Arab oil thing is scary. San Jose, before we moved here last fall, was a nightmare."

"Congress finally showed they're good for something, with those special rural allotments," Jim observed. "Otherwise we'd have lines, too. My pickup's not four-wheel, but I'm out in all kinds of weather because of the paper. In winter, I weight down the back with sand bags for traction, and I pour sand on the ice if I get stuck."

"It's paying for propane that's killing us," Pat said. "That's gone up even more than gasoline, and we have to heat the office downtown and our drafty old house. Because Stevo does home-school, we can't let the place get cold."

"At least it's been a warm spring," her husband Jim added.

"Well, four-wheel drive or sand bags, Sandra and I have to do something," Ian stated. "I've already crawled around in the slop way too many times putting on chains."

"The first winter you're here is always the hardest," Molly said. "Try sand bags next year, and we'll loan you the Travelall if you get in a jam."

CHAPTER 4

The half-dozen surviving buildings of Pike City flanked the main spur off Ridge Road right where the pavement ended—or began, if you came from the direction Buck was. He loved driving the lower-elevation back roads this time of year. Mud about gone and too soon for dust. Up ahead he saw the grove of locusts in which the town was set and smelled the creamy, perfume-sweet blossoms clustered among their leaves. True or not, people said they were called Tree of Heaven in China, and thousands got planted up and down the Mother Load, wherever Chinese labor'd been brought in. There was nothing heavenly about locusts most of the year, but in spring, when they bloomed, that name made sense and you forgot about their thorns, scraggly bark and droopy foliage.

Buck eased into the shade of the largest tree, killed the motor, removed his sunglasses and waited. The silky air carried the twanging guitars and choked lyrics of three guys sitting on the porch of the old one-room school that was Pike's principal structure. Jeanne Potter, a hippie-queen type and her half-breed kids lived inside along with a shifting cast of other tenants. Something about *Casey Jones* drivin' some train was what they were singing, while a gaggle of tots looked on and a barefoot woman wrapped in a batik bedspread slowly twirled and danced. Buck wanted to be sure they saw him first and had plenty of chance to extinguish anything they might be smoking that they shouldn't be.

Across the way was the tumbled stonework of a long-gone Wells Fargo office, and in the near distance a frame house occupied by the Freemans, an established Pike family. In a grassy field between the two a pony grazed and swatted his tail at flies outside a large, knobby teepee set back from the road and partly hidden by a line of drying laundry. Set further back, on a low stone foundation, was a miniature version of one of those angled domes hippies seemed to like building.

The teepee was the home of Marvin Mavis, who went by the name Satya instead, and whose girlfriend and kids used Hindu-sounding monikers, too. He was leader, more-or-less, of the Pike tribe and somebody Buck thought he could communicate with. Be a bad break if the guy turned out not to be home. Satya had been around a few years and occasionally showed up at Board of Supervisors' meetings in Downieville and wrote letters published in the *Merc*. Also, as Buck understood things, Satya was on good terms with Om Gillette and the Darnell's hippie daughter Edna over in Goodyear Bar.

"Oh…oh…Sheriff…it's you." Jeanne Potter, trailing a couple of kids in her wake had come up to the car. She was built like Buck, dark and round, but ten years younger, wearing flip-flops, pajama-looking pants and one of those tie-died shirts. Her face projected uncertainty bordering on worry. "Thought you'd be Deputy Garland. What's up?"

"Nothin's up," Buck shrugged. "Gave Garland the day off. He's a good kid. I'm just cruisin' the county to be sure I stay in touch."

"No warrants, no beef?"

"Not a one. Relax. Person might think you had something to hide." For Buck, that was a howler of a joke, and she got the humor despite his straight face.

"Who, me?" Jeanne joked back. "I was worried something'd happened to Garland, that's all. We get along fine with him."

"Glad to hear it. You suppose Mr. Satya is home there in his teepee?" Buck asked.

"Not teepee," she corrected, "yurt. Double walled and as nice inside as any house in town. And yeah, he's home. Talked to him an hour ago."

"How about seein' if he'd like to come out an' visit? He's not expecting me, and I don't want to give the wrong impression knocking on the door myself."

"Sure," Jeanne answered. "Supposed to be private between you and him?"

"No, no," Buck said, climbing out of the car. "Anybody interested can gather 'round." He sat on the cruiser's hood and laid his hat beside him. He saw Jeanne look at his pistol, which had climbed almost into his lap from how he was sitting, and tried to give a smile. Buck felt like he was smiling, hoped he was, but he couldn't always tell.

"Hold on, I'll get Satya." She moved off, kids still trailing, a boy and girl, in jeans and their own little tie-died shirts.

BELONGING

Within minutes the tall, gangly, bearded, beaded Satya, his dishy, honey-blonde *old lady*, their kids, and the crew from Jeanne Potter's porch had relocated to the vicinity of Buck's car, along with Jeanne and her own brood. Buck waved to Beth Freeman down the street, a second cousin of his mother's, who had come out in a housedress with her hair pulled into a bun, and was tending her roses. He saw that she and her husband had a Buck Thompson poster in their window, but Beth didn't walk over to join the group.

"Just a social visit, then?" Satya asked after they'd finished their hi's and howdys.

"That's the size of it. Since people vote for sheriff, they ought to see what one looks like now and then." Buck scratched his ear in the spot that itched him when he was in situations like this.

Satya cleared his throat. "Well, Jared Smith probably was wondering what a sheriff looks like...you know, that day last month the FBI snatched him out of the Quartz Cafe so fast he was jailed in Sacto before the cheese sandwich he ordered came off the grill."

"Believe it or not," Buck said, "I was hoping that'd come up."

"Yeah, bet you were," said one of the guitar players, whose instrument was now slung behind his shoulder like an M-1 with a macramé strap. Openly sarcastic, he continued, "One long-hair bounces a couple of checks and it's too hot for Sierra County to handle?"

Several of the hippies shuffled their feet and signaled approval with nods and other body language. In the following silence, Buck could hear bees swarming in the locust flowers dangling above him and a heavily distorted electric-guitar version of *The Star Spangled Banner* drifting from an open window further down the road.

"Wait...gim'me a chance, now," Buck said softly. "That Jared Smith business fried me more than anything since I came home here as Undersheriff four years ago. I have a beef with you, you'll know it. I don't need the FBI to cover my fanny. Never in Curt Foley's years or in all my daddy's did the Feds come into this county without giving us a heads-up and having us make the collar."

"Guess the Feds don't have faith in our top law enforcement officer these days," Satya stated, eyes on Buck.

"Could mean that," Buck admitted. "Doubtful, but if so, it's for the right reasons. I don't necessarily go by the book like they do. Course neither has any other Sierra County sheriff this century.

26

Folks think they want professionalism, it'll look a lot more like the FBI than me sittin' in Pike on the hood of my car."

"If Jared's bust doesn't mean what Satya said about lack of confidence," Jeanne Potter asked, "what does it mean? He and Om are friends of ours."

"Look, I'll level with you. Probably means one of two things. The Feds have an informer here, undercover narc or something, they don't want any of us knowing about, even me, and whoever it is ratted on Jared. Or...or, Jared himself was a narc, and the bust was to pull him and shield him from suspicion before some real action goes down."

There was general disbelief. "Jared a narc?" one voice said. "Man, you trippin'," said another. "Om would'a known. She'd never stand for that," someone else added.

"What did happen to Jared?" Satya asked. "All it said in the *Merc* was passing bad checks. That's no federal rap."

"Still in jail, far as I know," Buck answered. "But in Oregon, where he's from. Federal rap was interstate flight. He'd already skipped from a minimum security hoosegow there before he and Om hooked up, wherever that was."

"Marin County," the guitar guy said. "Same place I'm from. Om swears she didn't know about any fugitive rap."

"Possible," Buck said. "She seems like a good sort, and he'd've been pretty dumb to tell her. But she's lucky the FBI didn't haul *her* in, too. Very lucky. One reason I don't rule out my second theory."

"Shit," said a voice. "Bad news either way."

"Doesn't have to be...I mean for you folks. Live careful, watch who you talk to, and we'll all have plenty of happy days.

"What I'm sayin'," Buck continued, "is I don't look for trouble. And I complained plenty to the Feds about what they did. My family settled here in the 1870s with the same ideas you have today. Elbow-room, personal freedom, find a way to have the land support you...above ground with orchards or timber, below ground with mining. What you do inside your own households...however you define 'em," Buck added pointedly, "is pretty much your business. You don't steal, you don't abuse your kids, you don't try to mess over your neighbors, all you'll see of me and young Deputy Garland is we'll drive by and wave.

"I also read up a little when the first of your kind started showing here. Book called *The Greening of America* by some Berkeley egghead. Or *tried* to read it. Anyway, I know some of the, aah...*sacraments* you smoke, and those sugar cubes and mushrooms you use for...*religious* purposes. Again, what you do at home is your business, but don't be sharing that stuff with the local teenagers, and don't, for god's sake, try making cash crops out of 'em. You get people riled, or make me look bad because I started out by cutting you slack, you've got trouble. I can be nasty as hell when I'm mad."

"Why Sheriff," Satya's dishy girlfriend gibed, "you sendin' a message there?" She had pert little breasts under her ribbed tank-top, and those unshaven armpits Buck thought were gross, but erotic, too—the mark of women who really would do anything.

"If I was runnin' for office or not, it'd be the same message," Buck nodded. "I don't bother another man's religion if he don't bother mine. Chant all the Vishnu you want."

"Actually, we're into Native Indian more than East Indian these days," Satya said. "*Black Elk Speaks*, Carlos Casteneda, and like that. Built us a geodesic sweat lodge over at my place." He pointed to the low-lying dome Buck had noticed earlier on.

"Sounds interesting," Buck replied. "Fat as I am, I see the use of a good sweat. There's no Indians left this side of the pass that I know of, but there's quite a few in Sierra Valley...Washoes and Paiutes. I respect their ways, and they know it. Talk to any of 'em, and ask."

"What about nailing the Chilcutt boys last Friday?" Satya pressed. "I was over to Downieville, and that Drew Ormond at the welfare office said you'd locked 'em up. They're Washoes, right? You have a warrant?"

"Right, and bet your ass I had a warrant," Buck shot back. "We head through the door of your...your...tent...uninvited, that is...I'll have one then, too. What I hope is that day never comes."

"Fair enough," Satya acknowledged.

"Hell," Buck went on, "I had word months ago those two were hanging around with low-lifes over in Quincy. I warned their people we'd have 'em both on a short leash. Did everybody a favor slowin' 'em down before they got in deeper. I'm not supposed to talk politics in uniform like this, but believe me, I won't lose one Indian vote over how we handled that little situation. Wasn't the FBI made the bust, either."

"Well, we hear a lot of rumors around this county," Jeanne Potter said.

28

"Still got to understand who your friends are," Buck countered.

"Not just the FBI thing," she went on. "All due respect, Sheriff, but you weren't a model citizen when you lived here before, and later when you were down in...what was it...Redding?"

"Eureka," said Buck unhesitatingly.

"Wherever...but there was a lot of boozing, from what I hear, and it doesn't go down well with a strong-minded woman like me that you roughed up your wife."

"They *say* I did. That's old, old stuff, but you'll hear it, 'cause I've got enemies different places same as anybody else. I wouldn't accuse Mr. Pritchard himself of keeping it alive, but people close to him are. And Jesse Foster down in Alleghany don't care for me none. You run into her at Hogan's, she'll put out something mean, especially with this election coming up."

"So?" came the only word of the afternoon that Buck could attribute to the second guitar guy, whose instrument was nowhere in sight. He was skinny and shirtless under a black leather vest, and had wispy sideburns.

"So," Buck answered, "I used to like the sauce. Been stone dry near six years, but bourbon and water was my poison...not that I was averse to beer. Never went on benders, really, except once or twice. Always thought I was under control. But I was plenty drunk after work and weekends for a lotta' my life. Drunk and unhappy. All that's changed. Ask around. Anybody who knows me can set you straight. Never interfered with my work, neither."

"And bein' drunk excuses beating up women?" Jeanne challenged.

"Course not. You hear me say that? I'm not gonn'a lay out details, but I'll say this much. You can believe me or not. I wasn't the only drinker in the family, and Luann... that's my ex...don't have any better right to be grieved than me, if you're talking red marks on somebody else's skin. Doesn't excuse it, I could'a controlled myself better, and I could'a got out sooner, but that's water under the bridge." Buck tried for eye contact, one at a time, with everybody, and succeeded with most of them.

"Word is you roughed up your daughter, too," said Ms. Frizzy Armpits, who'd been the last to meet his eyes. "Charges were filed, we heard."

"That's a plain lie," Buck affirmed. "You check in Eureka. No charges on file. I never hit either of my girls except some swats on the rear up to first grade or so."

"You're right about Jesse Foster," Jeanne Potter said. "She has a different story than yours."

"Look, I was there, Jesse wasn't. Most a' this comes from Luann's custody fight over Ginny, the little one. Jesse was Luann's friend all through high school. She took sides against me, and so did Cindy, my older girl. Said a lot of things that weren't true. All I can say is Ginny, who's sixteen now, spends a month with me and my mother in Downieville every summer. You think the courts'd allow that if they believed I'd be beating on her?"

"Got an answer for everything, don't you?" guitar guy number one said.

"Hope so. Doesn't mean you'll accept it, though."

"Something to think about, anyway, Sheriff," Satya concluded, stretching his arms behind him. "Glad you came by. I'm gonn'a head off and do some yoga." He shook Buck's hand, backed away while his girlfriend and their kids grouped around him, then they all turned to cross the road.

The rest of the group, grunting various good-byes, also dispersed, with the kids heading over to pet the pony and the guitar guys getting into a new song that had *Mandolin Wind* in the chorus. Jeanne Potter stayed with Buck an extra minute.

"The newer folks here probably aren't registered to vote, you know," she said.

"Figured not," Buck responded. "Deadline's next week. You willing to encourage 'em if I get Marilyn Pezzola's office to bring up some forms?"

"Well, OK. No strings, right?"

"No strings. Marilyn's working with Edna Darnell to do the same in Goodyear Bar. By the way, you know any of those so-called rebirthing hippies who took over the old Camden Hot Springs in Sierraville?"

"Yeah, why?"

"What're they up to?"

"Very mystical. You float in enclosed tanks of body-temperature mineral water to re-experience life in the womb and be reborn in a pure state. They'll have themselves a nice business going for tourist season. I've been invited over sometime, and so've Edna and Om."

"Huh. Wha'da'ya' know? Another cut on sweat lodge, I guess. But when ya' do go, you might let 'em know Kenny Pritchard has been telling the town biddies in Loyalton he's gonn'a close down the rebirthers after the election. Health code violations, or something. Guess their kind of born again's too weird for the old guard."

Jeanne looked at Buck with a half-smile. "Thanks. You know, Sheriff, I might get over to Sierraville sooner than I'd thought."

Buck considered shifting to the subject of posters, but no, he didn't know her that well, and he'd pushed the Pike hippies pretty hard already. "OK, then, nice to see you. Thanks for helpin' bring people out." He slid back into his car.

"You're welcome," she replied, reaching through the window to shake Buck's hand. "Good luck."

"I'm no big-city cop and no lawyer," he said as Jeanne backed away. "Us Thompsons are plain folks, just like you."

CHAPTER 5

Flinching and squinting, Greg got the Travelall back into fourth gear as Molly scrambled to hand him his sunglasses. At the 6,700-foot summit they had abruptly gone from shade to full sun, not just in the western sky, but blindingly reflected from giant roadside drifts of grainy spring snow. Walled on both sides, the highway became a slot-car course gleaming with melt water.

They hadn't met another vehicle since starting their climb, an isolation that Greg was glad to have persist through the narrowest, most glare-ridden stretch. At least the downhill slope was less steep, with the pavement following the contours of a hanging valley forming the headwaters of the North Yuba River. After a bright red Corvette carrying Nevada plates and two youngish guys had dodged past in the opposite direction, conversation quieted, the miles rolled by and the snow-banks receded to open the vista as they lost altitude.

BELONGING

The thrusting mass of English Mountain, huge and elephant-shaped, its snowy flanks covered in dense fir and cedar, took over the skyline. Then when they reached Bassett's Meadow, the Sierra Buttes, a towering collage of rocky, snow-crusted spires that was the county's distinguishing landmark, loomed from the northwest to generate an emotional charge everyone seemed to share.

"It's funny," Pat Crandall said, "going east they're barely noticeable, but coming back, they just knock your eyes out. First time or fiftieth time, doesn't matter."

"Seems like you could touch them if the window was open," Molly said.

"I must have hiked a dozen trails up the Buttes and into Lakes Basin last fall," Ian put in, "and that didn't scratch the surface. It's fabulous there. I can't wait for summer."

"Here's what I don't get," said his wife Sandra. "Why would that Mrs. Cooper be such a twit about her recipe, and everybody act so weird because I'm keeping Torkin as my name, and Jerry Vargas treat me like a dummy if I don't know the exact term for some part at the hardware store? We're all here, new or old, because we love the mountains. Anybody new took a pay cut when they came. Everyone fights the same weather. I really don't get it."

"I didn't either...at first," Jim Crandall answered. "But I'm starting to. Not that I like it, or think it's fair."

"What do you mean?" Sandra pursued.

"Mainly, they're resentful. They've all lived through a disastrous economic dislocation. They lost young men in WWII like everywhere else, but when FDR forced the gold mines to close they lost their way of life. There were no jobs for their kids, a lot of whom moved away, and government jobs became more professionalized and more dependent on college training.

"Look at us...in this car. We're a mandarin class, with skills few or any locals possess. They feel diminished. Cheated. Now they're even losing their political power to Loyalton. No wonder the geezers at the Quartz Cafe track the London gold market on the shortwave in the morning. It's all they know, the only standard of value they've ever had. Why do you think I joined the Historical Society and run news on precious metals in the *Merc* every week?"

"The Quartz crowd must be creaming their jeans this year," Greg put in. "Gold's shot up faster than oil, and Nixon's pushing that bill for US citizens to own bullion. It hasn't been legal since the '20s, you said in the paper."

"$100 an ounce last week," Jim replied, "but still a flash in the pan, if you'll excuse the pun. It would take $450 to make those old mines pay."

"Yeah, but what does it take to be accepted here," Ian asked. "Really accepted. Can it be done?"

"Why should we care?" Molly put in. "Greg does, but I'm not sure I do."

"I'm tired of feeling like I don't count," Greg said. "I'm not a performing monkey. I teach their kids, for god's sake." And his faculty colleague—*former* colleague—Seth Holmes had felt the same way, but he wasn't going to mention Seth's name.

"Ian and I care, too," Sandra said. "It's a lot easier to go in front of a judge or a jury if you know they aren't suspicious of you for no good reason."

"So do Jim and I," Pat volunteered, "and not because we might sell more newspapers. We want to get beyond the people who butter us up just to see their names in print and feel really connected…be acknowledged as worthwhile."

"*We're* connected," Molly said. "Within our group, I mean."

"Sure," Jim conceded, "but does that have to be the limit? Pat's right about wanting acknowledgment, and I'm definitely willing to accord them *their* due."

"Well, maybe the acceptance thing can happen," Molly said. "Look at Ernie Warrington."

"The Search and Rescue guy?" Ian responded, eyebrows furrowed. "I know him to see, but don't really know him. Thought he *was* a native."

"Greg knows the story better than I do," Molly said.

"I know most of the story," Greg confirmed. "But wait, I want to pull off at Butte Springs for a drink. Molly and I never go by without stopping."

Greg eased the Travelall into a shaded parking area separated from the road by a waist-high fieldstone wall. He stopped, and dead ahead a pulsing froth of water six feet high and four feet wide poured from a notch in the rock buttressing the southernmost base of the Buttes. A lacy tangle of white-flowering dogwoods rimmed the boiling pool below the falls, itself the source of a small creek dashing off, parallel to the highway. Ferns crowded the water's edge, and on closer inspection, bright sparks of mimulus, phlox, allium and johnny-jump-up lined the ground as well.

Greg and the others got out to stretch their legs, while Molly reached in the glove box for the two Sierra Club cups she kept there. Even blindfolded, any one of them could tell they'd left the Alpine zone. Wafting velvety-warm up the canyon from thousands of feet down-slope, the air carried an indefinably fecund smell as though all of California was in estrus. And maybe it was. Despite their disagreements lately, he and Molly had been horny, and more eager than usual to get their son Ned off to sleep at night.

All six took turns dipping cups and sharing the water around. It was clear, tooth-numbing, and delicious. "OK," Greg said, wiping droplets out of his beard with the back of his hand, what do you want to know about Ernie? General bio?"

"Guess so," Ian replied. Outdoors, Ian typically wore a Baltimore Orioles cap, both to celebrate his hometown and protect his baldness from the sun, but here in the shade he twirled it in his hand.

"For starters, he's not a native. He's 25 or 26 now, and was about 5 when his parents arrived from the Bay Area. His dad sold insurance and dabbled in real estate. Early on, Sarah, his mom, started teaching kindergarten, which she still does. Ned'll have her next year, unless she retires like she threatens to every spring. There's an older brother, too, who's a career Air Force officer.

"So Ernie went all through school in Downieville and was the smartest kid anybody can remember. Got a full ride to Stanford, then graduated as a civil engineer. While he was in college his dad died, and Ernie married into the Sierra City branch of the Powell family. They have two kids and live in Sierra City themselves. Ernie does engineering work for local contractors and also heads up the county's Search and Rescue/Emergency Services Unit part time.

"A pretty fine guy, from what I can tell," Greg concluded, "but real private. He understands us, and he's not cowed by us, but given the choice, he'd rather be one of them. Or that's my take."

"Well put," said Jim. "But give Ernie a break. Rick Rodman's more of a newcomer than most of us, and Ernie's one of Rick's main backers in that Ore House pizza place." Jim put one foot on a low boulder and leaned to rest his forearms on his knee.

"Yay, Ernie!" Sandra said. "And another gem of behind-the-scenes knowledge from our ace reporter."

"I see what Molly was driving at," Ian acknowledged. "We can't tell Ernie from a native, they apparently can, but they're letting him pass. His kids, though…his kids'll be natives."

"OK," Jim said, looking at Ian. "What does it take to get accepted? That's what you asked, isn't it?" Jim always enjoyed offering analysis, and Greg could see he wasn't going to miss an opportunity.

"Piecing together what I just heard," Jim went on, "you need to graduate from Downieville High, you need to make your career in the county after that, you need to marry another DHS grad, you need to raise your kids here, and it doesn't hurt if your mom is a local institution in her own right."

"You left one thing out," Pat said to her husband.

"What's that?" Molly asked.

"The big headstone in the local cemetery," Pat replied. "The Warrington name must be Ernie's dad. I've been by there a bunch of times taking walks with Stevo."

"That definitely counts," Jim agreed. "But having a place named after you, like Rososco Ravine…or a plaque posted at some local landmark…is even better." Jim pointed to a bronze marker on the fieldstone wall behind them.

Greg turned. He'd seen the inscription during previous stops, but he'd forgotten the details. Moving forward, he read aloud: "In memory of Frank Pezzola, Jr., Sierra County Road Foreman, born 1930, died 1960, who loved this spot. Dedicated June, 1966, Department of Public Works."

As each of them had learned by the end of their first month in town, Frank Pezzola, not usually referred to as Jr., father of three and Downieville hero of the first magnitude, had been run off the road by a tourist in a daytime mishap at Convict Curve, downriver toward the county line. Somebody in the hardware store or the post office or The Forks bar inevitably brought it up. If you lived in the county, you were supposed to know.

"With all due respect," Ian said, "that's too tough a standard. You have to die first."

"Sorry, time's up," Greg broke in, interrupting the mood. "We should roll. I'm on for tennis with Henry later, if there's still daylight and he's not out being *Dr. Segal* on some emergency." By now Greg had completely unbuttoned his Pendleton in response to the warm air and planned to take it off for the remaining ride. His previously soaked foot was pretty much dry, too.

Below Butte Springs Highway 49 made a sharp, straight descent to Sierra City at 4,500 feet before dropping further into the canyon for a more gradual descent to finish their trip. Local pride was such that you could probably get punched out in Sierra City for suggesting that it was a suburb of Downieville, but by 1974, that was the case.

No longer having any jobs to speak of, no school, no real stores, just a chainsaw repair shop, some resorts open only in summer and not much else, it got by as a pretty spot with a colorful history and a huddle of mixed brick and wood buildings facing the highway or the two short cross-streets. The now absent Seth Holmes had lived there, and his soon-to-be ex-wife, Karen, continued in residence with the Holmeses' adopted Nicaraguan son, Juan.

Goodyear Bar, a few miles below Downieville, was even smaller than Sierra City and another de-facto suburb. The three communities had evolved into an organic whole, but there was no public transportation, so you had to have your own wheels to be a full citizen. And thanks to its bucolic, off-highway location, Goodyear Bar had also become Sierra County's center of hippie culture.

Driving the Yuba canyon always had a strange effect on Greg. While his body traversed the land, his mind offered a bird's-eye view. No other place had ever touched him the same way. He was glad, however, that the group's earlier discussion of cars and gas mileage had stopped on the note it had. He didn't want to deal with anyone's wondering how he and Molly could afford two nice vehicles and a spacious home on what, until her recent half-time slot at the clinic, had been his teaching salary alone. The fact was, Greg's parents in Sacramento had bought Molly the VW hatchback, and had made a significant down payment on their son and daughter-in-law's house.

Greg was fine with it himself, because he knew his folks had the money, and helping gave them pleasure. Molly was less comfortable, thinking she and Greg should be self-sufficient, and that he should give up the Travelall so they could pay for the VW themselves. True, the inconvenience of Greg's going carless would allow them to meet their transportation costs, but without some kind of subsidy there would still be no housing options that didn't involve a lot less space and comfort.

Besides, Greg's folks had been terrific. They never made needling remarks about cars or finances, nor behaved during their occasional visits as though Greg and Molly weren't the real homeowners. And now, with gas and propane way up, Greg wasn't feeling that flush. Molly sure didn't like it when the checkbook forced a postponement of their periodic trips to the Bay Area to buy books and catch up on urban pleasures.

CHAPTER 6

Now that hadn't gone bad at all, Buck thought, watching Jeanne Potter walk away toward the pony to join her children. And technically, he hadn't told the Pike City hippies a single lie. Running the motor almost at idle, Buck angled his cruiser across the road to where Beth Freeman, his mother's cousin, was tying rosebush runners to the outside of her picket fence. Seeing him stop, she stepped forward and leaned to brace her forearms against the car's door, her face at eye level to him through the passenger window.

"Howdy Beth," he said. "Thought I should visit, bein' as I'm passing by."

"Howdy Buck. Good to see you. How's Norma gettin' along?"

"Mama's in and out, like she's been for a while. You know what I mean?"

"Yeah, a weak ticker'd be bad enough, but her mind wasn't much there last time Virgil and I dropped by. She never has been right the ten years since she woke up that morning with Huey dead right beside her."

"Took a long time to feel right myself after Daddy went."

"Sally still helping with Norma?"

"You bet. Could never think of running for Sheriff otherwise. Nobody else I could hire would be half that loyal."

"I know it broke Dot and Jerry Vargas's hearts when their Sally come up with polio years ago, but she gained more in spirit than she ever lost from having a crippled arm." Beth ran through this litany every time Buck saw her, which fortunately wasn't often. She wore glasses, had small teeth for a grown woman, and took an abiding interest in other people's troubles. As though to complete a motif, her faded dress bore a rosebud pattern in the same color as the ones she was tending.

"Mama loves Sally, that's for sure. Can hardly stand for her to go home at night."

"Hope you do well this June," Beth said. "You were a good son to come back and take care of your Mama like you did."

"You know the story," Buck stated. And she did, but he was clearly expected to tell it again. "There'd'a been no job for me around here wasn't for Curt Foley. And he saw how bad off mama was. If I'd'a known it, I'd've moved her to a rest home down by Sacramento. I was back drivin' truck, so was mostly on the road."

"God does provide, Buck. What you doin' here? Hopin' to win over my long-haired neighbors?"

"Sums it up," Buck nodded. "Think I did OK, too. How all of you getting along in Pike these days?"

"Compared to no neighbors," Beth sighed, "like we've had off and on, it's nice to have some. But rather they be normal ones. Mostly good folks, though. You get past their looks, and the kids with that pony are fun to watch." She gave a tentative smile.

"Like Huey always said," Buck told her, "takes all kinds."

"Buck, I know you've lived in Eureka and places, but I'm learnin' there's a lot more kinds than this tired country lady ever figured on."

Buck laughed. "Mighty sharp poster you got in the window."

"You don't look a thing like your daddy," Beth said, "but you seem more like him every day."

"Thanks. Probably the best thing I could hear right now. Need any more of those," he pointed, "pick up the phone."

"We've got a couple extras in the house," she said. "Now you've softened 'em up, I'll have Virgil see if the neighbors want one for their teepee."

"Called a yurt, I just heard. Some different kind of teepee."

"Well, take care, and remember me to Norma."

"Will do. Howdy to Virgil from me."

Buck accelerated smoothly onto the pavement and rolled southwest to connect back to the ridge road two miles ahead. He saw the locust trees and white-framed, green-shuttered houses of Pike recede in the mirror, while open meadows streamed by on both sides. The rest of the way to Downieville he'd be in the oak and pine forest, but not here.

A lot of politics was puttin' your own interpretation on things, which was mainly what Buck had done. That and leaving stuff out. His real theory on the FBI business with Jared Smith was that Pritchard had set it up on the sly to make Buck look weak and piss the hippies off. Jerry Vargas and Buck's other backers on the Elect HBT Committee were doing what they could to control the damage among the regular folks, but it fell to Buck to deal with the long-hairs.

He couldn't go around openly blaming Pritchard, because he had no proof, and the more Buck pushed the accusation, the quicker Pritchard could call his bluff. But on Pritchard's off-the-record threats to go after Camden Hot Springs Buck had a solid source, Paiute bigwig Hal Voorden, who didn't miss a trick around Sierraville.

Some of the leaving out Buck had done in Pike was that there were more ways to get in trouble around here than bothering your neighbors or dealing drugs. He and all the other locals disdained tourists, but tourism was the county's lifeblood. The hippies did anything to threaten that, he'd have to come down on 'em Katie-bar-the-door. And you don't mess with people's mining claims, either, or try high-grading tricks like those dummies over by Carson City last month. A few of the hippie men were working day labor in the Bumble Bee and the Eleven-to-One and the handful of other Sierra County digs still operating, but they'd better not be taking any slugs and fines with 'em at quitting time. The mine owners would catch on, cry conspiracy, and Buck'd have to search every damned yurt there was.

OK, and he'd also finessed the usual stuff regarding Luann. She *had* tried to file charges against him, but Buck's being on the force in Eureka at the time meant that the charges never quite got officially filed. On paper his record was cleaner than it was in fact, and the only way he'd been able to keep it clean, the time things really got crazy with Cindy that once, was to resign and turn in his badge. The judge's order letting Ginny spend a month with Buck every summer was conditional on Buck's mother being part of the household. No Norma, no Ginny, unless the judge reconsidered.

Feeling more numb than bitter, Buck started brooding on how Beth Freeman had asked to be remembered to his mother. Barring a miracle, she wouldn't remember Buck himself tonight, much less her cousin Beth. Now his Mama referred to Buck as either Huey or Cal, Buck's father or big brother, both dead, and remembered Sally mainly because she thought Sally Vargas was Sally Powell, Cal's fiancée from before the war, before Cal got killed at Anzio Beach. It had embarrassed Sally and Buck at first, but they'd gotten used to it. What he'd never got used to, and what made Sally leave the room, was when Norma would sit muttering over and over, "Never amount to anything, that Buck. People were right. Never amount to anything."

All the penance he could possibly owe for those wasted years he paid every time she got going. And hell, they were his years, too, not just hers. Worse yet, no sooner had Buck really gotten the booze and Luann out of his head and started to amount to something, when Curt dies and here's this election and it's up or out. Last thing Pritchard would do was keep Buck around, and Pritchard'd be right. If Buck wasn't politically dangerous enough to win office, he'd still be way too dangerous to keep. It was victory in June or rest home for Norma, no job for Sally, no visits from Ginny and good-bye Downieville. If that happened, it might be hello again to bourbon. Why the hell not?

See, Buck hadn't worked his way through the ranks, so he had no civil service protection letting him bump down to Deputy whether Pritchard liked it or not. Buck was Sierra County born and raised, but he'd come in as an outsider. The Undersheriff was a political appointee, serving solely at the Sheriff's pleasure. All part of Curt's plan, but it wasn't supposed to wind up this way.

The facts were: Buck had been a fuck-up in high school, got crappy grades and picked fights. Being Huey's son, he could get away with it. He graduated, just barely, and started driving truck, feeding logs to the old Cal-Ida mill. Come 1948, the second summer after he left school, he got 17-year-old Luann pregnant with what turned out to be Cindy.

Of course he hadn't known and she hadn't told him until into her senior year, when she started to show and told her parents first and all hell broke loose. Only good part was she didn't have Downieville roots. Blonde, cute, sexy, and later in a class by herself for conniving cussedness, she was the daughter of a state engineer living in a trailer at the end of Pearl Street while her daddy completed a highway project east of town.

Anyway, Luann was sent to stay with her grandparents in Sacramento to finish high school. Buck, determined to do the *right thing* for once, followed, got a job there and married her just before Cindy was born. Luann's parents hated him and he hated them. His parents tried to like Luann, but she never gave them a chance. Buck went in the Army, got assigned to Japan, not Korea, and returned afterward to Cindy and Luann in Eureka where she was working in a hair salon. They had one good month. By then Luann had started on the gin, and when Buck switched from beer to bourbon, the wasted years cranked up in earnest.

He drove truck, she set hair, they drank, they fought, he'd be away alternate weeks to LA or Seattle, and time was measured by empty bottles and Cindy's birthdays. Along the way Luann had another pregnancy in 1957 and Ginny was born, but even that didn't change how the next two years slid by. One day Buck walked out. He'd set aside some cash, gave it all to Luann, took a gas station job in Redding, quit the bourbon, put a few criminology courses at Shasta College under his belt, and had Huey pull strings to get him into the POST Academy where Buck became a top performer for the first time in his life. When a police job in Eureka opened up, Huey helped a little more and Buck suddenly had a career there in law enforcement.

Luann had talked divorce, but never done anything about it, so Buck went back to her and this time they had a whole good year. Buck could go home to Downieville, be somebody and trade stories with Huey and the rest of them, where he got to know Curt, Huey's newest and last Undersheriff. Turned out, though, the gin, bourbon and Luann's cussedness hadn't left for good, they'd only been on holiday. Buck got promoted to sergeant, but everything else was hanging by a thread. Then, bam, the impossible happened. Huey, who'd set himself a goal of serving ten terms—forty years—ran for an eleventh at age 68 over Norma's objections, won, but died with no warning in his sleep in 1964 halfway through that eleventh term. Curt took over, won an easy race on his own two years later, and prepared to settle in.

Buck, meanwhile, was undermined to where he flat couldn't cope. He slogged through police work in Eureka hung-over every day, things with Luann escalated until she all but abandoned the girls and started staying out with Homer, the sap she married later on, while Buck discovered just what it meant to hit bottom. By spring 1970, when Curt was facing a tough election and needed the Thompson name to pull him through in the west county, Buck was divorced, off the force, driving truck again, and had AA'd himself free of booze. Curt tracked him down by phone and offered a deal. Buck could be Undersheriff, get back into law enforcement, move home to take care of his mother, and all it would cost him was working for Curt politically whenever Curt asked, plus swearing he'd never run against Curt for as long as Curt wanted the job.

It was also understood that Curt could *un*-appoint Buck and find a new Undersheriff at any time. First drop of booze, or recurrence of problems with Luann, or something bothersome about the way Buck parted his hair, he'd be gone. And for insurance, Curt said he had papers nobody else had, based on the coincidence that Curt and the Eureka chief, Buck's former boss, had been in the Marines together and were long-time buddies.

Wherever those papers might be, and Buck doubted Pritchard knew they existed, if Pritchard got enough votes June 4, it was *adios* Buck, regardless. But if Pritchard somehow did lay his hands on them, and the story showed up in the *Merc* before the election, the ball game was not only over, the Thompson name wouldn't be worth jack shit anywhere. In fact, it had already proven less powerful than Buck had hoped. The Board of Supervisors had appointed him only Acting Sheriff instead of full bird, and at no increase in pay. He'd have to beat Pritchard to taste the real prize.

With the vote of the east- and west-county natives being so predictable, Buck's newcomer strategy could produce a win, but there was no margin for error. Marilyn Pezzola, a classy lady who was running unopposed for reelection as Clerk-Auditor, had helped him think it through. She was also an honorary niece of Buck's mother's, and had quietly arranged for her staff to be accommodating in registering new voters vetted by Buck while being less available — in various subtle ways — when Pritchard's people made similar requests. The other key to the newcomers was getting the *Mountain Merc's* endorsement, though Buck didn't have a clue how he'd bring that off.

Right now, it was drive and enjoy the scenery. Shows how rugged Sierra County is, he often thought, that you couldn't reach any of its four corners on paved roads and couldn't cross its western or eastern boundaries by wheeled vehicle, period. Having dropped southwest off Alleghany Ridge to pick up Highway 49, Buck was over the line into Yuba County for the moment, looking to cross back a few miles ahead. Then it would be down the long grade at Depot Hill, past a series of roadside seep-springs and waterfalls, to where he'd span the North Yuba at Indian Valley and follow it upstream eighteen winding miles. His watch said about 4:15, so the prediction he'd made as to when he'd be hitting the office looked pretty good. No need to call in. Hell, he hadn't seen Patty Hearst, and Sam, his dispatcher, wouldn't care how beautiful the dogwoods looked in this slanting light.

At the bridge, the river was really ripping with spring runoff. It'd be plain spectacular today above town where the canyon was narrower and the road hugged the water. Buck eased through the largely empty public campground, waving at the last few tourists who were packing their gear to head out. An impish boy, age 10 or so, stood at attention to give Buck a salute, which he returned by putting two fingers against his hat brim. Jack Murdock, a Forest Service guy from Goodyear Bar, was walking around checking fire pits. Buck saluted him, too, and drew a throaty chuckle in reply.

This place'd be mobbed next weekend for the trout opener. There'd be fights and drunks and lost dogs to deal with, and Buck would have his whole force plus the reserve deputies on duty both days. At least the water was so cold yet they wouldn't have to worry about people swimming. Tourist kids didn't have the sense to respect the current when it was like this, and adults could be almost as bad. Put one toe in before June, though, and even the dumbest of 'em'd jump back screaming. Wouldn't see many fishermen getting wet either. Without insulated waders, that water'd shrink up your nuts to a pair of freeze-dried raisins.

At the campground exit, Buck backtracked a hundred feet on the highway to cruise the parking lot at the Outpost store. Ouch! Gas up to sixty-nine cents at the pump with this Arab oil thing. Nobody knew if that would kill tourism this year, or boost it, because Sierra County was closer to Reno, Sacramento and the Bay Area than a lot of destinations people normally chose. Buck's poster was on display out front, but so was Pritchard's. Del Houston, the owner, was hedging his bets publicly, but Buck was confident that Del's and every other vote in the Houston family would come his way. Extra money on color posters wouldn't do Pritchard much good down here, and might piss people off by seeming too fancy. Buck stopped and sat in the car to clean his sunglasses.

BELONGING

Two girls, tourists, fourteen or fifteen years old, in tight T shirts and jeans came laughing out of the store arguing over how to share the bubble gum they'd just bought. Buck felt a twang in his pants in spite of himself. Kids they were, younger than his baby daughter Ginny for Christ's sake, but the asses on 'em and the way they moved and swung their hair so free gave him fits. Time for another trip to Mustang Ranch or a new *Hustler* for his nighttime supply. And this year he really would have to get Sally to talk to Ginny about that white bathing suit she'd worn every afternoon during her visit last summer. A skimpy two-piece number that went up the crack of her behind when she walked and seemed damn near transparent when it was wet against her golden skin.

Now she was sixteen, Ginny'd probably be even more stacked her next visit. Luann and Cindy never had tits like those. Seemed to happen overnight, too. Couple of years ago she was just a spindly thing. Buck had about gotten used to her suddenly provocative wardrobe by a few days after her arrival and stopped paying attention, until he'd overheard two of his deputies talking about her stretched out on the rocks at the town swimming hole with her halter straps loose and how they'd decided to patrol that spot more frequently the rest of the month.

He hadn't been sure then if Ginny knew what signals she was putting out, exactly, but by this summer she'd absolutely know. Buck hoped that knowledge would cause her to tone it down a bit. Funny thing was, she still sounded like daddy's little sweetheart on the phone. Since he didn't want to talk to Luann, and Cindy wouldn't speak to him, talking to Ginny was something Buck looked forward to.

He took off again on the highway and slowed to pass the two tourist girls walking along the shoulder away from him. Turning as he approached, they jokingly held out their thumbs, giggling and blushing at their own bravado. Buck went on by, but shit! Couple of little minxes, and one had a face reminded him of that Georgina Spelvin from *Devil in Miss Jones*, the horniest porno flick of Buck's life, which he'd seen the last time he was in Sacramento. *Deep Throat* was something, but this new one, Jesus! Taking it up the butt like that for the whole world to see.

Buck had gotten into whores and porn in Japan and never really gotten out. He wasn't a handsome man, was awkward around women he was attracted to, and generally felt that sex was dirty and should be treated that way. He'd stayed married to Luann mainly because husbands had rights and he deserved his for all her crap he put up with. But that didn't mean he wouldn't take in a sex flick when he was on the road or that he didn't occasionally go for hired pussy in the truck-stop parking lots. Of course, when he was drinking heavy, his appetites had been dulled and it hadn't taken much to keep him satisfied.

Besides, in law enforcement, you had to be damned careful. Whores he'd only do two or three times a year now, at legal brothels over in Nevada. These wild new porn flicks were legal, too, apparently. The theaters where Buck saw them advertised in the Sacramento paper like they were showing Walt Disney. But lately, it had pretty much been Vaseline and *Hustler* that were keeping Buck on an even keel. And with Sally almost live-in help these days because of Norma, he had to make sure everything was put away real good when he wasn't in his room.

Wouldn't the biddies who raised such a stink about the name of the Ore House pizza place have a field day if Sally ever came across Buck's magazines and blabbed? There'd been ore houses and whorehouses both up in this country not so long ago and only damn fools would deny it. And speaking of fools, what about the Board of Supervisors voting 5-0 to protest the Ore House's name and write the State Alcoholic Beverage Commission requesting that the beer and wine license be pulled? Must've taken the commissioners longer to stop laughing than to deny the request. Rick Rodman, the newcomer guy who owned the place, was so pissed he attended the next supervisors' meeting and read the state's decision into the record verbatim.

As far as Buck was concerned, anything he did off duty and in private was way better than what Seth Holmes had done to Janet Carr right under everybody's noses. A teacher, for god's sake, and a married man going on forty, taking advantage of a nineteen-year-old kid. OK, she turned twenty later that summer, and she hadn't been Holmes's student since before he left for the Peace Corps, but Holmes was still lucky her dad didn't shoot him or worse. Old Leland was known for his temper and had made some wild threats.

Janet came home from college down at Chico last June, told her folks she was going to room with Edna Darnell in Goodyear Bar, which they went along with but didn't like, and next minute Holmes had abandoned his wife and their mestizo kid and put his dick in Janet like he thought he was nineteen himself. Thank god Zack Brennan, the school superintendent, took Buck's advice and pressured Holmes into resigning and leaving town. Janet up and went with him, there was a full-scale shit storm, but no blood was shed and gradually things had calmed down.

Sad part was Karen Holmes, who got dumped, seemed like a fine woman, the kind Buck would marry in a minute if he ever had the chance, and that adopted son of hers was as cute as they came. The kid reminded Buck of somebody, but he couldn't place who. Now Karen was suing Holmes's worthless ass for alimony, divorce, and the whole nine yards, while Holmes was suing Zack and the school board for *unfairly* yanking his contract. The only ones happy were that lawyer couple with the mismatched names, since people bickering was what kept 'em employed. She was representing Karen in the divorce while her County Counsel husband would be defending the school district.

Most of the town assumed Buck would end up marrying Sally, and he knew Sally'd say yes if he put the question. Even with her withered arm, he could do a lot worse, but he didn't feel the spark with her he wanted if he took another wife. Just because Buck'd be doing Seth Holmes a favor to marry Karen and get her off Holmes's worthless tail didn't make it a bad idea. The real problem was her being one of those college-grad newcomers who might not give Buck the time of day. But Karen needed more chance to get over her hurt, and for political reasons, too, it would have to be after the election before Buck'd dare try. At least she was more down-to-earth than the rest of the crowd she and her ex used to run with.

God, that social worker Ormond, and Segal, the new doctor, and the *Mountain Mercury* people, and that other teacher, Holmes's buddy, Greg Fulton and his wife, they all thought theirs didn't stink! Wonder whose side Fulton would be on in the divorce? He was supposedly also mixed up in Holmes's lawsuit against the school district. In fact, Buck thought Fulton himself was a scandal waiting to happen—coaching girls' basketball and giving big hugs to all the players like he did every game. A lot of people believed at this point that Seth Holmes and Janet Carr had been playing touchie-feelie back in her school days. Why else would she jump in the sack with him first chance she had? And Janet was no more of a looker than some of those basketball babes of Fulton's.

So what if he was a hotshot on the town's rec-league team and had played college ball at SF State? So what if the girls went undefeated? The school district still should've found a woman coach. Buck was glad Ginny wasn't exposed to that sort of thing in Eureka, not that Ginny was into sports. She'd tried out for cheerleader and almost made it, which Buck thought was darn good. But in the first year ever for girls' competition in the Feather River League, what did Downieville do? Turned red-beard Fulton loose on those kids. The boys' team had an OK season under Coach N, going 2 and 10. Smallest school in the conference, what did people expect? Hell, the town went ape years back, whenever it was, that the boys went 6 and 6.

Then Fulton starts hugging away on the boys' sweaty cousins and sisters along the sidelines this winter and puts up 12-0. Made Coach N's team feel like shit, Buck'd bet, and all that hugging really raised some eyebrows. Coach N's daughter played for Fulton, and Coach N hadn't looked too pleased during the girls' games Buck went to. Neither had Fulton's wife if Buck knew what he was seeing. Only reason the PTA hadn't been all over Zack to put a stop to it is the girls won the championship. The Holmes mess should've wised people up, but everybody was so crazy over winning they made excuses instead of demanding that things be set straight.

Buck also suspected Fulton and his crowd were smoking the old Mary Jane at their parties. What kind of example was that for a teacher to set? If they weren't careful, or if any kids got involved, Fulton would be run out of town—assuming he wasn't jailed instead. Hippies in Pike or Goodyear Bar were one thing, but no way could Buck have townspeople smoking dope right under his nose. And it wouldn't matter that Zack Brennan was a good guy and had been superintendent a long time. He'd be run out too. You had to draw the line somewhere. Zack had bet wrong on Holmes, and Fulton was looking like the next dose of trouble.

From years of handling big rigs and police cruisers Buck was a good driver, but coming into Convict Curve, where he was now, he always checked his speed and made sure he was away from the centerline. The cliff crowds in from the left and the road cuts back around the nose of it so sharp that you couldn't see cars coming at you till they were three feet away.

Buck hadn't been through this spot one time since Frank Pezzola's fatal crash here in 1960 that he didn't wince thinking of him, and today was no exception. Goddamn, life played rough. Frank and Buck had been the same age, born in 1930, and both Downieville natives, but that's where the similarities ended. Buck was part of a prominent town family, while Frank came from a hardscrabble, Italian-American ranch up Pauley Creek at Second Divide.

But Frank had been like Cal, Buck's brother—popular, poised, a basketball star, natural leader, all the things Buck wasn't. You couldn't explain it, but kids like Cal or Frank would come along, maybe five or six years apart, and light the whole place up. Smart, accomplished, good-looking, nothing seemed to get them down. And their stars didn't dim when they left school either. Frank came after Cal, and next after Frank came Marilyn Koontz. When she finished up at junior college and returned home to marry Frank Pezzola, it was like a royal wedding.

A few years later, right on schedule, had come Gina Conrad, now Peterson, who was in her own election battle this year to stay on as County Treasurer. Then Gina was followed by Ernie Warrington, maybe the smartest of the lot, who wasn't a local exactly, but might as well be. Janet Carr had been next in line, which made what Holmes did all the worse. When Cal had died, or Frank, both so young, or when Janet threw her gifts away and left, the town seemed barren as winter.

Tough enough in Buck's case to grow up with a father who was sheriff and on his way to being a legend without having a brother you could never measure up to, and then that brother died and left you wrestling with a ghost. Might have been only five years ago Buck even started feeling like his own man. Sure, Frank Pezzola and Buck had been friendly as classmates, but Buck's only real friend in high school had been Stan White, the minister's son, who carried a lot of the same burdens.

How much of a goody-good were you supposed to be when your pop was preaching sermons at Community Methodist Church every week, or when Huey drove around sporting a two-pound badge? It was cigarettes and beer and not taking shit from anybody that Buck and Stan went for from ninth grade on. Whatever qualms they might've felt over their sneaking and lying had seemed a cheap price.

According to Reverend White, Stan was overseas in the oil business someplace. Buck hadn't seen him since Frank Pezzola's funeral. They'd sure had their laughs in the old days though. If jacking off really could stunt your growth they'd each be a foot shorter and probably still have acne. But later on, when Buck got Luann to fall for him that summer and he told Stan she was pregnant, Stan had gotten so agitated you'd think he'd fucked her himself. Buck was such a jerk back then it hadn't occurred to him that that might be his last memory of their friendship.

His consciousness having turned inward with these thoughts, he didn't really notice as the next mile or two slid by, but Sam Beals' call about a possible drowning abruptly snapped him back to the present. Moments later, by which time Buck's flashing and siren-pulsing cruiser was racing toward the intersection with the Goodyear Bar spur road, his radio gave an additional shot of static, again overridden by Sam's tense voice.

"4:45 p.m. It's the Crandall boy, Toby's his name, 12 years old, who's in the Yuba. Search and Rescue's gone out like you said."

Buck slowed and cut off his warning devices. "No! Goddamn! A local?"

"Yeah, swept in from the Downie say eight or ten minutes ago."

"How'd it happen?"

"Such a warm day that him, the Stark kid and another one got the idea to ride inner tubes." More crackling broke in, followed by an audible breath from Sam. "Thought they'd stop behind the motel, right before the main river. We think two of 'em got out OK, but can't say for sure yet. Crandalls' boy didn't steer to shore quick enough. Went on by, was thrown off his tube the first fifty feet in the big current and ain't been seen since."

"Sweet Jesus!" Buck said. "You have a look at the river this afternoon?"

"During lunch break, and its probably wilder now. Worst thing you can think of. I got grandchildren around here for god's sake."

"OK, I'm just about to Goodyear. Keep me posted and send the van down to work up from there."

"Gotcha. Will do."

CHAPTER 7

Everybody in the Yuba canyon hated the tourist idiots who roared through the towns as though the entire county was open road. As always, Greg crept through Sierra City, and his passengers found people to wave to, who then waved back. This was especially true near the Ore House, which had opened the previous month and thrown the county's moral guardians into a tizzy with its name. Featuring popular host Rick Rodman, good food, cheap beer, and a line-up of acoustic music on weekends, the place was already the newcomers' favorite haunt.

Greg had his window down, and immediately after exchanging greetings with patrons on the Ore House's porch he heard a shrill voice call his name, "Gregory! Hey, Greg!" It was 6-year-old Juan Holmes, across to the left, running his little legs at top speed in an attempt to keep pace. Greg pulled toward him and stopped under a bare-branched locust tree by the sporadically gurgling town fountain. Juan closed the gap and approached on the driver's side.

He was a handsome boy, with olive-brown skin, black hair, bright eyes, a square jaw and an old-fashioned bowl haircut probably authored by Karen, his mom. Moreover, Juan's English was now so good, and his mannerisms so completely colloquial, it was impossible to believe that only four years ago he'd been an orphan in a village in the hinterlands of Central America. An extraordinary kid.

Ned Fulton, Greg and Molly's 4-year-old, loved Juan, Greg loved him, Molly loved him, Karen loved him, and so, Greg was sure, did Seth. Which must be partly why Seth was gone—to let the scandal die down and minimize its impact on *Juanito*. Seth hadn't said so, but that's how he would think. Yet what really mattered was that none of the events disrupting Juan's life this past year should have happened.

Puffing and gasping from the exertion of his run, Juan looked up at Greg as everyone leaned out the car windows to say hello.

"Where's Ned?" Juan asked.

"Ned's home today," Greg told the boy. "Toby's taking care of him. We went to a meeting in Sierra Valley."

"I love Toby," said Juan.

"He loves you, too," Pat Crandall said. She was Toby's mother, so Juan accepted that she could speak for him.

"Can I go play with them?" Juan asked. "And Jojo?"

Jojo was the Fulton's Labrador Retriever. "Next weekend, OK?" Molly replied. "It's too late now. Where's your mom?"

"Working. At the Ore House."

"Well," said Greg, "That's news." He knew Karen Holmes needed money. Why not the Ore House? She'd held a variety of odd jobs since Seth left, probably a further reason that her hair and eyes had lost some of their luster and that the newcomer group was seeing so much less of her.

"She lets me come there, too…and I get…pizza!" Juan bounced up onto his toes twice in rapid succession. "That's where I'm going."

"Be sure to say you saw us, OK?" Molly said. "I promise to call her this week."

"OK, bye-bye." Juan turned and trotted off.

"What a doll," Sandra said with finality. Both she and Ian had professional reasons not to segue into casual discussion of Seth and his family. Greg and Molly had personal ones. Greg held his breath, hoping that everyone's reasons would be respected.

"He is," Pat nodded, aware of all this and gently taking up the slack. "It's great to see him doing so well."

No one had a word to add. Relieved, Greg resumed his westward route, downshifting to take the curves as the Travelall dropped toward the river. The encounter with Juan had again put Greg's mind ruminating, but this time his focus was people, not geography. And somehow, despite their being almost too new to think of as close friends, Ian and Sandra headed the list.

They were the first two-lawyer couple he'd known, doing their best to endure the local disapproval provoked by Sandra's calm insistence on retaining her own name. "Not really married, you know," was the rumor that never died among the town's understimulated dowagers. It was nothing like the firestorm Seth had triggered, but a woman's not automatically claiming her husband's identity was still of note.

Both from the Atlantic seaboard, they had reached Sierra County after employment sojourns in urban California. Since Jim Crandall was from Chicago and Pat from Santa Barbara, with or without the presence of Peace Corps alumni like the Holmeses, the newcomers thought themselves a worldly bunch. The Fultons might have traveled the shortest distance from their roots, because they'd grown up in the Sacramento area, but they had met as VISTA volunteers in New Mexico and had lived in Berkeley. Greg got his teaching credential there while Molly, as primary breadwinner, had been a section chief for the city library.

At 45, their friend Drew Ormond, the County Welfare Department's lone social worker, was the oldest of the current newcomers and had been around longest. These factors as well as his garrulous empathy for the adjustments they were all going through had made him their indispensable social nucleus. And when the Holmeses came back from Nicaragua to reclaim Seth's teaching position, it began to seem a golden time.

Greg had heard about Seth Holmes and Seth's unpaid leave from Downieville High long before meeting him. Nonetheless, Seth's charisma and his reputation as the school's all-time best teacher had not prevented Karen and him from having felt so isolated during their initial stint in the county that they had almost decided not to return. While they knew they'd miss the mountains and the pristine air, Seth could easily have found another job. Now he was faced with finding one, and Greg was responsible for some of why it hadn't turned out to be easy.

Overall, however, the group continued to flourish. Henry and Meg Segal, the west county's new, young physician and wife, had been in town nearly a year, and without intending it, more or less replaced the Holmeses. And to complete the roster, Drew had enlisted his hippie neighbors Edna Darnell, Om Gillette and her boyfriend Jared Smith, who had more in common with the straight, college-educated newcomers than they did with anyone else around.

At first Greg's having a neatly trimmed beard had itself been mildly shocking—for a teacher, that is—yet now the free-flowing, drop-in parties at the Crandalls or at Drew's cabin in nearby Goodyear Bar could probably qualify as shocking to those bent on being shocked. Everyone's limits were honored, but dope was discreetly smoked, wine flowed freely, the music was loud, anti-establishment politics were continuously debated, joking never stopped, and sexual innuendo was thick. Or put another way, precisely Greg's definition of fun.

As for children, in the core group the Crandalls had three and the Fultons and Holmeses one each, with Edna Darnell's son from Goodyear Bar frequently around as well. Moreover, an additional child was on the way, since Meg Segal was visibly and nervously pregnant—so nervous that Greg and Molly enjoyed teasing that she'd have never dared to reproduce if her husband weren't a doctor. Nor was she the only one to find comfort in that. He was the town's first MD in some time, placed via an NIH grant after interning in Texas.

The group's attitude toward the kids was inclusive and tribal, with childcare readily traded and activities like fishing, hiking and swimming automatically shared, though ten-year-old Stevo Crandall, bright, but wheelchair-bound and heavily speech-impaired due to cerebral palsy, was a special case. He adored his brother Toby, who could understand him when no one else could, and provided steady part-time employment for Om Gillette on the days and nights that Pat Crandall was helping Jim meet the newspaper's weekly deadline.

Eventually the Travelall reached the canyon bottom and drew even with the river. The highway through this stretch was an underappreciated feat of engineering, sometimes cantilevered above the streambed and sometimes running on benches blasted into the granite of what had been box canyons. Greg checked his watch. It wasn't quite 4:25 and they had a half dozen miles to go. Here partially leafed-out oaks and maples outnumbered the pines, while vertical patches of lupine and poppies shone in the angled sunlight wherever there was soil enough to take root.

But it was the water that commanded attention. Swollen with the peak of the day's snowmelt, the North Yuba was wilder now than at noon, when they'd been heading east, and even then they'd all commented on its raging force.

Bank-to-bank, the carved, boulder-strewn bed was fifty or sixty feet wide, though summer flows, so pleasurable for swimming and fishing, filled no more than half that space. Spring runoff took it all, surging nearly to the pavement in some places, geysering upward where submerged or barely visible obstacles created resistance, and alternating elsewhere between the purposeful, taut, glassine surface of a milky-green ocean wave about to break, and the hurling, rushing foam of that same wave finally broken. The sound, too, could suggest the ocean. In Downieville the Yuba's storm-fed churning, with boulders driven downstream like bowling pins, was sometimes so loud it roused Greg from his sleep.

"How the hell are our beloved tourists from the flatlands going to fish in *that* next weekend?" he asked, not expecting an answer.

Facing backward, Pat had a quiet interchange going with Sandra, which Ian ignored while craning to observe more of the scenery. At Greg's side Molly seemed lost in her thoughts. From behind, though, Jim was ready for conversation.

"Oh, they'll wet a line somehow, and maybe drown doing it," he replied. "I plan to dust off last year's story, tweak the headline, and pop it back onto page one. Right next to *Two More Chilcutt Boys Busted* you'll read *Yuba Ripe for Trout Opener.*"

"I'd rather you did that than list my favorite side-streams," Greg laughed. "But why not forgo the bullshit and make it factual?"

"What? Like *Crummy Fishing Expected This Year?*"

"No, just skip the whole thing. Until some year when conditions *are* ripe."

"Because, my friend," Jim said with slight harshness, "the tourists need to see an upbeat headline and an upbeat story to ensure that they patronize my big advertisers... who, as you know, are the motels and Jerry Vargas's Downieville Hardware, where every bait and lure known to mankind just happen to be for sale. No reader has ever complained that the *Merc* misled them, some bozo always catches something, and I enjoy cashing the checks of the aforesaid advertisers."

This brought Molly out of her reverie. "God," she said, "how cynical."

"Practical or cynical, take your pick." Jim responded, still with an edge. "What the *Merc* needs is to keep its friends and not add to its enemies."

"Maybe you're right," Molly said. "Practical is important. Endorsing Ken Pritchard for sheriff will be tricky enough."

"I'm voting for Pritchard," Jim stated. "Who says I'll be endorsing him?"

"What?" several voices exclaimed at once, Pat's not included.

"Shows what you know about practical," Jim shot back. "And it figures. Pat and I are the only ones in the car who don't draw a government paycheck."

"Oh, come on!" Sandra jumped in. "Cheap shot." Her cheeks were flushed.

"Not so cheap. Stop by my office and look in the files. Go back four years, to the last local election, when the Newfields owned the *Merc*. Yeah, they endorsed, but who? Candidates running unopposed, or the sure-thing, west-county winners. In the close races, where east-county influence was strong, no endorsements. Just pabulum about 'may the best man win'…and those candidates *were* all men, by the way. Loyalton already had Foley in as Sheriff by then, but 1970 is when they took over the DA and the Assessor.

"I could do the same this year, endorse shoe-ins like Marilyn Pezzola for Clerk-Auditor, and stiff both Buck and Pritchard. But I'm not. Pat agrees. The *Merc* isn't endorsing at all. I'll run some boilerplate about saluting the democratic process. It's more honest than what the Newfields did, and maybe Buck and his cronies will be a little less pissed off if I don't single them out."

"Buck! What do you care about Buck?" Molly demanded.

"I care that his cronies keep buying ads," Jim said. "And he has tons of cronies. He's Huey Thompson's son, for god's sake. Huey was sheriff in this county for forty years."

"Christ, Jim!" Greg implored. "You're going to look the other way on Buck's drinking, and on his beating his wife and daughter?"

"Listen, I checked that all out. He's clean on the drinking. Quit five or six years ago. And there's nothing on the books anywhere about spousal abuse, which would've been years back, too, before his divorce. Nobody I can find will even talk to me, much less on the record. Not that I doubt the rumors. His older daughter seems to hate his guts."

"There's got to be something somewhere," Ian said. "What got him kicked off the police force in Redding or Eureka, wherever it was? I hear he was driving truck when Curt Foley picked him up."

"I told you, nothing on the books. Good service record and a voluntary termination. The truck-driving part's true, and if I had anything else, I'd run it as news, not opinion. Let people draw their own conclusions."

"And you would run it?" Molly pressed.

"Hell, yes. I'm not that big a whore. We have stringers county-wide and work hard to cover the whole place…fairly. Reading the *Merc* every week may be the one thing the west and east have in common. I'm sunk if I let that slip away. Damn! Why'd we get onto this? Let's shut up and look at the river."

"Well," Sandra said peckishly, "if it's legal back-up you're worried about, and you do get something on Buck, I'm your girl...pro bono. I'd love to have a go at him."

Since spirited discussions were common among the newcomers, Greg wasn't worried about a damaging personal flare-up, but looking at the river is what he wanted to do. They were near the end of their trip, and it was more spectacular here than in town, where the canyon walls opened up at its confluence with the smaller, more placid Downie. This would be his best chance for the rest of the week to watch the Yuba really rip, so any attention he could spare from the last mile of highway he gave to the frothing, roiling water.

Coming in from the upcountry wilderness, tourists and locals alike found Downieville, with its population of 325, a bastion of civilization. The river and highway made a sweeping right-hand curve, and suddenly, against a background of piney slopes, were overarching elms and a row of the town's grandest houses, set among hydrangeas, lilacs, lawns and picket fences. Also in that block stood the prim, white saltbox of the Methodist Church, sagging out of true from the strain of supporting a three-story bell tower on a foundation of century-old logs. And as with the Sierra Buttes, Greg could feel the effect that the sight of Bridge Street had on him and on his passengers by being so familiar, and yet so distinctive, a part of their lives.

To the right at the end of the block was Pearl Street, which would take them to the Crandalls', a few doors up, where he'd drop Jim and Pat. Further along he'd cross a one-lane bridge over the Downie River before leaving Ian and Sandra at their place. Then would be the drive through town and home to call Henry Segal.

Virtually every structure on that whole route, he realized absently, without knowing whether it had significance or not, was occupied by someone whose name he could recite as he passed, which his mind often did. But there would apparently be plenty of light for tennis, despite the fact that he and Molly were running late. Of course Ned, who was always thrilled to have Toby Crandall to himself for an afternoon, would think his parents had gotten home too soon. Slowing, Greg began to negotiate the corner.

"If any of you are cooking tonight," Pat said, launching into the planning for another potluck, "come cook at our house. We'll all be on the job tomorrow, so let's enjoy while we can. I'm nearly sure Drew and Om are available." She paused. "Oh, Greg ...invite the

Segals, since you'll be seeing Henry. Tell them Meg can come anytime. She doesn't have to wait for him to get off the courts. I really
haven't..."

Greg was partway onto Pearl Street when Pat's voice was
eclipsed by the screeching decibels of the emergency siren in the
town plaza near the post office. Deafeningly, two longs and a short,
two longs and a short, two longs and a short, with dozens of unseen
dogs howling accompaniment. That meant search and rescue, not a
fire. At least nobody's house was going up, and a weekend rescue at
this time of year was most likely a tourist. Greg regained speed, but
Pat didn't resume her thought.

In the street outside the Crandalls' house stood their social
worker friend Drew Ormond, waving frantically for Greg to hurry.
Next to Drew was Stevo Crandall, in his wheelchair, thrashing
wildly, his ears apparently in pain from the siren.

"Oh, god! What's Drew doing with Stevo?" Jim said to Pat.
"Lisa was supposed to take care of him today, while Toby babysat
Ned."

Greg exchanged a look with Molly. Lisa was the Crandalls' oldest, a high school sophomore. It was hard to think that his innocent
and compliant son would one day present the same kind of problem, but Greg knew from his own growing up that when Ned
reached the right—or was that wrong—age, any number of lapses
could be expected, some more major than this.

"If she's ditched," Pat said emphatically, "I'm going to raise
hell. Damn teenagers! They turn fifteen and think they're twenty-
one."

CHAPTER 8

The instant Greg stopped, Pat and Jim jumped from the
Travelall to converge on Drew and Stevo. By the time Greg, Molly,
and the lawyer couple, Ian and Sandra, followed, Pat had knelt near
the wheelchair to comfort the boy, stroking his head and crooning
that everything would be OK. Stevo ceased thrashing, but quietly
mumbled a repeating string of words Greg couldn't understand.

BELONGING

Drew Ormond hugged Jim, a usual greeting where Drew was concerned, but his face was drained of color and he pulled Jim toward the porch steps to sit.

Jim resisted. "Where's our daughter?" he demanded.

Drew took a deep breath. "Lisa's fine. I told her to go, that I'd take Stevo."

The lanky Drew, in a workshirt, jeans and open nylon shell jacket, stood several inches taller than anyone. With his Van Dyke beard, sharp features, and long, wavy, graying hair, he had always struck Greg as a '70s country cousin of *The Three Musketeers*. But none of his normal jauntiness was present. In Drew's social work job Greg had occasionally seen him at school, and it was that on-duty persona being projected now.

"Told Lisa to go where?" Jim insisted.

"Jim," Drew said, "Lisa's not the problem. Please, please sit down. Pat, come over here. You sit, too."

"For god's sake, what's happening?" There was a hint of panic in Pat's tone.

She stood and wheeled Stevo a few feet to the porch steps, pausing to wipe some of his saliva from her cheek with the sleeve of her blouse. Drew steadied the wheelchair with one hand and pushed Pat onto the middle step with the other. Jim squatted near her but didn't sit. Greg and the others pressed closer, agog at Drew's behavior.

"I'm...I'm...so sorry," Drew's voice broke. "Toby's lost in the river. I'm so sorry. If I'd only known, I could have stopped him!"

Pat said nothing, but her upturned face showed the bewildered pain of a pietà.

"My son?" Jim asked, dumbfounded. "Which river?"

"The Yuba," Drew blurted. "Eight or ten minutes ago. Search and Rescue's going out. That's what the siren was."

"My god, no!" Pat shrieked. "No! No!"

Molly threw herself into Greg's chest and latched on. "Ned! Ned!" she moaned. "Is Ned all right?" Greg's knees nearly buckled with her extra weight and the shock of what he'd heard. If Toby Crandall, the Fultons' babysitter, was in the river, where *was* their son Ned?

Pat began to weep uncontrollably, grasping Jim with such force that he more fell onto the steps beside her than sat. Stevo, agitated again, raised the pitch of his monotone babble, and Greg realized that he'd been saying "Oby, plash, plash...Oby, plash, plash..." again and again. Sandra looked helplessly from Pat to Stevo, while Ian, Orioles baseball cap down to his ears, sought details.

"Jesus, Drew! Tell us what happened! What can we do?"

Drew struggled to compose himself. "Molly, Greg...Ned's OK. He's with Om at your place." Tears ran from Drew's eyes. "She and I met Toby and Ned in the laundromat. They'd walked downtown for candy. Toby was invited to play with some older boys. They said Ned couldn't come, so Om took him home. Toby planned to be back in an hour. It all seemed so routine."

It *was* routine, Greg thought. Exactly how their group always functioned. Everyone looked out for everyone else. Molly, recovered somewhat but still forcefully leaning into him, turned to face Drew. Huddled together, Jim and Pat listened intently, their expressions deformed by disbelief and horror.

"What about the river?" Molly asked, prodding for more.

"I only know what Lisa told me." On the verge of hyperventilating, Drew could barely go on. "She'd taken Stevo for a walk, and crossing the main bridge over the Downie, she saw three boys floating toward her on inner tubes. The third was Toby, paddling to catch up. He recognized her and waved. They went under the bridge and she watched the first two swing onto the beach behind the motel. Toby was too far out in the current to get to shore."

"I heard screaming," he continued hoarsely, "and came out of the laundromat just as Lisa rolled Stevo by calling for help. Toby got swept into the Yuba and was thrown off his tube right away. I took the wheelchair and told Lisa to find the other boys. I ran to the motel office with Stevo, had them call the Sheriff, then ran back here to call again. Just as I got off, the alarm sounded. Oh, god," Drew finished, "I'm so sorry!"

Jim jumped to his feet. "We should be at the river! Below town! He's hanging onto a rock or snag. Somebody's got to pull him out!"

"People ran down that way already," Drew said, now collapsed on the steps with an arm around Pat. "They're having Search and Rescue try everyplace from here to Goodyear Bar."

"I'm going, too!" Jim exclaimed, twitching and reaching for his car keys.

Stevo began wailing, and Pat freed herself from Drew to tend to her son. Her surviving son, Greg thought. It was inconceivable that any human being could come out of that water alive. A thousand-to-one shot, or worse. Greg shuddered, but tried to hold steady for Molly's sake.

"Jim, no!" Drew protested. "It's too late. There's nothing you can do but stay put till the sheriff calls. Be here for Pat and Stevo. I'll bring Lisa home." Drew rose and forced Jim back down.

"The historical society!" Jim yowled in anguished frustration. "We were at the fucking historical society!"

"Molly," Drew went on, "you and Greg see after Ned. He and Om probably don't know yet. Ian, run to Henry's and have him bring his medical bag. These people will need sedatives."

"I'll stick with Pat and Jim," Sandra put in. "Ian, scoot! Scoot!" she said to her husband, who dashed away to find Henry Segal.

"Drew's right," Molly agreed. "That's what we have to do." She strode from Greg to embrace Pat. "There's hope. Really. I just know they'll find him."

Drew departed on foot while Greg and Molly got in the Travelall and Greg, feeling he was in suspended animation, laboriously turned it around in the narrow street. When they reached the main bridge over the Downie, they had almost overtaken Drew, who veered off the sidewalk at the far end to follow a fishermen's path to the river along the back wall of the Gold Pan Motel. Greg stopped halfway across the span to observe.

On the rocky beach, with the swollen Downie at her feet and the terrifying Yuba raging across from left to right, was Lisa Crandall, her blonde hair flinging as she convulsively yelled downstream, toward Greg and Molly's house at the other end of town. Drew reappeared, stumbling among the rocks past two discarded inner tubes and two hysterical, shivering boys in soggy jeans and soaking white T-shirts. Billy Stark and Lou Bishop. Greg knew them from school. A door thumped and Pete Lowry, the owner of the motel, started down the back stairs with blankets under his arm.

In a daze, Greg continued a short block on Bridge until it dead-ended at Main, opposite the plaza, the post office and the hardware store, where he turned to follow the board sidewalks and vaguely New-England storefronts past the Quartz Cafe and the Hi-Grade Market to turn again on Prospect Street. There would be no tennis or anything else normal tonight—for anybody. Immediately ahead was the rusted steel bridge across the Yuba that led to Greg and Molly's neighborhood, and to the courthouse, the health clinic, and the Forest Service station.

Greg couldn't bear to look at the water as they crossed, knowing that it had carried a flailing, desperate Toby in its crest only moments before. Molly, biting her lip, was as silent as outer space. Even so, they couldn't avoid seeing figures in orange Search and Rescue vests walking slowly along the brushy levee where the river channel curved out of view near Rososco Ravine. Below there, the canyon narrowed again and was so deep and wooded all the way to Goodyear that even getting in on foot was tough and trying to scan it from the highway would be useless.

Greg took the turn into their driveway at such a poor angle that he grazed the wisteria arbor before slamming to a halt behind Molly's VW. Om Gillette and Ned Fulton were on the porch, and Ned came running to Molly's door of the Travelall the moment it opened. She fell on her knees to engulf him. Greg plunged around and crouched to do the same, while Om watched from a few feet away. Through a distorting film of unshed tears, Greg could read puzzlement and concern on her face. Then the Fultons' black Lab Jojo, tail wagging happily, nuzzled in to block Greg's view.

"Mommy, Daddy," Ned said, pulling away. "Something happened."

"What did happen?" Om asked as she stepped onto the lawn. "We heard the siren, and Jojo was yiping his head off."

Greg looked up at her, framed against the tangle of budding Virginia creeper that hung from the porch railing. Beyond the fact that Om didn't know, she would blame herself horribly when she found out. Greg smelled the stink of his own armpits.

Copying what Drew had done, Greg rose from his crouch, left Molly and Ned, and led Om to the porch steps to sit. His nostrils now also registered the mix of herbal oils she used as perfume. He sat, too. Jojo dropped himself at Greg's feet.

Om was from Tucson and claimed to be part Apache, though part Gypsy would be as good a guess. She favored hoop earrings, scarves tied in her long black hair, flowing hand-made skirts, and a multiplicity of metal bracelets.

Although her face and body were pleasingly round, Om wouldn't be called overweight, but she was secretive about her age. She could be as young as 25 or as old as 35, and Greg's sense of where she fell in that range varied from day to day. But among hippies or straights, she had no enemies, and her patient, engaging manner was a constant.

BELONGING

Molly and Ned walked hand-in-hand toward Greg. "Om," he began, "we don't know how to tell you, but the siren was for Toby."

"What?...How?" she gasped.

"When is Toby coming back?" Ned asked.

Tears showed on Molly's cheeks. She tried to say something, but couldn't.

"Toby's lost in the river," Greg continued for her. "They're searching all the way down to Goodyear."

Om was stunned. "But I just saw him," she said. "He went with those older kids, Billy and Lou, for an hour. That's why I'm here."

"We know," Molly managed to say.

"Wow! Toby got to go swimming," Ned exclaimed.

"Om, somehow the boys decided to ride inner tubes in the Downie. That was crazy enough, but..." Greg went on to tell Om and Ned what he knew, while Molly cried softly and hugged them both. As the story sank in, Om put her face in her hands, wept, then sat barely breathing.

"Why are Om and Mommy crying?" Ned asked.

"Because they're afraid Toby will stay lost," Greg answered.

"You mean like Juan's dad?"

"No, that he'll drown...that he'll be dead."

"Toby's a good swimmer," Ned insisted. "I saw him last year."

"I know, son, but the current is very strong now. And super cold. Even Daddy couldn't swim in it. That's why we never, never go near the river till summertime."

"Oh...will Toby be OK?"

"Maybe...maybe. But Mommy and I are really scared for him."

Ned thought for a moment. "What's for dinner? I'm hungry. Can Om stay?"

Molly found her voice. "Sure, if she wants. I'll make spaghetti. Drew and Sandra are with Toby's mom and dad. Om needs people with her, too. The only thing we can do is wait till he's found."

"And pray," Om said in a despairing whisper. "God," she went on, "how will I ever face Pat? Or Jim? If I'd just done my laundry this morning like I planned, Toby would've had to stay with Ned. This is all because I rode into town with Drew two hours ago."

"Om," Greg said, "it isn't your fault. You couldn't have known. You did exactly what Molly or Pat or Jim or I would have wanted. Drew is going through hell himself, but it's not his fault either. The boys never said anything about swimming, did they?"

"No," Om sighed. "Not a word. They were going to catch frogs in some ditch. Billy's mom knows how to cook frogs' legs."

"I wanted to go but they wouldn't let me," Ned announced. "I was mad."

"Thanks for the invite," Om said, somberly linking arms with Molly and Ned, "but I'm going to Crandalls'. I've got to see Pat...and Stevo. Tell them it will be OK. We can't lose Toby like this. We just can't."

"You're right," Molly agreed. "There *is* hope. We have to believe."

"Let's all go to Toby's," Ned said. "We can be there when he comes home."

Greg picked up Ned and held him. "No, Mommy wants to cook here tonight. Pat and Jim don't feel good now, so Om can help Stevo." The life so obviously coursing in his son's body was a gift beyond measure.

"OK," Ned squirmed disappointedly. "But stop, Daddy. That hurts. You're holding me too tight."

* * *

Buck sat in his office with the lights off trying to think. It was past 8:30, and it'd been dark outside for an hour. From the lobby area he could hear Donny Remo, the night dispatcher, relaying something to a deputy in the east county. Search and Rescue had brought the Crandall boy's body into the morgue from the lower end of Rososco Ravine a short time earlier, and young Ernie Warrington, the team coordinator, had just left after briefing Buck on details. A miracle that the body had even been recovered, with the river the way it was. Of course, they'd all been hoping for a greater miracle, but the deck was so stacked against it nobody'd really believed the heat packs, the oxygen mask and the syringe of adrenaline in the rescue van would end up being used. And they'd been right. A body bag and a stretcher were the only equipment needed.

Rick Conrad and Alex Darnell had spotted the kid's white T-shirt in a rockbound eddy just east of the Kohl orchard, across the canyon from the highway and a hundred or more vertical feet down through the forest canopy from where the Jeep track ends. Because it was dusk, they'd thought maybe they were seeing foam or a loose piece of cloth, but the boy turned out to be there too. They'd radioed the find to Ernie, who'd put the van in four-wheel and gone to make the retrieval. By then Buck had turned his cruiser into a command post a mile downstream at the Goodyear bridge, which was where Ernie found him to confirm that the search was over.

Since the river'd been hissing past the bridge at better than twenty miles an hour the whole time, and there was a yard-high standing wave down the middle of it like the ruff of an attacking animal, Buck had figured the body might've gone on by without anyone knowing. At least this way they had an answer, but he still had to get positive ID, then break the news to the family. Ernie would keep things quiet until Buck made it official.

This was the worst part of the job and made Buck wonder why he ever wanted to be Sheriff. But all those years when Buck was growing up Huey had notified the families, in person if humanly possible, and he'd driven the county in some pretty ridiculous weather to do it. Curt had been less conscientious, but Curt'd still done his share. Nowadays, though, not that many people died of unnatural causes in Sierra County, and none in Buck's experience had been local kids. If it had hurt like it did for Frank Pezzola or his brother Cal going in their twenties, how much more would it hurt if they'd been twelve? An unanswerable question, but Buck was about to off-load a corner of his distress.

Neither he nor any of Ernie's search team knew the Crandall boy well enough to ID him, and it shouldn't fall to the parents. That'd be cruel, especially with the body beat-up like Ernie said. Besides, a bereaved family deserved certainty. When they heard from Buck, they shouldn't have to go through twenty minutes of false hope that it was some other kid, not theirs. In other words, the red-bearded Mr. Greg Fulton was about to have himself a little chore.

The guy lived a block away, had plenty of past contact with the boy, and would certainly want to spare the parents. Of course Fulton might pass out or pee his pants in the process, but Buck wanted to see what the guy was made of. Buck stood and went into the lighted lobby.

"Be gone about an hour, Donny," he said to the dispatcher. "Got to ID the body and go tell the family. I'll check back with you before I call it a night."

"Don't worry about this place, boss. Head home when you can and get some sleep. We need you rested for campaigning."

"Depends on how I feel. Might rather talk."

"OK," Donny nodded. "Your choice."

Buck let himself out and walked down the wide courthouse steps, past his cruiser and across the dark, empty parking lot. To his right was the road department, in a converted miner's cottage beneath the town's largest hawthorn tree.

About the time of the election it would be so dense with pink flowers everything nearby would seem to change color. Straight ahead was the health clinic, in another converted miner's cottage, adjoining two vacant lots. Just up from the second lot was Fulton's driveway. There were a million stars and no moon. The river, its flow gradually diminishing as night slowed the upcountry melt, had begun to sound benign and familiar, a music Buck remembered from outside his bedroom window all those years growing up. The air was warmly sweet, too, like the breath of that one geisha he had met in Japan, and that he thought about every spring.

Who the hell was Fulton kidding, Buck wondered. Newly hired at the high school, second teaching job of his life people said, and he buys a four-bedroom house, the nicest in this part of town, with a river view, where the assistant manager of the Bush Creek Mine had always lived. That mine produced truckloads of ingots worth more than you could imagine, and had stayed in business most of a century. Buck made $13,500 a year as Undersheriff. What did Fulton make? Two-thirds that? You don't buy any four-bedroom house on a salary of under $10K. Think how the other teachers lived. That wife of his probably came from money. She looked it. And they had two nice cars to boot.

Buck lived the opposite direction, across the river, up behind the Hi-Grade Market, in his Daddy's old place. Three bedrooms, counting the addition, but not half the square feet Fulton had. Huey Thompson had been a legend around here. There was no young teacher deserved a nicer house than Huey, especially a teacher living off his wife's money. You add that to how Fulton carried on with his basketball girls, and Buck was hoping he might smell something funny being smoked when he knocked on the door. If he did, he'd do a follow-up investigation—after the election, that is. As he'd said plenty of times, where teachers were concerned, you couldn't let things get out of hand.

CHAPTER 9

Since Jojo was asleep, there'd been no warning bark, and Greg hadn't heard footsteps on the porch, so the sudden knock startled him forward in his chair. He and Molly had leadenly finished eating, gotten Ned off to bed, and were in the living room trying to watch *Upstairs, Downstairs* on PBS, afraid to talk and afraid to think. Grading student papers for tomorrow was impossible as well.

"I'm too drained," Molly said when a second knock quickly followed. "You go."

"OK." A stranger would use the doorbell, Greg thought as he got up. This was probably Ian sent by Sandra with an update.

She had walked home from Crandalls' and called during the Fultons' dinner, confirming Om's arrival to help and the continued lack of news. Pat and daughter Lisa had accepted medication from Henry Segal, while Jim and Drew were quietly consuming a bottle of Scotch. The idea had been not to call in or out on Crandalls' phone so their line would stay open.

Bracing himself for the worst, he went into the hall and swung back the door to reveal, bizarrely, Sheriff Thompson.

"Sorry to bother you," Buck said, "but I could use some help."

"Huh?" Greg was disconcerted to have the County Sheriff right in front of him, and holding the door open emphasized the river noise, echoing up through town. It was the beautiful spring night of a beautiful spring day, which seemed oppressively wrong under the circumstances.

"OK if I come in?" Buck asked with his strangled smile, another thing about the guy that always turned Greg off. Buck was the last person Greg wanted to see.

"It's business…heh, heh," Buck went on, adding an awkward laugh. "But no warrant or anything."

Greg was used to being taller than people he dealt with. He wasn't that much taller than Buck, but with Buck's girth, and his saucer hat, and with the porch a step below the threshold, Buck might have been a uniformed dwarf — or troll. "Sure, welcome,"

Greg said reluctantly, standing aside. "Molly," he called. "It's the Sheriff. Business, he says."

"Nice place you got here," Buck said, once he was in the hall amidst Greg and Molly's new floor-to-ceiling bookcases. "Must have caught old Clarence Dunkirk in a good mood when you bought it off him."

"Thanks. We did all right. Lucky, I guess."

What was this, Greg wondered, a campaign visit? And in uniform, yet. After that stupid crack about no warrant, it would have been tasty if they'd had a Pritchard poster lying on the foyer table. Accompanied by a curious Jojo, Molly came up behind Greg and looked guardedly at Buck, who was rocking on his heels and loudly breathing in through his nose.

"Mrs. Fulton," Buck nodded, removing his hat to acknowledge her. "Guess, that's spaghetti sauce I smell. Reminds me I haven't been home yet for my own dinner."

"What kind of business?" Molly replied. "Is there word on Toby Crandall."

"'Fraid that's what brought me."

"How do you mean?" Greg's gut twisted and he heard Molly draw a sharp breath.

"Family doesn't know yet, but we found a body below Rososco Ravine. It figures to be him, but I'd like Mr. Fulton to help with ID before I trouble the parents. You folks knew the boy, and it'd be a big help."

Ned came to the top of the stairs and called down, "Who are you talking to, Daddy? Did Toby come home?"

"You should go," Molly said, squeezing Greg's arm. "I'll get Ned back to sleep." Then, starting up the stairs, she said, "It's somebody from Mommy's work, sweetheart. I'm coming for another kiss. We don't know about Toby yet." Greg had never seen her move so stiffly or look so pale.

Though what he was agreeing to do hadn't entirely sunk in, Greg said, "Sure, Sheriff, lead on," and followed Buck outside. They cleared Greg's driveway, dog-legged a short distance down the street and started across the deserted courthouse parking lot. The building's only lights were in a left front window, where Greg saw a deputy, striped by the slats of the venetian blinds, sitting at a radio console wearing a headset.

Buck didn't make for the main door. He went down the side of the building ahead of Greg in the dark, leather belt and boots squeaking with each step. Walking easily despite his growing apprehension, Greg could hear the squeak of Buck's gear more than see him, but Greg still couldn't ignore the absurd way the guy moved. Maybe his underwear was too tight, or he had hemorrhoids, because Buck didn't stride forward, he pivoted—left, then right, left, then right—legs apart, in a linked series of semicircles, yet he covered a lot of ground.

"Morgue is back this way," Buck said over his shoulder. "In the basement."

By the time Greg caught up, Buck had descended a short concrete ramp, unlocked the heavy door, and flipped on a sparse row of buzzing fluorescent lights in the corridor. Racks of custodial supplies and extra police equipment lined the walls.

"Excuse the mess," Buck said. "We got 1970s government all crammed into a 1934 courthouse."

Squeak-squeak, pivot-pivot, Buck preceded Greg to an interior door and unlocked that. The only sound not made by his escort or the overhead lights was his own breathing.

They entered a small bunker of a room with a grated drain in the concrete floor beneath a flat stainless-steel table. The end wall held three shiny metal doors, each about thirty inches on a side. The lower two were at knee height, while the upper was shoulder high and off-center to the left. To its right, where a fourth door would be, was a deep recess in the wall, at the mouth of which sat an open cardboard box labeled Rubber Gloves - 500 Pair. The upper door had a file card taped to it and so did one of the two below. Standing at Buck's shoulder, Greg could make out that the lower card read JOHN DOE - April 21, 1974 and the upper, FLYNN - ECV.

"Done this sort of thing before?" Buck asked companionably.

"No." Dread welled through him, and Greg's tongue had trouble managing even that one syllable.

"Never get used to it, I don't think."

"Probably not. I helped carry a corpse on a stretcher, back when I was teaching on the Navajo Reservation. An old woman who'd collapsed in her garden. We didn't know for sure she was dead at the time."

"This'll be different. I haven't seen him yet myself, but I'm told he was beat up bad on the rocks. Won't be pretty."

"I'm ready when you are." Greg's eye began twitching and he fought to control it.

Buck leaned over the JOHN DOE door, released a catch with his thumb, and pulled out a drawer containing a child weighing no more than a hundred pounds with his feet pointing away from Greg, his face and neck uncovered, and his body draped in a double-folded bedsheet. He knew instinctively it was Toby. The facial structure, the hair, the lips and the shape of the forehead left no room for doubt. Yet the longer he looked, even when he stepped closer, the less of Toby he saw. He gasped quietly, expecting tears he might not be able to hide, though none came.

"Jesus," Buck said. "Breaks your heart. It him?"

"Yeah, it's him."

"Positive enough to sign papers?"

"Yeah, whatever you need." Greg moved a step closer. It was Toby — the warm-hearted boy who had always been so solicitous of Ned, such a welcome fixture in their lives — yet it wasn't. More accurately it was a hideous wax-museum replica, blue-green from lack of oxygen, blotched with bluish-yellow bruises, showing a welter of bloodless cuts and a deep vertical gash behind the ear and up into the scalp. The eyes were open, the jaw locked in an expression of terror like the model for Edward Munch's famous painting. Greg experienced a rush of dizziness and felt his gorge rise, but he was determined not to lurch into Buck or provide any clue.

"Can I close 'er?" Buck asked. "I'm guessing a bunch of broken bones, too, from what I saw before putting the sheet over him, but that don't relate to your purposes."

"Sure, go ahead and close." Greg also concealed the relief he felt. "That's all I need …more than, actually."

"Know what you mean. They're always a nasty color, the drowning victims, but I never seen one so beat up." The drawer slid again and clicked shut.

"You'll have to come upstairs for the papers," Buck went on. "We don't do autopsies or that down here. There's a mortuary we contract with in Nevada City. They'll pick him up tonight now we've established ID. Then bring him back for the funeral, if that's what the family wants."

"When does the family find out? And how?"

"In ten minutes, say. Soon as I'm done with you I'll go over and tell 'em…face-to-face."

Greg was impressed. "You always do that?"

"Try to. Hate it, but I try like hell. Just like my daddy did. Seems the only right thing."

"I agree."

"To end on a lighter note," Buck tapped the shiny surface of the upper drawer, "let me tell you about Flynn. He's on the coldest setting, embalmed in a used tuxedo, waiting for the Clampers to stick him in the ground over in Poker Flat once the Jeep road's free of snow and mud. Died this January but I won't be shut of him till June."

"Saw a death notice in the *Merc*. Who was he, anyway?"

"Cory Flynn? The oldest of the old-timers. Lived 92 years, all of 'em at Poker Flat, scrabbling nuggets out of Canyon Creek. Never married, drank a shot of whiskey with breakfast every day, always carried a pistol, and only started coming into Downieville for winters after he turned eighty. Crusty, tough, funny. Hundreds of folks called Poker Flat home the year Flynn was born over there, but he already had the place to himself while my daddy was still Sheriff.

"Amazing. That mean you knew him?"

"You bet. Came to visit my mama for an hour last Thanksgiving. He was boarding with Leland Carr a few months...you know Leland, Janet's pop." Buck gave Greg an odd look, as though Janet Carr, because of having run off with Seth Holmes, was some great friend of Greg's.

"It was Leland got me into this pickle," Buck went on. "When Flynn knew he was done for, he made Leland promise to have him buried in what's left of the Poker Flat cemetery. Leland promised, but yours truly got stuck with interim storage. The Clampers say they'll pay the electricity bill, but I'm not holding my breath. They'll run a hell of a funeral procession for him all the way out there, though, I'll guarantee that." Buck gave a snorting laugh.

"Biggest problem for me," he continued, "is we've only got a three-drawer morgue. Every year Curt Foley and I put in our budget for a fourth drawer, and every year the Supervisors take it out, saying they'll reconsider if we end up storing bodies in the hall. Been lucky so far, but it could happen. Let's head for my office."

Buck led them out the way they'd come, locking the doors behind him. Greg met Donny Remo, the night dispatcher, whom he recognized from around town, waited while Buck found the papers, signed where instructed, and was leaving for home in a matter of minutes. Buck walked him to the middle of the parking lot.

"Thanks," Buck said, offering Greg a hand to shake. "Needed the assistance. Hope you can put that out of your mind."

"Hope so, too," Greg replied, taking Buck's hand and receiving a firm, warm grip. "I was glad to help." Greg also knew his mind would never, never erase what he and Buck had just seen. "Wouldn't trade places for your next stop, though."

"Goes with the job," Buck shrugged, turning back toward his cruiser.

Molly had heard Greg's approaching footsteps and was waiting in the hall when he came in. Wordlessly, he took two steps and held her, repeatedly kissing her hair and down the side of her face to her neck. "It *was* Toby," he finally said, in a choked whisper.

Molly gently pulled away, taking Greg's hands and walking backward to lead him into the kitchen. "How bad?" she asked. Fresh tears marked her cheeks.

"Very, very bad," Greg answered. "The worst thing I ever saw." Something cold gripped the coils of his intestines.

"Come on," Molly said. "Sit at the table by the window with me and have a little brandy."

"Exactly what I need. But here's a sidelight you won't believe."

"What?"

"I actually had a conversation with Buck Thompson. The guy's human after all."

"You're right. I don't believe it." She wiped her face with a tissue before turning to the cupboard.

"And no phone call to Crandalls." Greg lowered himself heavily into a chair. "He's going over to notify them in person."

"Well, that counts," Molly said quietly. "But shush. Ned keeps waking up. If he does again, I guess we should tell him."

* * *

That poor Crandall kid was beat all to hell, Buck thought, standing near his cruiser outside the courthouse. He'd half-believed Ernie Warrington had been exaggerating, but no. And Fulton had handled himself OK. A fairly decent sort, beard and all, to Buck's surprise, and Buck hadn't smelled any funny cigarettes while he was in the guy's house. Maybe, if Buck talked to Zack Brennan, the school Superintendent, Zack could get Fulton to shave, change his MO around the basketball girls and stay clear of pot smokers like Drew Ormond and the rest of the Goodyear Bar hippies. If that's who he picked as friends, and vice versa, people were going to assume they had interests in common.

What the hippies themselves did was different, if they kept it low-key and nobody complained. Fulton didn't seem to grasp that he had to meet a higher standard, just like he didn't realize that anybody who cared could check with Marilyn Pezzola's County Clerk office and find out exactly how much Clarence Dunkirk had gouged Fulton for his house, and the whopping down payment Fulton had come up with. What was it the guy'd said? "We did all right"? Now there was a belly laugh.

Another thing was those shelves in the hall, obviously new since Clarence's time, which held more books than Buck had ever seen in one place except a law office or a library. College or not, Fulton and his wife together couldn't possibly have read even half, so it must be just for show. But who around here did they—or mainly she, he'd bet—think they would be scoring points with? The kind of business her husband and Buck had just gone through was what really mattered.

He looked over to where Greg had disappeared behind the road department headquarters and thought of Gina Conrad. Local politics were always where his mind went when he needed a break from things that couldn't be avoided. And she was a lucky gal to have married Bud Peterson, the road chief. Bud had Loyalton roots going back three generations, so the east-county muckety-mucks had never run anybody against her the way they were this year with Pritchard against Buck. Not that Gina wasn't in a peck of trouble as County Treasurer, but you couldn't say it was her own doing.

How was she supposed to know this Arab oil thing would hit and interest rates would skyrocket? Investing county funds was one of Gina's main jobs, and she'd locked in what looked like good payoffs only to lose big when she had to dump the notes mid-year because the county needed extra cash to meet its fuel bills. Buck didn't understand all the ins and outs, exactly, even after Marilyn Pezzola explained it to him, but to make up for those losses, the damn-fool Board of Supervisors sold off part of the county's famous gold collection, which went down with folks like a cup of carbolic acid.

But did the board take the heat? Dream on. They turned around and blamed it not on the Arabs, but on Gina. And with all their scape goating, this jackass fertilizer salesman who'd recently retired to his family's property in Sierra City decided he could do better and filed against her. It'd take that guy — Farrell was his name — four years to remember the combination to the vault from what Buck could tell, but people were so pissed about gas prices and interest rates he might win anyway.

Fact is, when Buck thought about Gina or about what the drowned boy's parents were up against, his own problems didn't seem so major. Pritchard hadn't seen the whole Thompson arsenal yet, not by a long shot. But for the next half-hour, Buck would really be walking on eggs. The Crandalls were bound to be desperately hurting, so who knew what fault they'd find with how Buck's staff had handled the search. It was more than the usual business of telling people the very thing they didn't want to hear. That was always bad, but these people owned the newspaper, for Christ's sake.

Should he walk or drive? All the main part of town was close enough he could leave his cruiser at the courthouse, and regardless of his mission it was a real nice night. No, better not. He'd be recognized either way, and that he was in uniform this late might help with the campaign. But walking, he'd have to talk to whoever he bumped into, and he didn't want that. In his car he could at least be alone to prepare his thoughts.

CHAPTER 10

The next twenty-four hours were as dismal as any Greg could remember. His sleep after seeing Toby's corpse had been riven with nightmares, he'd had to beg off on grading papers he'd promised his students they would have, the whole school was in shock, and the flag outside flying at half mast was only the most visible sign.

Billy Stark, Lou Bishop and Lisa Crandall were all absent, while Toby Crandall's name—what choice did they have—was dropped from the roster. Toby had been too young to be in any of Greg's classes, but the empty seats of Billy, Lou, and Lisa dominated the room during every period they missed. Even though all the kids were grieving to some extent in such a tight-knit student body, Greg understood that the absent three were more torn by guilt than by grief. Grief likes to be shared. Guilt doesn't.

Yes, Billy was culpable, because he was the oldest and had apparently gotten the idea. But his intent had been innocent, and he'd taken the same risk himself. Could Lou have stayed closer to Toby and helped bring him in? No one knew, and no one could know. And Toby had certainly had it drummed into him how dangerous the rivers were. It was a case of kids exercising poor judgment, because they *were* kids, which is part of what kids do. Every course Greg had taken getting his teaching credential after his return from VISTA had made that point repeatedly, and it had just been made again.

Lisa Crandall had been blameless in every respect, but according to Drew, that didn't seem to count much in helping her cope. For Om to feel guilty, perhaps with better reason, didn't impress Lisa either. She'd been left in charge of both her brothers the previous day, and wouldn't be contradicted on what that meant.

Molly planned to be at Crandalls' during the afternoon, so Greg looked forward to a further update when she got home. Until then all he had to go on was a chance meeting with Drew by the school playground during lunch break. Lisa had refused medication after Buck's visit Sunday night, and had been crying almost ever since. Pat was continuing with tranquilizers prescribed by Henry, while

Jim remained drunk. Om had moved in full time to bolster everyone and see after Stevo. How this week's *Merc* was going to get out was a big question, but Jim's father, a retired magazine editor, was supposedly on his way from Chicago and might be able to take over. Drew would use a couple of vacation days from his social work job to pitch in as well. The funeral was set for 3 p.m. Wednesday, the day after tomorrow.

Greg stayed late at school to be sure he caught up with his backlog, but Molly still wasn't home when he arrived. A note from her said that Ned was playing with Juan Holmes in Sierra City and would be eating there, a familiar arrangement. Jojo was with them. What was unfamiliar was Greg's having the house to himself, though he settled in, opened a beer and put on an Eagles album. Molly had bought Joni Mitchell's new *Court and Spark* on their last trip to Sacramento, but the vocal style was too melancholy for his mood. *Witchy Woman* was a better idea, and it had almost given him a fresh toehold on the day when Molly came banging in.

"Turn that down...please!" she said, annoyed. "Couldn't I come home to something peaceful?"

"Yeah, OK," Greg responded. What was he supposed to play, Rachmaninoff's *Funeral March*? He turned the music off, not down.

"Thanks," she said. "Sorry I snapped at you, but things are worse than we thought."

"What things?"

"Crandall things. Pat and Jim are broke, for one."

"Impossible."

"I was shocked, too. Follow me into the kitchen, I want a glass of wine." Molly left the room. "How about leftovers tonight so neither of us has to cook?" she called back from the hall.

"Fine." Greg got up to join her. Out the large kitchen window were the rooftops of town, the ungraceful spire of the Community Methodist Church and the wooded flanks of High Commission, the humorously named ridge that bounded Downieville to the northeast. As he got closer, the foreground opened up to reveal the riverbed, fifty feet downhill from their deck and swirling with what looked like cake icing from this distance.

"Grab me another beer, will you?" Greg asked.

"Sure." She passed a can to him over her shoulder.

Molly brought her wine and they sat. Her face and eyes said she hadn't slept any better than Greg had last night, and before coming to bed she'd spent a long time crying with Ned in his room because they'd decided that telling him then was the right thing.

"Henry needed me past three at the clinic today," Molly began, "so I didn't get to Pat and Jim's till four. Thank god Ned's OK now and could go to Karen's with Juan."

"Jim still drunk? That's what I heard from Drew at school."

"Yes. Drunk and morose. He's in terrible pain...and not just about Toby. From how Pat is, tranquilizers beat liquor any day. And Om's been fantastic. She says Pat has never cast blame and won't let Om blame herself. They're like the best two sisters you'd ever see. Jim barely talks, but he's not blaming anybody either."

"And Lisa?"

"Didn't see her. She won't come out of her room. Drew is the only one she'll talk to, but he's gone to Sacramento to pick up Jim's dad at the airport. Om thinks Lisa's doing better, though. She's stopped crying. Om wants to get her involved with Stevo as soon as there's a chance."

"That might work. I'll go over later and see Jim myself. With Drew, his dad and me there, maybe he'll get a grip. But cut the suspense...what's this you said about broke?"

"Om got Pat to open up. Jim was at the other end of the table looking like he's the one who died. Finally, all slurred, he said, 'If my father finds out, I'll kill myself. I mean it!' He scared me. We really have to keep this part quiet."

"Wow. What the hell's going on?"

"Mainly, they paid too high a price for the *Merc*. It's barely profitable after they meet the overhead and make their loan payments. They've been living on the royalties from Jim's book, but those have slowed way down. And it's April. You know how tight things are for us because of paying taxes and propane. Om's donating her time, Jim will get more royalties, and the *Merc* always does better in the summer, but right now they have a lot of credit out and not much cash. You know...for the mortuary, a gravesite, gravediggers, headstone. It's awful."

"Oh, god...*worse* than awful. But look, together we'll pull them through. You know...the two of us, the Segals, Drew, Ian and Sandra. How much do they need?"

"I had the same idea, and Pat thought $2,500, even if they delay on the headstone. But she doesn't know how they'd pay us back. The tranquilizers didn't keep her from crying while she told me."

"Ouch! Way more than I figured."

"Then, just as I was leaving, the phone rang. It was Buck Thompson. Pat talked to him, and you'll never guess what happened."

"He called to see how they were doing, I suppose."

"No, he said he was donating a gravesite along the edge of the Thompson family plot, and that Ernie Warrington would organize volunteers to dig the grave. So all Pat and Jim need is maybe $1,000 for the mortuary to tend and transport the body."

"Unbelievable! Our group can handle that. We'll make it a gift, not a loan."

"Exactly what Om and I told Pat. I was sure you'd agree. Jim had his head and arms down on the table and was groaning."

"Jim better dump his pride and deal with his grief. Any idea how Buck got in the picture?"

"I wasn't there yet, but right before Drew left, he called Phil Bosley. Besides being president of those damned drunken Clampers, he's in charge of the cemetery, and there's hardly any gravesites left. The old families have the place pretty much tied up, so the few available are expensive. Money from new sales covers maintenance and stuff. Drew got pretty hot. Said Crandalls couldn't pay that much, and what the hell were they supposed to do with their dead son, leave him on the sidewalk? When Bosley claimed his hands were tied, Drew called him a prick and hung up."

"Means Bosley brought in Buck, I guess, and Buck brought in Ernie. Amazing." Greg smiled in spite of himself. If anybody in the county was more of a redneck than Buck, it was Phil Bosley.

"Amazing? Oh, Greg! I didn't want to discourage Pat, but it's all part of the election. Don't you see? Nothing's too smarmy for the Elect Buck Thompson Committee."

"I wouldn't be so quick to say that."

"You and Buck must have sniffed butts and become great pals."

"I wouldn't say that either," Greg laughed.

"Crandalls may need help right now, but they won't fall for it as far as the *Merc* is concerned. Buck's wasting his time."

"Buck is a more complicated guy than we give him credit for. The way he behaved seeing Toby's body last night was no act."

"It's sweet that you're naive, and I know it helps you relate to students, but sometimes it drives me nuts." Molly stood and went to the fridge to get out leftovers.

"What you say about the election being involved might be true. Probably is. But I'm sure there's more."

"You have to believe that, don't you? Just like with Seth." As Molly well knew, Seth Holmes was a loaded subject between them.

"Don't get going on that," Greg replied angrily. "I had a crappy day myself."

"Well, every day is crappy for Karen since he left. I know how destroyed my mom was when my dad ran off with *his* bimbo...and what it did to my brother. When Karen was picking up Ned this afternoon she asked again about a time for Sandra to develop your testimony on the divorce."

"I still haven't decided if I should." This wasn't the first time Molly's father had been mentioned in the context of Seth, a father she could still barely bring herself to see.

She was holding two dinner plates, which she now put on the counter with a sharp clack. "Greg, I'm wondering, and our friends are wondering, what kind of guy you really are. Do you approve of what Seth did?"

"Of course not. You know I don't. He knows I don't." Philandering husbands were the lowest of the low to Molly because of her family history, especially her younger brother's descent into drug addiction while she was away at college. Focusing blame on their father was apparently how she avoided blaming herself—though there was no earthly reason for the latter. It had taken Greg a long time to win her trust after they met.

She leaned on a chair back and looked at him accusingly. "Fine, you disapprove. Then why can't Sandra question you as Karen's attorney?"

"She can. Have Judge Sturdevant issue a subpoena."

"That's not the same. She and Karen want you as *their* witness."

"Right. Same as Seth wants me as *his* witness."

"You were on the phone with him a long time last month. You had me leave the room, but you said you turned him down.

"I did. He can subpoena me, too."

"That means you have decided about Sandra...and Karen."

"I wasn't sure, but yeah, guess I have. I don't want to be involved. Seth and Karen are both good people. What happened, happened. I can't fix it."

"That makes me sick."

"You be Karen's witness. Nobody's stopping you."

"I will," Molly said emphatically. "But I was nowhere as close to Seth as you were. You know things that could help Karen, and also help Juan."

"Maybe. I doubt it. Anyway, either side in the divorce can make me appear if they want. I've got enough trouble with whose side I'm on in Seth's new lawsuit against the school district."

"And what's my wonderful tower of Jell-O going to do there?"

"When I decide, I'll let you know. Thanks for the support and understanding," he said bitterly. "It's not your job or career that could be on the line."

"Oh, please," Molly groaned.

"Look, I'm not sure Zack Brennan was fair to Seth. That Seth really knew what he was doing. Would he have left town right after resigning if Zack had told him that the law gives teachers 72 hours to change their mind? Coach N and some of the longer-time faculty were talking about it, and last week I checked the *Ed Code* in the school office. I was Seth's back-up witness at that private meeting. He brought me."

"You were Zack's back-up, too."

"That's the hellish part, and only by accident, because Buzz Sieboldt, who was supposed to be Zack's witness, ran late because he hit a deer driving in..."

"I know the story, Greg," she interrupted. "Act like you remember who you work for, and your job can't possibly be on the line. You're a husband and father now, and it's you that brought us here. This was more your dream than mine. I'm the one who gave up a career. There's not a single paid library position for fifty miles. If you won't cooperate with Sandra, at least help Zack. He's your boss, and his attorney is your friend. It's Ian's biggest case yet."

"And sell Seth out?"

"No worse than he sold out Karen and Juan."

"Molly, you're not being fair."

"And neither are you, hugging those girls in their shorts and tank tops the way you did all winter."

"What!" Greg was shocked. "Where did that come from?"

"You think I didn't notice? Or hear people talk? Get your head out of the sand."

"You never said anything."

"I shouldn't have to."

"When did you turn into a small-town prude?"

"About the time I started wondering who you were thinking about when we make love, Brenda or Tricia?"

"You've lost your mind."

"They're both better looking than Janet Carr, and they're crazy about their coachie-woachie."

"There's nothing going on between me and any of my students, and there never will be. Never."

"Seth told Karen the same thing."

"I'm not Seth."

"You're a man."

"Spoken like a woman. How about you and Henry Segal? I have eyes too."

"Now you've lost *your* mind."

"He's a man. His wife is pregnant. Supposedly that's a common time we stray. Could he be immune to your adoring looks?"

"Adoring looks! Outrageous!" Molly stamped her foot. "I like my job. I like Henry. So do you, I thought. Or are you mad he always beats you at chess?"

"I get my revenge at tennis. Usually, anyway."

"I bet you remember the score of every game."

"Not any more than Henry does. You think guys go to med school because they hate competition?"

"Sometimes I don't know what I think."

Greg stood up. "Right now nobody knows what you think. I'm walking downtown for a burger at the Quartz, then over to Pat and Jim's. You eat the leftovers."

"That means I drive to Sierra City to pick up Ned?"

"Tonight, yes. Helping Jim is more important…if I can."

"Which conveniently lets you avoid facing Karen. Since I have to do the dirty work, what shall I say?" Molly's face was pinched and the little lines near her mouth were visible in a way she wouldn't have liked. But even without them, she wasn't a woman who looked prettier when she was angry.

"I'll do my own dirty work. Tell Karen I promise to call her by the end of the week with a definite answer. I'd appreciate your not saying more."

"Yee-ss, master," she mocked.

"Give it a rest, will you? Our problems are nothing compared to half the people we know." Fighting back his anger, he strode noisily out of the room to get his jacket.

CHAPTER 11

Greg eased the Travelall onto the grassy shoulder of North Main Street near the cemetery, balanced at a tippy angle above the ditch. Several other awkwardly leaning cars and pickups were parked in line ahead of him, all surrounded by a wild singing of frogs in the evening light. It was Tuesday evening, time to dig Toby's grave for the funeral tomorrow, and this spot must be where Toby and his two friends had planned to hunt for frogs' legs before a warm afternoon's impulse got them into bigger, colder water on their inner tubes instead. The thought made Greg ache.

He and Molly had patched things up last night, both sorry at how their frayed emotions had caused petty disagreements to escalate. That Molly was jealous in some way of Greg and his basketball team had taken him completely by surprise. He knew there'd been talk about the propriety of a male versus a female coach, but he'd dismissed it as nonsense. In fact, Greg had been surprised at his own remark about Molly and Henry. The words had felt genuine, but he had no idea where they'd come from.

Molly said that she had overreacted to everything because she was getting her period and because she'd found and plucked her very first gray hair that afternoon in the mirror of Crandalls' bathroom. Not only that, she thought her wrinkles were showing more than ever with the stress of Toby's death. Greg had reassured her on all counts, and also said he knew he'd been taking an inordinate time making up his mind about the two lawsuits, but that he'd never felt quite so caught in the middle in his life. The only practical conclusion, cliché notwithstanding, was united we stand, divided we fall, and they had both slept well afterward despite talking past midnight.

Greg's visit to Crandalls' immediately following his blowup with Molly had led him to sign on with Ernie Warrington and the volunteer gravediggers. His other friends were already helping as they could. Ian, Sandra and Drew, in company with Jim's father Colin Crandall and the two paid staff would put out the *Merc*, while Om continued to run the Crandall household. Greg had seen Lisa in the TV room with Stevo, apparently doing better and acting vaguely like her normal self. He knew her best as equipment manager for the girls' basketball team, and she had brightened a little with his presence. Numb and dazed, Pat had slogged around saying she was trying to accept fate and be what she called "realistic."

The newly arrived Colin, a widower, was clearly the source of his son's Kennedy looks. Colin also radiated charm, though he'd downplayed that in deference to Jim, who was still a mess. Jim's skin had been flushed and translucent, while his clothes, with a tattered bathrobe flung over them, had grown a size in relation to his body. Fooling no one, he had kept himself sloshed, drinking what Om told Greg was straight vodka from a coffee cup while periodically congratulating Om on what good coffee she'd made.

In a minor way this had suggested Jim's routine party-time wisecracks, so Greg tried to take it as a positive. Finding any kind of positive made him feel better, because Jim had ignored all Greg's attempts at real interaction. Accompanying Greg to the door, Drew had reported the same problem, and if Drew Ormond wasn't getting through, Greg realized there was little hope for him — or not for awhile, anyway.

Greg also wanted their group to be involved with the digging, and he hadn't been concerned about the difficulty of the work. But to actually get out of the Travelall once he was parked took effort of another kind. He'd done plenty of digging over the years, yet this was no barbecue pit or septic tank, it was a grave.

Male voices, including Ernie's, Greg assumed, could be heard grousing and laughing from above, beyond a large, outspreading oak. A retaining wall of rip-rap stood along the cemetery's lower perimeter, while the plots themselves ranged for more than an acre on a sloping shoulder of Oxford Ridge. Clamping his work gloves under his arm, Greg carried a mattock, a shovel and an unlit Coleman lantern through the open, scrolled-iron gate and up a path of crushed granite.

Distance and more laughter intermittently drowned out an unseen exchange which made Greg wince, when "...explains why you never got any off o' sweet little Janet senior year..." was followed by an equally anonymous, "Should'a known her horny old science instructor already had drilling rights..." and then a third voice adding, "Prob'ly told her it was biology lab."

82

"For her age," the first voice overrode the diminishing laughs, "that ex of his ain't what you'd term shabby. Wouldn't mind some drillin' rights there…"

"Yeah, but one o' them real short-term leases," came a joking reply. "You don't want that Injun-brown kid to start callin' you daddy…'specially in public."

"What's so high about your own pedigree?" a new voice parried with disapproval.

"Yo!" Greg cried, to announce his presence before rounding the big oak. It felt cowardly, but he decided against challenging any of what he'd just heard; not as an outsider, not here, not now. Yet if they'd been ragging on him and his students instead of on Seth, which Molly said she'd heard, he'd have made a scene regardless.

"Hey, it's Teach Fulton," waved Lonny Harris, jamming his shovel into a dirt pile and leaning on it while Greg drew closer. "Or should that be *coach*?"

"Can't call Fulton coach unless you've got a pussy," said Tommy Schoville, who stood waist deep in the hole they were digging. "But," he added quietly, as Greg gave him a level stare, "time to cut wising off about Holmes."

"Lonny *is* a pussy, even if he don't have one," said Scott Millard, drinking beer with Ernie Warrington under the tree, "or get much of it." At this Greg smiled and relaxed. Standard ribbing he could handle.

"Hey, Greg," Ernie broke in. "Hope you brought muscle power to go with that pick. Want a brewski?"

"Sure, why not?" Greg put down his tools and lantern to catch the can Ernie tossed him. "And call me anything you want…as long as my team has twelve wins a season. How's the digging?"

"OK," Ernie replied. "Almost half done. Good to have someone fresh. Rick Conrad and Alex Darnell just left. They were the ones who found the body, so they wanted to put in a little time."

"Plenty o' roots, but only one nasty boulder so far," Scott Millard said, nodding at Greg.

"And no accidental bones…Thompson or otherwise," Lonny Harris joked. "Toss me another beer while you're at it," he said to Ernie.

Lonny was a big guy, maybe 6'3", with straggly brown hair, who worked as a logger in the summer and drove snowplow in the winter. Between seasons he got drunk and hung around town in a long-billed cap and sweatshirt with the top of his butt-crack show-ing above his jeans. At the moment he was perspiring and shirtless, and his jeans were blessedly cinched higher than normal.

Though Lonny's bulging gut and bad posture gave no clue, he'd been the star center on a Downieville High basketball squad that had finished an amazing 6-6 back in the early '60s. Greg's girls going undefeated this year had undoubtedly rankled him, and per-haps the others, which would account for the sarcastic way Greg had been greeted.

In fact, earlier versions of all these guys could be found in the class and team photos hanging in the hallways at school if you knew where to look. So could earlier versions of Janet Carr and Seth. But rather than refining his guesses as to who had said what when he'd first come within earshot, Greg pushed that episode out of his consciousness. The work at hand was too important.

He was on good terms with Ernie, had a passing acquaintance with Lonny, and not quite that with Scott and Tommy. Younger than Greg, but too old to have been in school when he'd started teaching there, the latter two worked seasonal jobs for the Forest Service, and the blonde, clean-cut Tommy Schoville, if Greg re-membered right, was married, though he wasn't sure to whom.

Weekends and off-season, Scott Millard spent his time chasing gold, and supposedly had a nose for it, even in the picked-over streambeds and tailings left when the big mines had closed. A brawny Vietnam vet with an ugly shrapnel scar on his forearm, Scott was a loner and a mountain man who lived on a mining claim up the Downie River somewhere. You could say he was a 70s re-make of Cory Flynn, the old-timer from Poker Flat that Buck Thompson had told Greg about on Sunday.

On his way in Greg had passed the conspicuous gravestone of Ernie Warrington's father adjacent to the path, and he saw a second of equal size bearing the name Huey E. Thompson beyond the berm of fresh dirt from the large, rectangular hole Tommy was digging. To Greg's left was a line of the Pezzola family's markers, some stones old and indistinct, some with the inscriptions clear. Though he'd never paid attention to the layout, Greg had noted on past walk-throughs that the Powell, Cresta, Vargas, Koontz, Conrad, Carr, Murdock and a long list of other families were also well repre-sented.

The hole for Toby Crandall was six-and-a-half feet long, three feet wide, and needed to be six-and-a-half feet deep. With better than three feet down still to go, it was decided to put two diggers at a time inside and to spell them frequently. Greg climbed in with Tommy for ten minutes, then rotated to moving dirt away from the opening with Lonny, then rested under the tree to drink beer while two other diggers went at it and the two remaining guys moved dirt or cleared rocks. Greg had shed his warm-up jacket almost immediately and his T-shirt was soaked five minutes later.

As the sun disappeared behind City of Six Ridge, a hatch of mosquitoes began to swarm, and Ernie passed repellent around. Lonny had consumed at least a six-pack by then, which fueled his loud bad-mouthing of everybody and everything in Sierra County without slowing the pace of his work. They made steady progress.

"Hell of a perfect hole," Greg puffed, resting his shovel in the dirt pile as he'd seen Lonny do earlier. "Exact rectangle, sides cut straight. You guys know your stuff."

"Every one of us has earned pocket money digging graves," Scott said, "but Lonny the most. He can line up perfect holes anywhere."

"Don't need an engineering degree to dig holes," Lonny razzed, throwing a shovel of dirt onto Ernie's boots. Scott and Lonny were inside the hole, while Greg was above it moving earth and rocks with Ernie.

Tommy sat under the tree pouring the last of a beer down the back of his head and neck. "Damn, that feels good," he said.

"Don't take an engineer to find gold, neither," Scott put in. "Or run a pizza joint."

"These guys love to give me shit," Ernie Warrington laughed. "Must take an engineer for some things in this county. My phone keeps ringing and Leland Carr writes me checks."

Greg had no idea how busy Ernie was as an engineer or what his motive might be for bankrolling Rick Rodman's pizza venture at the Ore House. On the other hand, Ernie seemed to make a comfortable living and it had to come from somewhere. In addition to being Stanford smart, he was good looking, a trim, muscular six-footer with a stylish brown mustache overlaying his fine-boned face. And from knowing his mother as a faculty colleague, Greg didn't have to guess the origin of Ernie's deep blue eyes.

"Why Leland Carr?" Greg asked.

"Leland caretakes a lot of old mines for the investors who own 'em," Ernie replied. "They need engineering studies for their stock offerings and annual reports. With gold up like it is, Leland's my best client, but I mainly used his name to piss off Scott. Leland has more gold under his mattress than Scott'll see in his life."

"You think," Scott Millard shot back.

"I know," Ernie countered.

"Scott wins if you count pyrites," Lonny Harris joked.

"You always dig the same size hole?" Greg asked. "Seems awfully big for a kid."

"It's what Bosley has us do," Lonny said. "State law or something. You never know how big the casket'll be anyway."

"Lonny, you going to help dig Flynn's over in Poker Flat?" Tommy Schoville called from where he was sitting. "That'll be a party."

"Clampers buy the beer, I'll be there," Lonny answered.

"You know," Scott said, "once I got digging tonight, I forgot it was a kid. Kinda' shakes you up. With all the half-assed shit I pulled at that age, it's a miracle I'm not in here myself. They say he was a hell of a nice kid, too."

"He was," Greg said, forcing his throat to get the words out.

"You help ID the body?" Ernie said to Greg quietly. "Buck told me he was going to ask."

"Yeah," Greg answered. "You saw it yourself, didn't you?"

"Right," Ernie said. "Something I won't forget."

"Same here. But sure is strange, Buck letting go of this gravesite all of a sudden."

"Not so strange…kind of thing Buck would do."

Greg found himself arguing Molly's point. "With the election coming," he said, shrugging to convey irony, "and the *Merc* involved, a guy might…might…suspect an ulterior motive."

Ernie's eyes narrowed. "A guy who didn't grow up here, you mean."

"Oh? Why?" Greg wasn't impressed with that as an answer.

Ernie pointed. "Buck's brother Cal is over past Huey. You've heard about Frank Pezzola dying young? Well, Cal was a town hero in his day, too, but got killed at Anzio right when he turned 20. Buck's seen how it hurts."

"The *Merc* people are down on their luck for cash, too, from what I hear," Scott said. "Newfields had the same problem. Making a go of that paper is tough."

"Specially after what Crandall paid for it," Lonny added.

Greg gave a surprised look, to which Ernie bobbed his head sideways and replied, "Public record. Clerk's office is in the courthouse, and people are *always* curious."

"None o' that matters," Scott said. "Crandall's alright by me. Runs the best gold industry coverage the *Merc* ever had. That's why I'm here. He needs help, I'll help."

"Buck had some extra plots anyway," Lonny said. "Cal didn't leave no one, and Buck's kids never lived in the county. Doesn't figure they'd be buried here."

"Saw your father's grave down below," Greg said to Ernie. Having just added Cal Thompson to his store of local knowledge, Greg wanted to find a safer subject than the Crandalls' finances. Jim would be appalled at how many of his secrets were already out. Or could anybody *have* secrets around here?

"Yeah, that's the old man," Ernie answered, "but nothing like losing a kid. My dad was 48 when I was born and lived another twenty years. He had a full life."

"Pass that mattock, will you," said Scott. "We got more roots to cut."

"And a big-ass rock," Lonny added. "Shit."

"Take the long crowbar, too," Tommy said, walking toward the hole. "And the lanterns. Gettin' dark. Better fire 'em up."

* * *

The dry chill of the beer cooler at the Hi-Grade Market prickled up hairs on the back of Buck's hand. What would it be, Coors? Yeah, a couple of sixers, and he'd make it the tall ones. Funny how the soft-drink cooler, Buck's usual haunt, never felt this cold. Or maybe the lure of forbidden fruit was throwing him off. It was a minute or two before closing and Buck was the only customer in the place. Shep Conrad, the owner, had sent the younger help home and was waiting at the register. When the creaking floorboards announced Buck's approach, Shep looked shocked at what Buck was carrying.

"You willing to sell this stuff to a Sheriff in uniform?" Buck asked.

"Whole lot rather sell you Pepsi. Sure that's what you want?"

"Shee-it," Buck laughed. "Had you going, didn't I? This here's for the boys digging at the graveyard. Little thank-you gift."

"Bad business, that kid drowning. They're supposed to go to our funerals, not the other way around." Shep had just the right shape and demeanor to play Santa Claus at the town Christmas Fair, which he had done every year for a long time, though all the hair for that role was glued on. Shep's normal was a clean-shaven jaw topped by a graying GI close-crop, but he'd seen a lot of kids grow up around here starting from when they sat on his lap all the way to the ones who worked part- or full-time in the store.

"Bad is right," Buck nodded. "Worst thing in the world."

"He was a damn nice kid. Good you were able to *give* his folks that plot, so to speak."

"Seemed right. Then they can pay what they owe you."

"Not what I meant."

"Come on, Shep, I'm pullin' your leg. By the way, two of those election posters you have in the front window are real sharp, but the third's ugly as sin."

Shep finally broke a smile. "Which would that be?"

"Can't remember. Name starts with a *P* or something."

"Oh, Gina Peterson, the County Treasurer lady?"

"No, the other *P*, the guy...and quit playing dumb."

"I got a store to run, Buck. Sad to say, Pritchard might win. I got to be on the right side of you both."

"Hey, I understand. Long as it don't affect your vote."

"Nothin' to worry about on that score."

"How's Gina doing, you think?" Buck asked. Shep Conrad was Gina Peterson's uncle, and likely to know.

"The more campaigning that dummy Farrell does," Shep replied, "the better for Gina. *His* poster I won't put up. And even if he wins, it won't have the same impact as Sheriff. I'll be disappointed for family reasons, but I got no dealings at the Treasurer's Office."

"Tell you what else I heard interesting today."

"Yeah?"

"That Rick Rodman from the Ore House is still so pissed about the liquor license flap, he's running for District 2 Supervisor as a write-in. Hope he puts the fear of god into old Will Jeffers. Will's made enough enemies around Sierra City his last two terms, Rod-man could pull it off."

"Will's a loud-mouth ass for a Supervisor," Shep said, "but you really want a hippie with pizza sauce in his beard making decisions on the law enforcement budget?"

"Depends on the decision. Meanwhile I'll be kissing up to both of them just like you are with Pritchard."

Shep Conrad smiled again and handed Buck his change. "Well, good luck. You delivering these brewskis in person?"

"Yeah, right now. They're probably down to boulders and needing reinforcement."

Buck put the two six-packs on the back seat and positioned himself behind the wheel. The first dozen or so stars were up and the moon was showing in the notch of the Yuba canyon, as perfectly symmetrical a half as Buck could ever remember. Eight p.m. and town was so quiet you'd think nobody lived there. The locust trees weren't in bloom at this elevation like they were in Pike, but mock orange or something was perfuming the night. He started the engine and rolled slowly up Main Street toward North Main.

The Forks bar was on his right, with the St. Charles diagonally across the street, both hosting the usual weeknight boozers and losers. Nope, Buck didn't miss that life, though he'd always been more of a home drinker than a barfly. Since he was in the Sheriff's personal cruiser, not a standard unit, there was no steel grill separating him from the back. He could reach behind and stash one of those sixers under the seat for later, then drive out of town and help himself, but he knew he wouldn't.

Those days were past, and it wasn't just because he worried somebody might—no, probably would—see him or smell it on his breath. Those days were truly past. But knowing that he'd never get away with it around here had helped him through some rough spots. People, whether they were public officials or not, *should* be accountable to their community, and that worked best if they all knew one another face-to-face. For the first few hours visiting Sacramento or Reno out of uniform he enjoyed being anonymous, but then the lack of connection started feeling like it wasn't really him.

Next building past the St. Charles bar, the *Merc* office was lit up and busy. A silver-haired man in a ribbed golf sweater was leaning in the doorway smoking with Drew Ormond. Buck waved and simultaneously, so did they. Those'd be legal cigarettes, of course, and the unknown man was likely Jim Crandall's father. Word was he'd come from back east for the funeral and was putting out the *Merc* to give his son a break. From the way Jim had looked when Buck delivered the bad news Sunday night, a week off, at a minimum, would be essential. The *Merc* would have to cover the boy's drowning this issue and run a major fishing story for opening day, but Buck hoped the Chilcutt bust would still make front page. People needed to know his department was on the ball.

After the *Merc* office came the community center and then the turn-off to the school opposite the ramshackle, little historical museum his mother had helped found. God, how many times was it he'd traveled this block? With 365 days in a year, had to be going on ten thousand by now. The whole town had seemed like a prison to Buck and to Stan White when they were growing up, but lately, since Buck had come back, he looked forward to noticing the details that changed each time he came through. Tonight it was the mock orange and the *Merc* being lit up. Tomorrow it'd be something else.

Two hundred yards short of the cemetery, the figure of a teenage boy ducked off the pavement uphill into a vacant lot at the furthest reach of Buck's headlights. Stands of blackberry bramble immediately swallowed the kid, but Buck was pretty sure it was Billy Stark, who had to be hurting as bad as anybody over the Crandall drowning. Billy had been plain stupid to get in that water himself, was lucky to've survived, and now had to live with the consequences. Buck wished the boy'd stayed on the road so he could've talked to him and maybe help relieve his mind. There'd been nothing mean about what he'd done. You could just bet young Crandall had begged to go along, and people said he was a good swimmer for his age.

Half a block later a second figure, a man in jeans and a jeans jacket, was lurching down the middle of the road carrying a shovel. Ray Stark, Billy's father, apparently on one of his benders, intended to join the gravediggers, if he got there before passing out, that was. Buck slid up next to Ray and lowered his window. Ray was probably hurting, too, going over and over what he had and hadn't done to keep track of Billy that day.

"Get in and take a load off," Buck said, projecting his voice over a riotous chorus of frogs and crickets. "I'll take you the last block."

"Got no cause to bust me," Ray answered. "I'm OK." He'd been aware of the approaching headlights, but was wide-eyed that they'd turned out to be Buck's.

"Ain't no bust, but I *do* want ya' to get in. Been a while since we talked."

"Don't feel like talking." Ray straightened, leaning on the shovel but swaying anyway. His face was pouchy and red. He wore a white T-shirt under his jacket and his uneven butch haircut looked like it had been administered by his wife, recently and in a hurry.

Buck leaned over and opened the passenger door. "OK, no talk. We'll just ride. Lay that shovel in the rear."

It was completely dark. Coming around, Ray walked close to the hood of Buck's car, momentarily blocking the headlight beam, first on one side, then the other, so the only thing illuminated was a narrow swath of Ray's jeans at thigh level. In those instants Buck glimpsed a faint glow up-slope, in the graveyard. The guys were still working, and Buck knew the exact spot. There was no mistaking the spreading branches of the big oak where a plot was waiting for Buck's mama, next to Huey. Buck's own plot was farther down, next to Cal.

"Hey, you got beer back there," Ray said after putting his shovel in the car. He was making a maximum show of sobriety for Buck's benefit, but Buck caught the sweet, unmistakable smell of bourbon when Ray got in beside him and closed the door.

"It's for the cemetery fella's. You help, you'll get some, too."

"No time like the present." Ray groped his left hand behind him trying to snag one of the sixers, only half turning to watch what he was doing.

The car had barely begun to move, but Buck got Ray Stark's full attention when he tromped the brakes and threw Ray nearly out of his seat. "Like I say," Buck emphasized, "up at the graveyard." Buck let the car crawl forward again.

"Yeah, OK, sorry. Can't be drinkin' in this car, can we?"

"No, and forget *we*. I don't drink no more, period, and I'm better for it. Something you might think about."

"You said we didn't have to talk."

"Right...guess I did. You know what a man needs to do in this life just as well as me, and I know how hard it is sometimes."

"Can't argue that. You also gotta know it's been one hellish week at my house."

"Figures. Bad things happen, whether you deserve 'em or not. How's that boy of yours? Ain't been his best week either."

"No...but damn, he knows better. Could'a killed hisself and young Bishop on top of it. I set him straight, tell you what."

"You aware he was followin' you a minute ago? Darted up into Cresta's vacant lot and hid when I came by. Probably above us along the ridge right now."

"Little whelp!" Ray growled, turning abruptly to look out the back window. "Told him real clear to stay home. Wanted to come down and dig, if you can imagine."

"Might'a been a good thing. Wasn't all Billy's fault, you know. Not by a long shot. He's gotta start workin' it off somehow.

"He'll work it off. I'll see to that."

Buck sighed. "Don't make me sorry I let on about seein' him," he said. "Your wife calls my office later to restrain you, we ain't gonn'a be lenient."

"A family matter," Ray Stark said doggedly.

"Yeah," Buck answered, "but only to a point." He'd driven past the cemetery so he could U-turn at the wide spot where the pavement ended and return to park on the shoulder between the road and the ditch. Ernie Warrington's car had been first in line ahead of him, and it looked like Scott Millard, Tommy Schoville and Lonny Harris were part of the crew.

All of 'em turning out to be good men in Buck's way of thinking, but that Lonny still had growing up to do. The surprise was seeing Greg Fulton's fancy Travelall parked right behind. Like on Sunday night, it could be there was something to the damn guy after all. The semicircle of the moon had risen just enough out of the canyon to be showing over the shoulder of High Commission. It'd be easy finding their way up the path, but Buck had a flashlight in his belt just in case.

"See Scott Millard's here," Buck said as he and Ray fished the beer and the shovel out of Buck's cruiser. "You running that business with him again this summer?" Ray Stark worked locally as a carpenter when he could, and ran a makeshift plywood booth with Scott selling odd bits of gold to tourists outside the Quartz Cafe, May to September.

"You bet. Scott finds the stuff, I fob it off on the flatlanders. Starts next weekend. Gonn'a try wearin' a Gabby Hayes hat and red bandanna. Price of gold's way up, too."

"One plus to all this inflation, anyway," Buck said.

"How 'bout I have myself a brew now we're out of the car?" Ray asked.

"Sure, if that's what you need." Buck pulled a can free from the cardboard pack and handed it to Ray.

After propping his shovel against the cemetery gate, Ray felt for the can's tab-top. "These little items were sure a great invention." A hiss and a fizzing sploosh followed. "Damn, spilled some." Ray tipped his head, taking three long gulps. "OK. Let's go dig."

When Buck arrived with Ray, Lonny Harris and Scott Millard were in the bottom of the hole levering at an ovoid boulder about the size of a car engine. Above them sat Tommy Schoville, legs dangling into the cavity and his right bull-finger wrapped in a bloody kerchief. At each end of the hole was a low mound of dirt supporting a lit Coleman lantern. Ernie Warrington and Greg Fulton were carrying rocks to the upper boundary wall from the dirt pile that would be used for fill after the coffin went in.

"Hey, Sheriff," called Tommy. "Come to see if we're doin' it right?"

"You must be," Buck answered. "You're way along already. Hope you saved a little dirt for Ray."

Scott looked up briefly and nodded. "Howdy, Sheriff...Ray. Kinda' late, aren't you?"

"Could have used him an hour ago," Lonny grunted. "And Raymond, what's that shiny object you're carrying?"

"One a Buck's beers," Ray answered. "He's got plenty more."

"They cold?" Tommy demanded.

"Less'n ten minutes out of the cooler," Buck said.

"Great. Pass one over, would ya'? Need the cold for my finger. Mashed that sucker pretty good when the pry-bar slipped."

Buck walked around to Tommy, squatted, and put the sixers down. "Take two. One for cold and one to drink." Buck laid an unopened beer in Tommy's lap and popped another for Tommy's uninjured hand. "Think anything's broke?" Buck asked

"Nah. Ernie looked at it. Says it'll be OK."

Buck stood. "You switching from engineer to sawbones?" he asked Ernie, who had just returned from carrying rocks. "Thought we had young Doc Segal for that."

"You're the one sent me to EMT training," Ernie countered, smiling.

"Think you could you use one of these?" Buck handed Ernie a beer. "And how 'bout Mr. Fulton over there?" He motioned toward Greg.

"Thanks Sheriff, don't mind if I do. Call me Greg, by the way."

"Soon as you start callin' me Buck." He tossed Greg a can.

Standing in the hole, Lonny and Scott had stopped work to pop their own cans. "Hot damn, tall ones," Lonny said. "Thanks Buck." "Yeah, thanks," echoed Scott. Ray Stark, meanwhile, had finished his first can, stomped it and was popping open a second.

"Never get that boulder out unless somebody brings a hoist," he said, gulping more beer.

"No kidding," Scott Millard replied sarcastically. "But we ain't takin' it out, Ray. We're lowerin' it. You know...tippin' it up and diggin' under till it settles into the bottom."

"Smart," Ray nodded.

"Ernie's idea," Lonny Harris put in. "Learned something in college after all."

"You find any gold it's mine," Buck joked. "Thompson family property, remember."

"Long as you can prove out your claim," Tommy Schoville countered.

"Let me in to help," Ray said. "Come on, Tommy, scrooch over so I can get by."

"Not room for three, Ray," Scott said. "Stand away and let us finish."

"Goddamn!" Ray complained. "I come all the way down here to dig, I ought'a be able to dig."

Buck could see Scott Millard and Ray Stark had personal issues, maybe related to their gold business. Lonny Harris must have picked up on it, too, because he nudged Scott and said, "Take the bar, hold the damn thing, and let him dig. I need a rest."

Scott moved to take the bar while Lonny clambered out of the hole and Ray tumbled in. "Deep," Ray said, laughing to himself. "Make sure I'm out before you fill 'er up."

Greg Fulton sidled over to Buck from the other side of the dirt pile. "How'd it go at Crandalls' Sunday night?"

"What you'd expect," Buck answered. "Telling people the last thing in the world they want to hear, it never goes good."

"I went over myself late yesterday," Greg said. "She's gradually coming around and so's the daughter. Him I'm real worried about."

"Good you went," Buck said. "They all looked like hell when I saw 'em. That Jim's father...the silver-haired guy?"

"Yeah. Colin's his name. He's putting out this week's *Merc*. Good he's here for that, but I wonder...well, if Jim can really let out grief while his dad's around."

"Shit," Buck said flatly. "Fathers and sons. Who can figure that stuff? She got people coming tomorrow?"

"No, doesn't look like it. Pat Crandall's main family is a mom and a stepfather, but they're on an ocean cruise somewhere and might not know yet."

"Bein' rich don't protect you from losin' a grandkid," Buck said. Jesus, he thought, an ocean cruise. Who the hell from Sierra County goes on an ocean cruise? Nobody Buck ever knew.

"Guess not," Greg answered. "A very fine thing you did, though, giving Crandalls this plot."

"*Selling* it to them, you mean," Buck winked. "For what they could afford. One dollar's a fair price. I don't want Bosley over-charging just 'cause folks are new here."

"Lonny," Scott called. "Get back in and help put this booger down. Think we're done."

"Shit," Ray said. "I can do it. Forget Lonny." He flipped his shovel out onto the ground, barely missing one of the lanterns.

"Goddamn climb out while you can," Scott Millard said to Ray. "I'm not ending up with no split finger like Tommy's 'cause you let the bar slip."

"Bar's not gonn'a slip," Ray responded.

"Get out anyway," Scott said.

"Why's that?"

"'Cause you *know* why. I don't like workin' with you when you're drunk."

Lonny Harris lowered himself into the hole. It took Ray Stark several tries to crawl out, but he finally did. The half-moon was higher now, and Ray followed its path away from the lighted grave uphill to the encroaching darkness. With only the back of Ray's head and jeans jacket visible, it looked to Buck as though he was about to piss on one of Frank Pezzola's ancestors. Instead Ray held his hands out in front of his chest and called loudly into the woods above, sobbing after every few words.

"Billy! Go on home, boy!...Go on home!...I know you're up there...It wasn't your fault...I should never've hit you like I done.

Go on home...I love you, boy. It wasn't your fault. You know I love you...We'll all go to the funeral tomorrow like you wanted. I'll make you proud, Billy...Just go on home!"

Buck had seen and heard a lot in his forty-four years, but still his jaw dropped. Nobody else said a word either. Turning around to leave or perhaps rejoin the group, Ray stumbled in the tall grass and fell to his knees, head up and hands still outstretched.

CHAPTER 12

Toby's funeral Wednesday afternoon drew the biggest crowd Greg had seen in Downieville except for the girls' last home game, against Loyalton, when they'd gotten the eleventh of their twelve wins. Traffic was again tied up in all directions and people on foot were streaming toward the church the same way they had toward the gym, but much more subdued.

School had closed early and the weather stayed perversely gorgeous. That lilacs could be bursting and the sun golden for such an event underscored to Greg the indifference of the universe. Yet lousy weather would have brought its own problems. At this elevation, slushy snow was as likely as rain through the end of May.

While the traffic jam surprised them, Greg and Molly had never intended to drive, and were now walking across the Downie River bridge with Ned after having strolled through town. They'd held hands the whole way, Ned in the middle, and nodded quietly without waving to whomever they saw on the sidewalks or inching by in vehicles. Everyone seemed to have a dark suit of some kind, although most were years out of style, and especially on the men over forty, the jackets were shiny at the coattails and pinched at the shoulders and waist.

As for last night's beer, no ill effects as far as Greg was concerned. He'd sweat it out as fast as he'd drunk it, along with the big jug of water they had all shared. But his muscles were another story. No matter that he was in good shape from basketball and tennis, his back and shoulders were as sore as they'd probably ever been. Lonny Harris and Ernie Warrington were set to do the refilling after the interment, which was a family-only affair late in the day. Fine with Greg. He'd be happy never to see his shovel again, or to think about what it now signified for him.

Both rivers were calmer compared to Sunday, but still plenty dangerous. Greg kept his eyes away from the water and said nothing, filled with anguish that the decisive seconds of Toby's disaster had occurred a mere dozen yards from where the Fultons now stood. Though she didn't voice them, he was sure Molly was having identical thoughts. When they'd crossed the Yuba bridge earlier, on their way into town, she had fixed her eyes on the gas station at the end of the block. Only Ned had looked at the water, but he, too, had been silent. On this second bridge, he had a conclusion to share.

"I'm never, never going swimming anymore," he announced. "I'll just play on the beach with Jojo."

Molly, eyes shining, and looking exotic in her veiled hat, leaned down to kiss Ned's cheek. "Whatever you want, sweetheart. Mommy will make sure you're safe."

Greg gave Ned's hand an extra squeeze. "Did Mommy get lipstick on me?" Ned asked. "I don't like that."

Greg inspected and saw a slight smudge. He reached for a Kleenex in his pocket. "Here, Daddy will wipe it off."

The elms, roses and green lawns of Bridge Street lay thirty yards ahead, with people clustered everywhere and Buck Thompson's cruiser parked in front of the white clapboard church. As Greg drew closer, he could see Buck standing next to the car nodding left and right to make eye contact with passing faces. Even Buck had a dark suit, predictably tight at the gut, but he hadn't forsaken his Sheriff's hat or his black boots.

Unexpectedly, though, Greg was glad to see him, and what Buck was doing seemed perfectly OK. People must have witnessed this sort of thing before and could sort out for themselves the layers of politics that might be involved. Greg was more concerned with whether he and Molly were too late to get seats, or get inside at all.

"Hi, Buck," Greg said softly when they pushed by him into the churchyard.

"Afternoon, Greg," Buck nodded impassively. "Mrs. Fulton," Buck nodded again, touching his hat. "And you, young fella'," he said to Ned.

Molly gave Greg a pointed look. "Who's that man?" Ned asked as they hurried him along.

"Daddy's new best friend," Molly replied with scorn, which Greg resignedly let pass.

Teresa Powell, the most regal of Downieville's dowagers, materialized out of the throng and cut them off. Undoubtedly a local beauty in her early life, she wore a veiled hat cut like Molly's and a tasteful gabardine suit in charcoal gray with a two-inch circle of plain gold on one lapel and a dark purple iris blossom on the other.

"Hello," she said. "I'm so sorry we didn't visit together more at the Historical Society on Sunday, and who could have guessed we'd all come home to such tragedy?"

"Hello," Greg and Molly replied in tandem. "This is our son, Ned," Molly went on. "Ned, this is Mrs. Powell."

"What a fine young man." Teresa Powell bent to shake Ned's hand. Straightening, she continued, "You're the last of the people I was watching for. I'll take you to the side door, and we'll all go in together. You'll be in row two on the left, behind the Crandall family. They particularly asked for you."

"Oh...thanks very much," Greg said. "I was afraid we'd missed our chance."

Leading them on a curving path past the corner of the building, Teresa Powell looked back and briefly crinkled her nose. "You shouldn't have worried. A lot of these people really didn't know the boy, and they understand they'll have to pay their respects outside. But you were close to him...and his parents. It was like this for Frank Pezzola, too. Certain things just touch a nerve, and everyone needs to share somehow."

Inside, she proceeded toward the front, then stepped away to claim a seat with village elders Alf and Bonny Sennett and Maude White, the minister's wife. Reverend White himself sat stiffly in a wooden chair at the far edge of the platform, near the lectern, his cheeks more sunken every time Greg saw him. Muted organ music played by choir director Barbara Trabert soothed the rapidly filling room. A wide column of other attendees advanced through the main door, extra folding chairs had been set up in back, and people were already standing down the side aisles. The casket, as Greg already knew, would not be present.

A gesture from Teresa Powell had helped Greg locate the slumped backs of Lisa, Pat and Jim Crandall ranging leftward from the center aisle in row one, with Jim's dad Colin next to him and Drew Ormond as bookend. Having gotten his bearings, Greg surveyed the crowd while leading Molly and Ned to their seats. They were surrounded by everybody from Sierra City, Downieville and Goodyear Bar he could imagine knowing, including the graveyard crew's Tommy Schoville, still sporting a bandaged finger, and his hulking co-worker Lonny Harris, hair combed for a change and wearing a new navy blue sweatshirt. Stevo Crandall in his wheelchair was positioned in the center aisle, to Lisa's immediate right, and across from him sat a scrubbed and slicked Billy Stark in coat and tie.

At Billy's shoulder was his dad Ray, face still florid and pouchy from his recent bender, but otherwise alert and nicely dressed. Then came Billy's younger sister, whose name Greg didn't recall at the moment, flanked by Janice Stark, Billy's tense, big-boned mom who looked desperate for a cigarette, which she probably was, given how early they would've arrived to get those seats.

Lou Bishop, the other lucky survivor of the boys' reckless escapade sat between his parents and the Starks. Ernie Warrington, with his wife, mother and daughters, was a few rows behind the Bishops, adjacent to the town's commercial elite, hardware owner Jerry Vargas, grocer Shep Conrad, Pete Lowry who ran the leading motel, mining entrepreneur Leland Carr, and their families. Greg hadn't yet told Molly what Ray Stark had done at the cemetery last night, or about Buck's being there, but intended to once the funeral was over and his thoughts were more settled.

Sandra Torkin and Ian Dudley slipped into the last spots in the front row, next to Drew, while Greg preceded Ned and Molly into the second row where they joined Meg and Henry Segal, Meg now wearing a full-fledged maternity outfit, who were on the aisle behind Lisa. Molly had told Greg before they set out that Henry had prepared a special medication to keep Stevo calm for the service, and Greg halfway hoped that the rest of the Crandalls had taken some as well.

The bleak finality represented by the service made Greg's lunch sit in his gut like a piece of Ned's broken slinky toy, and he'd spent some of previous night dreaming that the big boulder in the bottom of Toby's grave was actually a bizarre predator awaiting the arrival of a meal, as though feeding time had come at the zoo. Equally disturbing was that Ray Stark's pathetic entreaties to Billy had transmogrified into Jim Crandall's desperately pleading with the beast that Toby be spared.

Doing his best to purge all such thoughts, Greg said a quiet hello to the Segals and reached his arm over the pew ahead, between Pat and Jim's abutted shoulders, touching both of them and whispering, "We love you. Don't forget it."

Jim responded by fiercely grabbing Greg's hand without turning around, saying, "Thanks, we know." Pat held Greg's forearm with both her hands, and in the light from the high windows lining the walls he caught a profile of her bereft face before she composed herself and turned farther to greet Molly. Lynn Reynolds, another of Om Gillette's Goodyear Bar friends, draped in a vertically striped black and brown caftan, drifted into the Fultons' row accompanied by some big-time hippies from Pike City, who Greg recognized but never really met. Just as Pat Crandall released Greg's arm, Satya, one of the hippie men, leaned forward to poke Drew on the bicep, and they exchanged a pumping, crossed-palm handshake.

"Where's Om?" Greg whispered to Molly. "And Edna?" He couldn't imagine those two from their core group weren't present, or that Om wasn't sitting with Stevo and Lisa Crandall.

"With the choir," Molly said, pointing back above her head. "Didn't you see?"

Greg shifted, extended his neck and there they were in the loft, spliced onto the end of the first row with hippie Jeanne somebody-or-other from Pike, the only ones not wearing robes. Om and Jeanne, in caftans like Lynn Reynolds's, almost matched their choirmates, but Edna Darnell, a true daughter of the revolution, had on a starched, olive-drab Chairman Mao suit topped by a black beret with an eagle feather along one side.

Greg felt his stomach relax and something like a smile form on his face, unquestionably his first of the afternoon. "Did you see Edna?" he asked Molly.

"Oh, yes," she replied.

Ned squirmed his knees onto the pew and also looked back. "Daddy," he whispered loudly, "Edna's like my GI Joe." And she was: the Army Ranger version Greg had tried, because of Vietnam, to keep Ned from buying with his birthday money, then had grudgingly assented to. As the church went from full to packed, Greg turned more times to look at the choir, savoring the view.

Plain-faced and freckled, Edna Darnell had grown up in Sierra County, gotten away to Humboldt State for some college, then returned pregnant with her now seven-year-old son Clyde and settled into Goodyear Bar as a hippie. Hanging around mostly with the newcomers, she took great pleasure in flouting every local social code she was aware of. Her Downieville family, from whom she was largely but not totally estranged, were no doubt cringing in the crowd below, but Edna had a nice voice, had reputedly been a choir mainstay during high school, and Greg guessed that Om had used the leverage of Pat Crandall's bereavement to finesse the three of them into a special appearance for Toby's service. For all Greg knew, maybe Om and Jeanne were singers too.

The crowning touch was that Tricia Nordstrom, an ultra-straight blonde who'd been the leading scorer on Greg's team—and in the league—was towering over Edna from behind, dwarfing both her and Barbara Trabert's hapless, crew-cut husband, positioned with the two other token men in the top row. It was common knowledge that Grant Trabert, who ran the propane dealership, couldn't sing and would rather not try, but with his wife the choir director and interested men in short supply, he'd been drafted years ago, protests notwithstanding.

Tricia, oddly shy for an athlete, looked extremely uncomfortable and began slouching back, either to avoid further notice or to escape the flamboyant Edna's patchouli updraft. Her eyes said she'd gladly trade places with anybody on the lower floor if she got the chance. Tricia's parents had done what they could to dissuade her from basketball, and it would be in character for them to push hard for anything related to church. Greg, facing forward again to relieve his neck, could bet the kid was up there only because she thought she owed them.

The lights went down, a hush fell over the room and Greg saw that Reverend White had gotten to his feet and was headed for the lectern. At the same time Karen Holmes arrived with a freshly bathed and clean-shirted Juan. They took places at the far end of Greg's row, behind Sandra, her lawyer in the divorce, whom she greeted warmly, and Sandra's husband, Ian, at whom she merely nodded. Never much of a churchgoer, Greg had been here just twice before, at Molly's urging, for Christmas concerts, after which they'd hosted friends for mulled wine and cookies. This would be different—very different—but he knew it was where he wanted to be.

* * *

101

By the time Buck squeezed into the back of the church and insinuated himself down the left side to stand against the wall, Reverend White was well into his standard *Blood of the Lamb/God's Mysterious Ways* oration. Jeez, the pants on this old suit of his were tighter than the coat and almost as tight as the old uniform pants he'd suffered in last weekend. He was sure glad his regular uniforms had come back from the cleaners in Grass Valley on Monday. Next load he'd send the suit for alterations while he was at it.

The death of a child, especially involving the river like this, was bound to cause a stir, but Buck was still amazed at the turnout. Not as big as Huey's, of course, but big. School had closed early and the courthouse was virtually deserted. A major portion of the folks in this end of the county were either here or waiting outside in the yard. Sally Vargas had also wanted to come, and she and Buck were going to bring his mama, but Norma Thompson turned out to not be having a good enough day to take the chance.

Sally even knew the Crandall boy. He'd apparently helped her carry groceries from the Hi-Grade Market one afternoon when he noticed her bad arm and she'd bought more than she meant to. Of course, she could have driven Buck's car. He constantly suggested it. Not his cruiser but his personal one, the Bronco. The thing hardly got used anymore with the hours he was putting in since becoming Acting Sheriff. He'd taken it down to Sacramento a couple times, and he planned on running it over to a Nevada brothel one of these nights if he could shake free to get his ashes hauled, but otherwise the thing sat.

Sally said the kid had been real bright, like Ernie Warrington as a boy, and sweet, and had stayed and drunk a soda with her and Norma after he brought the food in. That was a month ago, about. Sally didn't remember seeing him since, and now he was dead. Mysterious ways might be the official explanation, but cruel and rotten was more how it felt to Buck.

Across the room he saw Marilyn Pezzola with her dad, Charlie Koontz. They'd offered to save Norma a seat, which would've been fine, but Buck wondered if Charlie and Norma would actually recognize one another. Charlie Koontz was failing real bad now, like Norma, and it might not matter that the two of them had grown up together and she was stepdaughter to Charlie's uncle.

Painful as it was to see Norma reduced to what she was, with Charlie it might be worse. He'd been a legend most of his life: so strong he could lift a full oil drum off the back of a truck by himself—Buck'd seen him do it—and Charlie knew the country so well from his years of running pack mules out to the mines that he'd won dozens and dozens of five-dollar bets by lettin' people take him blindfolded to anyplace in the west county they wanted and he'd tell 'em within one minute after the blindfold came off exactly where he was. And as calm and helpful a guy as ever lived, besides.

Anyway, Norma hadn't been able to come and Sally insisted on staying home too. She understood that Buck needed to see and be seen at events like this for campaign reasons, but he would have wanted to be here regardless. He hadn't known the kid, except from a distance, but he felt a linkage with him after dealing with the body and going face-to-face with the parents. Even more so, in fact, since a chunk of the Thompson plot had become the Crandall plot.

Not that Buck felt remorse about having a dual motive. He'd never heard Huey say it outright, but Curt had been fond of quoting the old man as having told him in a sheriff's car one day, "Might be wrong to mix local politics into funerals and weddings and the like, but if a man has the chance to do it, and doesn't, he's a damn fool." Buck caught himself ready to smile thinking of it and made sure his face stayed neutral. Not the time or place for smiles, no sir.

By now he'd located the Crandall family, sitting down front with their newcomer friends, and damn if Satya, the hippie kingpin from Pike, and his tasty little lady weren't right there with 'em. This stuff was more than Buck could track. It used to be that the newspaper publisher was automatically a pillar of the community and ran with the kind of people on the Elect HBT Committee. Then the Newfields became pretty much absentee owners and suddenly sold to a guy with a JFK face who wanted to hang out with hippies. And finally, the new guy turned out to be short of cash despite having a father who looked like his pocket change was more than Buck made in a year. All of it had Marilyn Pezzola baffled just like Buck, and she didn't usually lack for answers.

Also, down front on the other side was Billy Stark, seeming more like the head of the family than his sad-sack father, even though Ray was doing a hell of a lot better at the moment than he had been last night when Buck dropped him off at home after his little performance at the graveyard. Maybe Ray could still turn his life around, but it wasn't gonn'a get easier as time went by. God, do you suppose that was how Buck's girls, especially Cindy, the older one, used to see him? He'd never been that bad, had he? Made his blood run cold at the thought.

But wait, with all Buck's ruminating and trying to block out the Reverend's platitudes, he'd nearly missed Karen Holmes and her kid sitting five feet away. A handsome gal, no question about it. She saw him looking and they exchanged nods. Her perky, dark-eyed son leaned around to see why she'd nodded, gave Buck an embarrassed wave, and ducked back. Damn he was cute, and Buck always felt as though he'd seen him before somewhere. Made Buck glad he was standing along the side like this, with the whole place in view.

Reverend White concluded his remarks, Barbara Trabert's organ music welled up, and it came time for the choir. Buck was sure they'd be doing *Amazing Grace*, a town favorite and one of their standbys. Perfect for the occasion, too. Buck raised his eyes to the loft and holy shit! Three hippies who didn't belong up there at all were right in front. And to make matters worse, not only were Om Gillette and Jeanne Potter, his new Pike City ally, dressed as A-rabs, get a load of wild woman Edna Darnell. She looked like that commie Che Guevara, for Christ sake!

Now Buck realized why Edna's folks were sitting way in back. It was so they wouldn't have to see her. They must have known what she'd be wearing and damn near fallen through the floor at the thought, but at least they weren't signing up for any extra kicks in the nuts. Not to mention what Stan White's dad, the hard-to-think-of-as-reverend Reverend, had just said, as he always did, "God never gives you more than He knows you can stand." He'd meant that to comfort the Crandalls, even if it flew in the face of how things were, but he might have ended up comforting the Darnells into the bargain.

One thing, though, Edna could sing, and so it sounded could her two pals. The rest of the choir, except for the Nordstrom girl, were the regulars, and they pretty much had *Amazing Grace* down pat, but they were harmonizing way better than Buck had expected. In fact, Barbara Trabert's happy face, the one she put on for holidays and special events, might be genuine this time, as long as she kept her eyes away from Edna.

Poor Tricia Nordstrom had the bad luck to be right behind the three interlopers, where everybody was staring. The kid looked scared stiff, and knowing her parents, they'd be more upset over Edna than the Darnells were. You'd never guess seeing Tricia try to sing that she was such a dynamo on the basketball court. Maybe she needed a hug from Greg Fulton to bring out her best. Fulton sure seemed to think so, and it couldn't be the worst thing about being coach. How Ruth and Tony Nordstrom had put up with it this year was more than Buck could figure.

But the simple melody and familiar words got to Buck, and he teared up when the whole place repeated the first two verses. It struck him that the choir had sung it for his brother Cal, way back then. Buck'd been how old, fourteen? The same age as Lou Bishop, two years older than young Crandall, and one less than Billy Stark.

He'd blubbered like a baby, like Lou and Billy were now, crying all the tears Huey and Norma hadn't been able to because they were so angry at what'd happened. The choir had sung it this way for Frank Pezzola, too, after his car wreck. Stan White and Buck, thirty themselves at the time, had sung along. In the mid-60s there'd been a different one for Huey, likely requested by Norma so she wouldn't have to bury her husband and her oldest son to the same music.

That was the last time Buck had cried till today, and it might've taken him those ten years to get his feelings back to where he could. He'd been devastated over Huey, way worse than for Frank and even worse than for Cal. Juan Holmes waved at him again and a jolt of goose-bumps went down Buck's arms. This half-hour of nostalgia and remembering had given him the key.

Juan, eyes flashing with intelligence and mischief, was the spit image of Frank Pezzola at that age, back when Frank used to come in from his family's ranch in a horse-drawn wagon on Saturdays to play kick-the-can in the schoolyard with Buck and the other town boys. Buck could check one of the old class photos in Norma's scrapbook at home to see if he was right, but he knew he was.

* * *

Amazing Grace? Greg understood that it was a traditional hymn, not something Judy Collins had originated in the '60s, and was one the choir regulars and their guests could probably perform with minimal rehearsing, but that didn't mean it fit. How could the phrase "wretch like me," a sinner marveling at redemption, relate to twelve-year-old Toby, particularly after Reverend White's endless references to innocence and "Blood of the Lamb"? Greg sang along half-heartedly when Barbara Trabert gestured for the audience to join in, and Molly seemed equally perplexed.

"I don't know the words," Ned Fulton fumed, having already been fidgeting and peeking past the grownups to make eye contact with Juan Holmes from every possible angle.

Still, the music was moving, in the sense that the Crandalls weren't close to dry of tears, and Billy Stark had streams of them running down his face. But there must have been any number of better choices available. Greg couldn't believe Pat and Jim had requested it, yet Barbara Trabert was glowing like she'd pulled a great coup. The crowd stirred as Reverend White stood again, probably to dismiss them with one last pseudo-comforting chestnut, but before he could, Om Gillette's voice came from the loft.

"Please...another few minutes. The three of us have something special for Pat and Jim and Stevo and Lisa. Oh, Barbara...if you know your Beatles' songs, we'd be happy for accompaniment."

At the mention of the Beatles, the stirring of the crowd became more pronounced. Greg saw a touch of alarm cross Reverend White's face. Edna, Om and Jeanne launched into a slow, perfect a-cappella rendition of a new pop classic, but with modified lyrics.

> Gee, Tobe, we sure feel sad,
> But from here on, we won't be bitter.
> You'll always be so alive in our minds,
> Helping us find a path that's better.
>
> Da, da, da...da-da-da-da...da-da-da-da...Gee, Tobe.
> Da, da, da...da-da-da-da...da-da-da-da...Gee, Tobe.
>
> We know your mom your dad and your sis
> Will forever miss you. So will your brother.
> But even when they...

In back, Greg saw the tearful Ore House proprietor Rick Rodman's teeth smiling so broadly through his heavy, brown beard that they seemed disembodied. Barbara Trabert, meanwhile, looked as though she'd swallowed a handful of choke cherries, and far from mounting an accompaniment, audibly closed the wooden cover

over the organ's keyboard. And she must have shared the cherries with Buck Thompson, or that was how he seemed to Greg. My god, the guy was a mixed bag. How would you ever know where you stood with him from one minute to the next?

Om and her two friends continued singing — verse, chorus, and coda — until a handful of the younger choir ladies also began to contribute and Tricia Nordstrom, blushing mightily, did the same.

Much of the audience sat bemused, while Greg's eyes finally blurred into a salty flood. He hadn't cried for Toby until now, and now he couldn't stop. His last clear view was of the Crandalls, overwhelmed, huddled together around Stevo's wheelchair, sobbing with Drew Ormond. The music went on and Greg completely lost himself. Though Meg Segal was just to his right, her loud spasms of weeping seemed to emanate from a distant source. Molly's hand, reaching over Ned to stroke the back of Greg's neck, became his remaining physical contact with the world.

When Greg returned, the singing had ended and Reverend White must have communicated somehow that people were free to leave, because the church was emptying and creaky boards and shuffling footsteps were the dominant sounds. The Crandalls had migrated away from Stevo, who seemed to be asleep anyway, and were engaged in a scrum of hugging with the Starks and the Bishops. Billy Stark, from the sight of him, might have cried more than anyone.

"That was intense," Molly said. Her hand, no longer moving, remained on Greg's neck.

"Why did you cry, Daddy?" Ned asked. Greg could tell Ned was worried.

"Because Toby's dead."

"But Toby was dead Sunday night. That's when Mommy and I cried."

"I don't know, son. I couldn't cry on Sunday. Today I could."

"Why, Daddy?"

"Because Toby's not coming back." A stray tear went down Greg's cheek and Ned wiped it off.

"Jesus came back, the man said he did."

"Not everybody believes that."

"But the man said!" Ned stood on the pew, his eyes even with his father's.

"Well," Greg paused, recognizing that this was not the time for theological discussion, "that's what makes Jesus special. Toby doesn't get to."

"Oh," Ned answered. "I'm really sad now, too." He hugged himself to Greg's shoulder and Greg held him there.

"I know, son. We all are."

Colin Crandall, Ian Dudley, and Drew Ormond separated themselves from the milling bodies near the altar and started up the center aisle. Colin and Ian were in well-tailored suits, and notwithstanding the thirty-year age difference between them, could almost be taken for contemporaries in the dim interior light, especially given Ian's lack of hair. Drew had hair enough for himself and Ian combined, and today looked more like D'Artagnon than ever in black slacks and a black turtleneck. The Segals were already gone, so Greg was closest as the three men came by.

"What's next?" he asked, tilting his head in their direction. Molly had removed her hand from Greg's neck and was moving away, taking Ned along.

Ian stopped to talk. "Colin's off to the interment with the rest of the family," he said. "Drew and I," Ian's face signaled irony, "have a weekly deadline to meet. I was a journalism major and editor of the *Vanderbilt Law Review*. You don't think I'd miss an opportunity to help put out the *Merc*, do you?"

"Guess not." Greg couldn't manage a smile, but seemed to have regained control of his emotions. "How's the front page look?"

"Well, there's Toby's death as the lead, of course, plus fishing season and the Chilcutt brothers crime spree. Also a new scoop."

"Scoop?"

"Yeah. Buck Thompson's race may not be the political Topic A anymore. Our pet bartender Rick Rodman is running for Supervisor against Will Jeffers in Sierra City. As a write-in. Don't you love it? Wish we lived up there to vote for him."

"That is a kick." Greg again tried to smile, but none came. "But Toby would be the lead." A wrenching detail Greg hadn't considered — the family's tragedy a banner headline in their own paper.

And could only three days have gone by? Greg's continuing sense of dread felt as though it had been with him for weeks. Maybe Ian, who had made clear he didn't intend to be a father, and the long-divorced, footloose Drew, whose children were grown and had been raised mainly by his ex, were more resilient because this didn't hit them as close to home. Nor had either one actually seen the body. Or maybe they just seemed more resilient. *Fake it till you make it* was one of Drew's favorite pieces of advice.

"Jim's dad wrote a beautiful eulogy to fill the editorial space," Ian went on, "with cautions about respecting the river's power."

"Rotten job for a grandpa," Greg said wearily.

"You're right about that." Ian lifted his palm in a goodbye wave and departed.

Juan Holmes and Ned frolicked noisily in and out of the side door, held open by Molly while she spoke with Sandra Torkin and Karen, Juan's mom. Greg still hadn't called her about his decision to stay neutral in the divorce, and he couldn't see himself doing it tonight either, however big an issue Molly made of it when they got home. Perhaps that was what the women were talking about. Molly might be fed up enough with his delays and for having to apologize on his behalf this past month that she was priming the other two for a go at changing his mind right now.

Wishing he were invisible, he began to slide down the pew toward them. Then it hit him. He hadn't been procrastinating since Monday because of Toby or out of embarrassment over his previous procrastination. It was because he really didn't have a decision. Staying neutral was clearly the most convenient posture for him, and probably the most practical, but it could also amount to dumping his ethics out the window. Maybe taking sides was the way to go, just as Molly claimed.

Miraculously, at the moment he reached the side aisle and took his feet, Karen, leading a reluctant Juan, left with Sandra. The bands of tension in Greg's temples and jaw slowly loosened. Still, he realized that awkward situations like this, and his powerlessness in dealing with the kind of destructive gossip he'd overheard in the graveyard last night, would recur and recur in a community as small as western Sierra County until he made peace with the entire Seth Holmes question.

Most of the current strains in his marriage were tied into it as well. But he must have been paranoid to think that Molly or any of the chatting women would jump him in front of Ned and Juan on such a touchy matter, and certainly not in these surroundings. Nonetheless, a way forward did exist, and an opportunity to pursue it was already on his calendar.

CHAPTER 13

Bullards Bar Dam truly was the cork in the bottle, Greg thought, slowing Molly's VW wagon a few miles past the county line as he traversed the stretch of road on the dam's top. An immense, flared-at-the-bottom slab of gray concrete, it contained to his right a long, narrow, gently lapping, forest-rimmed reservoir, dominated in the foreground by a powerboat marina almost at eye level. Across the road, and five hundred feet down, the North Yuba's residue flowed westward through a shallower, broader canyon cloaked only with scattered trees and manzanita.

During the time Greg and Buck had been in the morgue together, the sister molecules of those that had choked away Toby's life must have washed into the reservoir's upstream end. By now, ten days after the funeral, they were blended with the rest, waiting to be shunted through tunnels and pipelines for power generation or agricultural use, though some could already be in the modest releases at the spillway gate.

Lately almost anything could trigger painful thoughts of Toby, but experiencing so many aspects of the river from a single vantagepoint was still welcome. It was a sunny Saturday morning and Greg was on his way to a curriculum conference. He couldn't linger at the pullout because he might miss his registration deadline, but the recent return of daylight-saving time meant he'd have another chance at the view on his drive home. Most transitions between ecological zones were gradual. This one was pronounced, offering a vivid snapshot of why he'd moved to the mountains.

For fifty miles above here the North Yuba was wild, the fluid spine of a completely different life—for fish, plants, trees, animals, and people alike. From the dam on down, it was tamed, and he began to drop first through acres of open, rolling pasture, followed in turn by fruit and nut orchards, some still in bloom, then by low-lying fields of nascent row crops and finally into the modest Central Valley conurbation of Marysville/Yuba City.

His plan was to leave the conference a bit early, making sure not to jeopardize the units needed for his credential, and meet Seth at a hole-in-the-wall Mexican restaurant they both knew. If Molly was suspicious when he got back, he would say the afternoon session had run long, he'd been hungry, had stopped to eat, and service was slow. The real challenge had been setting it up, although a teacher pumping coins into the pay phone outside the gym at breaktime wasn't unusual. You weren't allowed to do personal business on the school line, and everything from scheduling dental work to arranging for furnace repairs had to be taken care of somehow.

But catching Seth at home when Janet wasn't, and then swearing him to secrecy, had taken multiple calls and hang-ups over several days. On top of that, Greg had to ensure that no passers-by could overhear. You'd have thought he was lining up a call girl, for god's sake, which he'd never done, although it seemed a transgression that lots of guys fell into. But once he did reach Seth, the details had come together and the stakes for Greg were high.

In the name of loyalty to Karen, Molly had insisted after Seth's departure last summer that Greg never socialize with him again. Greg had agreed, had given his word, in fact. Later he'd even agreed to stonewall Ned and Juan if they asked about Seth, to avoid interacting with Janet Carr in any way, and never to expect Molly to interact with either of them. Infrequent phone conversations, if initiated by Seth, were declared OK once Greg began to get enmeshed in the legal cases, but Molly often hovered within earshot to guard against overly friendly exchanges or active cooperation.

Sure, the Crandalls, or the Starks, or Karen and Juan themselves had problems that were infinitely greater, but for him this had become an insoluble conflict. He'd fudged matters the past week by telling Molly he was leaning toward giving voluntary testimony in the divorce after all. He said he wanted to sleep on it a night or two, and since a court date hadn't been set, there was no rush. As he'd hoped, she became so sure he would join the Karen-Sandra team, she stopped pressuring him.

She had also known for months about today's social science conference, yet she'd asked again recently if Seth would be there. No, Greg had reiterated, given that Seth taught biology and math, plus being jobless other than subbing, and was in financial straits. Greg could only go because the school district was reimbursing the cost. Moreover, Greg would honor his pledge to keep Seth at a distance in the unlikely event he did show up.

She'd accepted that answer, which until a few days ago had been the whole truth. And when it no longer was, and he'd undertaken to go back on his word, he certainly should have told her regardless of how she might react.

But he couldn't stand more strife at home over anything right now: not while Ned was still so fearful and upset because of Toby, and not while Molly was so wound up on good versus evil in the Buck Thompson and Rick Rodman elections, and not with the thought drumming in his head that his conduct with the basketball team had been circulating in the town rumor mill.

Greg needed peace in his marriage, yet he simply had to hear — face to face — Seth's version of the divorce and employment termination cases and share his own perspectives in reply. Having a major blowup with Molly over Seth Holmes — the minor ones they'd already had were bad enough — would only happen because Greg was fully confident that Seth's was the right side to be on. If yes, he'd back Seth to the hilt and take his chances on everything else. Otherwise, no more ducking and running. He'd oppose Seth on all counts and the reasons for a big blowup would be gone.

It seemed logical that Molly would be more forgiving of today's sneaking around if it led to his adopting the stance she'd always argued for. On the other hand, were he to side with Seth, she'd be so angry that the sneaking couldn't add much to it. A force-five storm was a force-five storm. But either way, he'd promised himself that as soon as he had a decision, he'd tell her everything. His choice in the meantime, however hackneyed, had been peace at any price, and his increasingly torn, guilty and apprehensive feelings as the day drew on were apparently part of the price.

* * *

Cafe Centrál occupied the middle of a shabby Marysville block backed up against the Yuba River levee, a twenty-foot berm of weedy dirt and rock bounding the city to the south. To Greg's dismay he had arrived first, time he actually owed his employer. Nursing a bottle of Bohemia and munching on chips and salsa, he waited at a small formica table near the back. He was nervous, more so than he'd expected, and the fact of having driven Molly's car to an encounter she would so thoroughly disapprove of had begun weighing on him as well.

Colorful *serápes* and *sombreros* decorated the pale green walls, dusty *piñatas* hung in the corners, and the smell of corn tortillas cooking in hot oil emanated from the kitchen. Perhaps half of the fifteen or so tables were occupied, the customers a wide mix of ages and genders but mostly speaking Spanish. Some appeared to be trades people and others, agricultural workers. It was a language Greg had studied, and he enjoyed eavesdropping for fragments of sentences that he could pick up, though he understood the children far better than the adults.

After ten minutes the door, draped with strings of painted ceramic beads, swung open and Seth entered. Greg stood momentarily and waved. Seth, in jeans, a button-down madras shirt, and carrying a worn leather briefcase, waved back. "*Mr.* Fulton," he called, with an uncertain smile, continuing their running faculty-room joke of greeting each other formally.

"*Mr.* Holmes," Greg replied in kind, automatically making his accent a slight impersonation of Dr. Watson. His own smile also felt uncertain.

Approaching, Seth glanced at his watch and said, "Sorry. I know you're on a schedule, and it's not like I had a conference myself or big distances to cover."

Six years older than Greg, he was of medium build and height, his fair coloring and animated expressions suggesting Johnny Carson, the TV personality. What Greg hadn't been prepared for was that Seth's hair would be swept back and shot with gray, its length and color both new since he'd last seen him.

"Yeah, gray," Seth nodded, having obviously tracked Greg's eyes. "Shows the stress I've been under, and none of it attributable to my sweet young thing in Chico."

If not directly, Greg thought, *then indirectly*, but he said, "So, that's not a total antidote for aging?" They shook hands warmly, the physicality of it reassuring to Greg, and Seth settled into one of the table's chrome-legged, red vinyl chairs. His briefcase went on a second chair nearby.

"She probably *has* kept me younger," Seth offered, "other things being equal. But what's Juan like now? I'm dying to know. Tell me everything you can think of."

Which Greg did, mentioning Karen only obliquely, while Seth ordered a beer and they each decided on different combination plates. With the proprietor, who doubled as their waiter, Seth operated entirely in fluent Spanish, seeming to earn real approval as he rattled on about the weather and a local boxer who was doing well in Sacramento. Janet Carr subscribed to the *Mountain Mercury*, so Seth already knew about Toby, but Greg filled him in on more of the background, plus a general update on the rest of the gang. By then their food had come and they were eating.

"God, what a shocker," Seth sighed, around a mouthful of enchilada. "But I know how scary that river can be. Extra tragic, because Toby was such a sharp young guy. He might have been the next Janet, or an Ernie Warrington, though Ernie was out of school before I started teaching there."

"I got the same sense. It would've been great having Toby in class." Acknowledging that amplified the loss, but somehow made Greg feel better.

Seth raised his beer in a toast. "I really appreciate this. Bad news or not, I've been starved for contact with everybody...especially you. How I wish I could have helped Pat and Jim. Also Billy Stark. He tries so hard to be a good kid despite everything."

"I've missed you, too. A lot...and not just at school. There's plenty more we need to talk about."

"For sure. I think of Juan every day, but I don't want to subject him to a tug-of-war between me and the Dragon Lady...oh..." Seth looked sheepish. "...me and Karen, that is. At the moment, I'm completely shut out, and she had Sandra get Judge Sturdevant, the small-minded bastard, to back her up. All I'm allowed to do is send money. You'll probably take a hit from Molly for even being here."

"Yeah. I'm going to tell her soon, but for god's sake don't breathe a word to Janet or anybody who could blab. Seriously. Everything between us today is off the record. Just know that the newcomer women are unanimous against you...and most of the locals."

"Got it. And I admit what I did was crappy. Karen deserves to be pissed. But it had to happen. It really did."

"Whatever you say."

"Sounds like you've never been in love, never consumed by it."

"What about you and Karen, back when you met?"

"Not the same, if I even remember. The question was to you."

"Well, I have. You weren't around when Molly and I got together. And I still am, in a way…if you count Ned."

"Ouch! Kind of a low blow."

"If you're free to state your feelings…I can state mine."

Seth reached for his briefcase, then paused. "No, let's order another beer and finish our meals before getting to the legal stuff."

"OK." Looking at his watch, Greg nodded and beckoned to the waiter.

"You heard my congrats by phone on the great B-ball season," Seth said, "but wow, I'd like to have seen some of those games. Two wins over Loyalton! The town must have been completely ga-ga. I was counting the days till the next *Merc* arrived."

"It was pretty exciting." Greg felt himself smile.

"Same with the election. Just think, in Sierra City I'd be writing in Rick Rodman. There's enough newcomers in that precinct, he might pull it off. What a poke in the eye for the people there who deserve one…and plenty do. The good part is I don't live where a bozo like Buck Thompson could end up as sheriff."

"I see problems, but the guy does have redeeming features." Internally, Greg debated going into specifics and decided against.

"Oh, come on! Any week now Jim will tear him a new one when the *Merc* endorses Pritchard. Buck's got a finger in every backward thing that goes on…not to mention a smarmy past."

"Don't hold your breath. Jim and Pat aren't endorsing in any of the races. Something they decided months ago, I'm told."

"Well there's a bunch of crap! Dumb, besides." Seth shook his head and gave a sharp exhale. "And I'm too far out of the picture now to talk them around."

"Molly and Karen aren't any happier about it than you are."

"See, I do have common ground with them. But, jeez, you'd think Chico was in a parallel universe from how little of the connection we all had still exists."

"To be alive is to make choices," Greg said pointedly. He was more and more convinced of that, despite his current difficulty in making them.

"Ouch, again," Seth replied.

"Applies to me, too. The biggest reason I'm here."

* * *

"This same lawyer," Seth said, further rearranging on the table the papers he'd brought, "is handling both cases. The divorce, *I'm* paying for, and dissolving the marriage per se is straightforward. The tricky parts are the division of property and child support/child custody. The wrongful termination is on a retainer from the CTU." Seth reached for Greg's hand. "Here's his business card, for future reference."

"Arnold Caldwell, JD," Greg read aloud, noting to himself that it was a Yuba City address and phone number. The CTU was the California Teachers Union. No logo indicated that affiliation, but Greg knew they frequently used outside attorneys to support members in rural areas. Greg himself was a member.

"That's him. But he goes by Arnie. And he's been frank with me. Doesn't do that many divorces, but has tons of expertise on school employment. Since so many of the facts overlap, I'm getting a bargain on what I owe. Right now, I'm strapped big-time."

"So?"

"So I need to level with you, too. At first our...you know, Arnie's and mine...idea was to lock you in on my side right up front. If you were a main character witness in the divorce, you wouldn't take a dive on the next one...how your boss Zack Brennan screwed me that night."

"Makes sense...just kind of unpleasant being the target."

"Well, here's the latest. I know it sounds Machiavellian, but after you said on the phone how much pressure you were getting from Molly, and how you'd rather stay neutral in the divorce, he thinks you should go on and testify for Karen."

"What!"

"Yeah."

"I'm not signing up to spy for you in the enemy camp."

"No, that isn't the point. Think about it. We weren't going to ask you for dirt about Karen...unfit mother, that kind of bullshit. None of it would be true anyway. She is who she is, and I know she loves Juan and treats him right. All we'd ask is that you affirm as strongly as possible that I love Juan and I've always treated him right. And that he loves me. Which he does, you've seen it."

"Yes, I have."

"Well, Arnie can put those same questions and get those same answers on cross examination no matter whose witness you are. Besides, you know Janet's reputation from when she was in school, and the fine person she is. Which you can say, too, along with whatever nice you say about Karen. I'm not afraid of the truth."

"I'll be damned. And the fact is, I don't know one bad thing to say about any of you along those lines."

"And you're not going to perjure yourself to oblige Sandra and Karen, right?" Seth jabbed his finger at one of the sheaves of paper.

"Of course not."

"Then we're there. Go forth and do good."

"Not so fast. I don't see how it all fits, how it's Machiavellian?"

"Your testimony goes strictly to the child custody aspect. I want joint custody, but where I'm at is zero. In any fair hearing, the least I come out with is guaranteed visitation rights, the more the better.

"The child support and property aspects don't concern you. I *want* to provide for Juan, and I will. Arnie'll just make sure I don't get taken. And on the property, the issue is an inheritance I received just before we went to Nicaragua, which Karen claims I've co-mingled, so it's no longer mine alone. She's wrong, though, and Arnie says we have a slam-dunk on that." Seth pointed again to some of the papers in front of him.

"But for now," he went on, "those assets are frozen pending a settlement. Which is why, along with the fact that Zack has kept me from getting a steady job, I'm so strap…"

"You're putting a lot of faith in Judge Sturdevant," Greg broke in, "who's a big buddy of Janet's very pissed-off father, as I recall."

"No, we're getting a change of venue to down here on exactly those grounds. It's already in the works. For both cases. But when you support me against Zack after already having been an opposition witness in the same courtroom, which Arnie will play up, it'll have that much more zing." Seth gave a self-congratulatory smile. "Now are you reminded of a certain sly Italian nobleman?"

Uncomfortable, Greg stayed with the previous topic. "How do you avoid the moral turpitude aspect? You're living with a woman not your wife, she's the better part of twenty years your junior, and was not too long ago your student? Even down here that's going to count against on child custody."

"Not as much as you think. For one thing, I haven't been there flaunting my life of sin in Juan's face. For another, Janet and I will *be*

117

married as soon as the dissolution goes through, most likely before custody is decided. If not, I'd stipulate to delaying the date of whatever custody I get until we are married. There's also not one shred of evidence...not one...that I ever touched Janet while she was my student. On top of which, I was in the Peace Corps the first two years she wasn't my student."

"You know damn well Sandra will look for witnesses."

"Let her look...and dare to put them on the stand."

"Are you sure?"

Seth had been getting steadily more agitated, and he now flushed vividly. "What are you saying?" He stared at Greg. "What the hell are you saying!"

"Neither you or Janet were in town when I started teaching there, but a lot of ugly rumors are going around."

"The town sport," Seth growled. "Like what?"

"You were apparently alone with her in science labs after school any number of times. Also, that you drove her home in bad weather. Sandra could have a field day with it. I won't mention names, but not everybody on the faculty is a fan of yours either."

"That's outrageous!" Seth's voice grew in intensity. "Janet was an honor student, for Christ sake! Naturally she had extra projects and labs. And every bit of it was in broad daylight with the door open...OK, not the car door, but I gave lots of kids rides...boys and girls...when they needed one."

"Maybe you don't really understand how angry Karen is. What if she tars you up and down with innuendo more than I...or anybody...can rebut?" In the corner of his eye, Greg saw a few heads turn in their direction.

"My friend Greg," Seth said disgustedly, quieting his tone. "The worry wart."

"I am your friend, which is why I'm giving you and Arnie my best guess on what to expect. Since Sandra and I haven't talked about any of this yet, I'm not violating her confidence. But I want you to tell *me* something. Look me square in the eye and say you and Janet never so much as held hands or made the slightest representations to each other before last summer."

"You're on." Seth leaned across the table. "Catch this: never. N-E-V-E-R."

"Did you write her letters from Nicaragua?"

"A couple of postcards. Touristy ones. Letters, no."

118

"And that's it?"

"As far as anything overt, yes. But Greg, you know how it is. Girls get crushes on male teachers. It's not hard to detect. You feel it, and sometimes, when they're juniors and seniors, you have to fight yourself not to respond. Jesus, their skin, tits, the short skirts. We're all human. Don't pretend you don't know what I'm talking about."

"I know what you're talking about." He felt the hair on his arms prickle. And like it or not, his behavior had raised similar concerns, as Molly herself had pointed out, even though he hugged all of the players every game, no favorites based on sex appeal, and in public, loosely, with his upper body only.

"So did I feel something with Janet?" Seth was saying. "Yes, absolutely. Did I respond in any physical way? Hell, no. But did I respond other ways? Probably yes, unconsciously. With her it was different. Night and day different. I didn't write her letters from Nicaragua, and she wasn't the only person receiving postcards, but I dreamed about her over and over down there. It was nuts. And she says her first two years at Chico, she was dreaming of me.

"Remember how I was goosey about coming back to Sierra County after the Peace Corps? Well, it wasn't only because of the closed attitude of the locals. I was also afraid that what did happen would happen…if Janet and I got in proximity again.

"But Karen insisted. I had a guaranteed job and she loved the mountains. OK…now she gets to keep them. But my god, when Janet showed up in town last June, looking like the gamine Truffaut would cast in his next film, and she let drop that she still hadn't had a serious college boyfriend, I was done for…" Seth gazed across the room, having either lost or suppressed his train of thought.

"Alright, I'm persuaded." Greg said at last. "I'll sign on with Karen to answer as completely and truthfully as I can whatever questions Sandra…and later Arnie…put to me. If that ends up helping you…without damage to Karen…I'll be glad."

"Thanks," Seth said, drinking from his beer. "All I could ask. And thanks for pointing out the tactics she may use. Forewarned needs to be forearmed, especially Arnie. My own time in front of the judge sounds like do or die."

"Also," Greg emphasized, "this is it for us till everything's over. No more meetings or phone calls."

"Understood. It's strictly Arnie you'll be working with on the school district stuff. But we may have more uniting us than you realize, old buddy. I've got a heads-up for you in the same vein."

"Oh?" It just couldn't be, Greg thought. Not the toxic baloney about his coaching.

"Yeah, from Janet's dad."

"He talks to you?"

"No way, but he calls to yell at her from time to time and she picks up the phone by mistake. If we guess it's him we don't answer, and he clicks off if I do."

"So?"

"According to him, a certain teacher who also happens to be a very successful coach has been hugging female players when they come out of the game, and decent citizens don't think they have to put up with it. My would-be nemesis Leland Carr's not on the school board now, but he was, and he's happy to hear complaints. He wants his daughter to know, that because of her, Downieville's become a moral sinkhole." Seth looked as pleased with himself as he had when making his Machiavelli reference.

"Shit," Greg said flatly. "Spare me. There's not a thing to it."

"As I well believe," Seth replied, nodding, "but watch your ass. They could make a move on you. We both saw how little it takes. Zack never informed me of my rights... which was no accident.

"He knew that I felt so guilty...over Juan...and everything... and then being called into his office at night...he probably could've gotten me to climb the Sierra Buttes and jump off. My mood swings were impossible to deal with."

"Well, I *don't* feel guilty...and I'm *not*."

"Under the wrong circumstances, and in a weak moment, you might lose that certainty. Think of my resignation, the way it was all drawn up before we got there. When Zack handed me the pen, how could I weigh the consequences? You know...the stigma of being on the teacher job market that late in the summer. It looked like I'd been fired, and who knows what bad-mouth rap he's putting out when somebody asks for a reference. I have it on pretty good authority that the other administrators are out of the loop. All queries about me are supposed to go through Zack."

"As for rumors, that's not one I've heard," Greg said icily. Whether or not Seth was deliberately trying to manipulate him, he didn't like how this felt. "The rest you've alluded to on the phone."

"Keep your ears open for me, 'cause Zack's vulnerable if it's true. Not only did I have no chance to change my mind the way the law allows, Arnie says they could never have fired me on the facts involved. Obviously there was a PR problem. To keep things cool in the west county, I'd've accepted a transfer to Loyalton, where I could either stick it out and live closer to Juan, or cut loose after a year if my job search around Chico paid off. The whole thing makes me boil."

"You wouldn't be living with Janet right now under that scenario."

"We'd've adapted. I could spend every weekend and vacation down here, or she'd transfer to Nevada-Reno and one of us would commute across the state line. Lots of people drive to or from the east county for jobs."

"Stop. That's as much as I need to know. But add one more to your list of regrets...why you agreed to go ahead with that meeting and have me as sole witness. It's right at the top of my list. Zack should've had his own somebody."

"Yeah, he outfoxed us both. Arnie says the same thing."

"Seth, I've heard your side of the story, and I know what I saw and heard between you and Zack. I haven't heard his side. I'm going to work with one of your attorneys and face the other in court, but I honest to god don't know where I am with it. Arnie'll be going up against Ian, by the way. And he or Zack will have to outline their case for me before I decide."

"Bullshit! You're kidding?"

"I'm not."

"I can't believe it! We hand you a pass on the divorce, I tell you the shit Leland is putting out, and now this? Where's the goddamn gratitude?" Seth pounded a fist on one of the sheaves of paper, eyes glaring and his voice the loudest so far.

"You can lay off the pressure. I've gotten immune. But whoever's side I come down on, yours or Zack's, I'll never do anything to give you the shaft." Greg scraped back his chair to leave and noticed the proprietor and many of the patrons staring at them. Standing, he reached for his wallet.

"Here's ten bucks to cover my meal," he went on. "And don't call me. When I have an answer, I'll be in touch." After extracting the bill from his wallet, he tucked in its place the lawyer's business card. "Sorry, but I can't keep Molly waiting any longer."

Rarely at a loss for comebacks, Seth had one now. "Ah, yes... the seemingly dutiful husband."

"Let's hope appearances count for something. I really wanted all this to be clearer for me by now...regarding you, I mean, and what I need to do. Too bad that part didn't work out."

CHAPTER 14

It was 6:30 on a Wednesday in late May, time for the evening rise, and Greg's personal trout season was about to begin. He'd parked behind the lumber yard, along the Downie just above the Main Street commercial strip, rigged his fly rod, climbed into his waders, negotiated the brushy embankment, and was stepping carefully into the water. In a smooth, wide, clear and fairly shallow stream like this one, careful was how you kept from spooking the fish, and careful was also how you avoided a cold bath from slipping on submerged rocks.

Across the way were the houses of Pearl Street, with Crandalls' mostly hidden by Grant Trabert's barn-like garage, and the steeple of the church showing among the treetops off to the right. Perfect. The middle of town and Greg had the water to himself. He never liked competing with weekend crowds, and this year he'd decidedly not been in the mood to fish until recently. Nothing about the Yuba or the Downie had seemed inviting.

Toby's funeral had been a month ago. Sandwiched between that and his unsatisfying visit with Seth and Seth's schemes, the official season had opened. Of course, since Greg was a fly fisherman, early conditions were never right for him anyway. Stream flows had to drop and there needed to be enough sustained warm weather to bring the bugs out. With the late sun throwing long shadows, and a hatch of what Greg recognized as small-to-medium stone flies just getting underway, tonight's prospects should be good. When he *was* looking to fish, he hit this stretch several times a year.

Actually, Greg could have fished any night during the past week, but he'd been too busy. Thank god he wasn't coaching a spring sport. Regular classwork was plenty, on top of final exams to prepare, papers to grade, anxious seniors to help with choosing their colleges, a bad fuel pump on the Travelall, and Ned's coming down with a cold and cough when the weather had turned cruddy again after April's teasings of summer.

Then, this last weekend, he and Molly had been lead chaperones at the junior-senior prom. The kids had used the theme of the popular Redford-Newman movie *The Sting*, with the girls as high-class molls and the boys impersonating card-sharks, complete with recorded ragtime piano whenever the country and western band hired from Grass Valley took breaks.

And to Molly's great credit, she'd been OK with Brenda Lowry's asking Greg to dance, even though Brenda was by far the best looking girl on Greg's team and the music was a slow ballad. The result of his saying yes had been very much at arms' length, of course, with both Greg and Brenda making sure of that. But Molly's forbearance was tested even further, because Brenda told him that Tricia Nordstrom and the other basketball girls attending the prom planned to do the same thing—and one-by-one, they did. Whatever Molly really thought, she said at the time it was *cute*, and so far hadn't varied from that.

To compensate Greg had tried nudging a few of the boys to dance with Molly, but none found the courage to do it. Tricia Nordstrom, who'd sung at the funeral, was a junior and would be back next year. Brenda Lowery was graduating and would attend University of the Pacific, a real achievement. One of the mixed joys of teaching was accepting that your biggest successes would depart and not return, especially in a community like this. Greg knew that was true of parenting, too, and in a much more profound sense, but it was a long way off yet with Ned. For high school teachers, saying good-bye was an annual event.

The Downie's seasonal flow was now rushing past Greg's knees and he'd moved far enough from shore that his back-cast would stay clear of the brush. He laid out a crisp, twenty-five-foot probe into a pocket eddy beside an upstream rock. The anticipation he felt during the first seconds his fly was on the water never got stale no matter how many times he cast. Greg had learned how to handle a fly rod from his dad, in the American River, near where he'd grown up, and the technique involved was as familiar to him as putting up a jump shot.

He got a nice little drift at the start, but no action, after which his line bellied out in the fast-moving current and the fly, trailing the V-wake of a tiny motorcraft, skimmed away from anywhere a trout might reasonably lie. Greg brought in line to cast again, taking three steps upstream at the same time.

His standard MO was to work his way at least to the next bridge, clamber out at a vacant lot, and walk back along North Main. Few of the locals were fly fishermen and this stretch of the Downie couldn't really be fished any other way. It was too shallow and swift for bait or lures to be that effective, and from shore the casting angles were too awkward. But Greg nearly always caught fish, though he usually released them. In fact, he used barbless hooks, and when he came home empty-handed, people thought he fished such lackluster water because he didn't know what he was doing. It was his private joke not to contest that assumption.

Another half-dozen casts and position changes produced no action either, but Greg began to see trout flashing and breaking the surface as more circling insects settled on the water to lay eggs. Since he thought he'd matched the hatch with the stone fly imitation he had on, Greg braced himself in the lee of a boulder and changed to a smaller size of the same pattern. Right away he got a follow from a nice rainbow, and on the next cast pulled in and released a beautiful nine-incher. Continuing to move upstream, Greg picked up four more on about ten casts, keeping the last one for Ned's breakfast before sitting on a half-submerged tree trunk to rest.

He was just offshore of the Starks' backyard. Their ramshackle house, not visible from where Greg sat, stood thirty or forty feet away, above a retaining wall. To the right of the wall a rutted path he'd never noticed before led to the water through a low-lying copse of willows, undoubtedly the route Toby had followed with his inner tube before meeting a horrible death. It still wrenched at Greg, at the kids at school, and at everyone who had known Toby, although things had superficially returned to normal.

Pat and Jim had gone back to work at the *Merc*, but only as monochrome images of their former selves. Greg and their other friends were using a platoon system to provide pretty much continuous company and activity, and didn't plan to stop. Jim, however, was drinking far more than he previously had, and Pat resignedly ate whatever meals people brought over without showing any of the flair for organization and adventurous menus that had been her trademark. This phase would pass, they all assured one another, yet no one could guess when or how. The most positive developments were that a royalty check had finally come in from Jim's publisher to resolve the family's immediate financial worries, and tourism-related *Merc* advertising was picking up, too.

Hearing a voice that sounded like Janice Stark yelling at Billy's sister in the yard, Greg was taken back to the pathetic scene Ray had made at the cemetery. Of course, seeing the back of the Stark's property and the adjoining streamside path, Greg could understand more of what had prompted Ray's behavior. Not only had his son been implicated, so had his home and, quite possibly, Ray himself. Who could say that he hadn't been inside drunk and not paying attention when the boys scrounged tubes out of the garage, pumped them up and headed for the water? Maybe he had grounds to feel more than indirectly responsible for what had happened.

But perhaps the oddest thing about the guy's boozed-up visit to Toby's gravesite was that Greg still hadn't mentioned it to Molly, or to anyone else. Not that Greg's silence would spare Ray and Billy from embarrassment. Lonny Harris didn't seem the type to keep his mouth shut, and there had been other witnesses. Molly wouldn't be as likely to launch it on the grapevine as they were. Greg's problem was how it reflected on Buck. He was the one who'd brought Ray, and who had fed an obviously sloshed guy more alcohol. Molly would note both those points in a flash, and Greg had no exculpating answers. Maybe the real problem was, why should Greg care?

With the election two weeks away, local politics had heated to a virtual frenzy and the Fultons' front lawn was sporting a Pritchard sign. Molly had seen to that a few days ago. In fact, there were signs, posters, and fliers for candidate nights of one sort or another pretty much everywhere. In addition to all the county offices, two seats were up on the school board along with any number of state offices and ballot initiatives.

Molly had also planted in their lawn a sign supporting Proposition 9, to regulate political campaign practices and funding. It was being sponsored by Jerry Brown, the current Secretary of State, who the Fultons and their friends were all backing for Governor. Still, it was a pain that Greg couldn't turn on the TV or radio, or have a conversation, without being bombarded by political opinion or the smarmy details of Watergate—one more plus about having an evening to spend alone with his fly rod.

Yet the Pritchard sign at home notwithstanding, Greg knew he would mark his ballot for Buck when the time came. It was tied in with Toby, of course, and the only thing giving Greg pause was the memory of Buck and Ray's arrival at the cemetery with those big cans of Coors. True, Buck had been stone sober himself, and had driven the guy home. But what the hell could have been going on between them before, when teetotaling Buck had bought the beer in the first place? If not for that, Greg might be open about his intended vote and see how Molly, Pat, Jim and the others would react.

Greg had even been hoping the Crandalls would initiate a discussion of their feelings about Buck and the way he'd helped them with their loss. Did they think it had just been to curry favor with the *Merc*? So far they weren't saying, and it would be way out of bounds for anyone else to bring it up. That left Greg with a secret he wasn't sharing, not only because he feared it would be unpopular, but because it was based on a kind of male bonding in the face of death that was too corny to defend. Actually, he'd ended up with two secrets, counting the one about meeting Seth in Marysville.

Molly and Sandra had been delighted to have Greg—*finally*, they said—declare himself on Karen Holmes's side. All to the good, but small comfort given that their approval had been earned by his taking what Seth had called a *pass*, a word that didn't sit well. Students, as supplicants, got passes from teachers to go to the restroom. Regardless, he hadn't yet spent any time with Sandra strategizing and preparing testimony, because the change of venue predicted by Seth had thrown the court schedule into limbo. Greg would do it when called, but had no idea when that would be.

For similar reasons, the Zack Brennan case was also on the back burner. The school board was happy enough to wait, and the new judge in Yuba City seemed in no hurry. Greg had told Ian he wanted a recap of the law involved before he threw his hat in with either camp, to which Ian had agreed. But sooner or later that part of the Holmes saga would become unavoidable as well. Just today, in fact, he'd received a phone call from the Superintendent.

Changing to a fresh fly, Greg stood, waded a few steps upstream toward the Pearl Street bridge, and snapped out another cast. As his tippet descended to the water, he brought his head down to follow intently the fly's smooth float back to him, drawing in line and prepared to react at the smallest bump or nudge from a trailing fish.

* * *

There'd been some fool wading in the Downie when Buck crossed the old bridge between Pearl and North Main on his roundabout way to the *Merc* office. Funny time of year to see a tourist with a pussy-ass fly rod out there on a weeknight, but no local would bother with that shallow, rocky stretch up from the lumber yard. Besides, anybody with a lick of sense knows trout can smell and they'll pick up on good bait or a baited lure long before they'll go swallowing feathers.

Buck moved slowly past the house of the new lawyer couple with the mismatched names and waved out the window to Charlie Koontz a few doors down, sitting hollow-eyed on the porch of his unpainted bat-and-board cabin. Charlie's rusty, ribbed-metal roof looked like it maybe had one more year in it, and Charlie looked like he'd be lucky to last a year himself. The old guy waved proudly in response, but Buck wasn't sure Charlie knew it was a sheriff's car much less who was driving. Sad. What a man he'd been, and not just for knowing the backcountry trails and hoisting oil drums around. He was the only one a lot of people trusted to pick safe mushrooms for 'em in the woods or could count on to find wild spring onions for their breakfast potatoes.

Buck remembered that Charlie used to fish with flies, little ones he tied himself, but that was always in late summer, when the water was low and Charlie was the only one catching anything in the rivers. Everybody else, tourists or locals, would've headed up to Lakes Basin by then to score with worms and salmon eggs. Charlie must have been on top of the world to see his daughter Marilyn marry Frank Pezzola, twenty years back if you were counting, and to have her become such a star as County Clerk after Frank's death. Young as Frank was when they buried him, Charlie had three fine grandkids to show for it, too.

Buck was looking forward to this Jim Crandall meeting. He'd put it off longer than he should, with all the poor guy'd been through, but now was the time. Marilyn Pezzola and hardware bigwig Jerry Vargas, Sally's pop, had already talked a little politics with Crandall and felt him out about endorsements, but the word was that the *Merc* would be ducking the whole thing. That was better than having the *Merc* against him, Buck knew, but not near what he really wanted.

Buck waved again, this time as he passed Mel Cresta, who was taking his evening constitutional along Main Street wearing his daily wardrobe of cardigan sweater and a beat-up Panama hat. When the weather wasn't right for that outfit, Mel stayed home. He and his brother Nick had owned the lumberyard for years and now care-took the place for Feather/Yuba Industries, the new owners. Nick was divorced and Mel had never married, so they'd ended up roommates in a double-wide trailer parked in the yard's back corner. There'd been quite a dust-up with Jerry Vargas over the sale, too, but Buck figured the two oldsters were reliable Thompson votes and wouldn't take it out on him that Jerry chaired the Elect HBT Committee.

Well into their 70s, the Crestas had also become Downieville's strongest living links with its past. Nick liked to travel and Mel didn't, so you saw Mel a lot more. Mel had even evolved into the town philosopher, which was to say he, his hat, his pipe and walking stick spent a lot of time on the wooden bench in front of Johnson's Mercantile, and Mel didn't mind talking to drunks. Strange, in a way, because Mel had never been a drinker. Buck parked in the small gravel lot between the newspaper office and the beauty parlor and pointed his feet to the short length of sidewalk that would take him to the *Merc*. Doing his best to look the part voters expected of him, he kept his posture straight and was in full uniform.

Mountain Mercury–Founded 1858 the side of the building read. Across the street in a pin-striped apron, toupee-wearing Dick James, owner and bartender of The Forks Grill, leaned against a post outside having a smoke in the spring air. Thinking that he'd stop there for a burger and some serious hand-shaking later on, Buck exchanged just a wave and a howdy with Dick. Buck had been eating out at one place or another nearly every night lately, even in the east county, hoping to make inroads. The sheriff's race was going down to the wire as far as Buck could tell, but Pritchard and his backers might get lazy thinking they still had a big lead.

CHAPTER 15

Fixing his glance on it, Buck saw that the *Merc's* door was unlocked and slightly ajar despite the closed sign. He took a deep breath, then gently shouldered his way in.

The cramped, unlit room he entered contained piles of papers, maps, books, file boxes and stray telephone sets virtually engulfing four unoccupied desks. Crandall had said there'd be nobody around unless something had gone haywire with tomorrow's edition and staff were working late. But Buck knew that haywire could be as usual as not when the paper went to press, so he was relieved. He'd been counting on a private one-on-one, and not having people in the outer office who might walk in or overhear would be a help. For further insurance, Buck clicked the door lock behind him.

"Mr. Crandall?" he called into the quiet. "I'm a little early. You available?"

Jim Crandall stuck his head out of a lighted, partly glass-walled office at the far back. "Oh, Sheriff," he said. "Be with you in a minute. I'm on the phone."

"No problem," Buck replied, propping his rump on the nearest desk. He couldn't remember if he'd been in here since the Newfields sold out, but it looked the same as ever. He would far rather take law enforcement, he reflected, where you never really knew what was coming, than deal with an inexorable weekly deadline.

"OK, I'm off," Crandall said, striding toward Buck in a sweatshirt, sneakers and jeans. "Come on in."

They shook hands among the vacant desks and Buck looked Crandall over as closely as he dared before following him to the office. No, the guy wasn't recovered yet, and why would he be? It'd only been a month. Buck thought of some old-time miners he'd known years ago, who'd had silicosis, and that's how Crandall looked—clothes hanging loose, dispirited, but with a twitchy, intermittent energy.

"Have a seat," Crandall waved, after dropping into a chair behind his own littered desk. Affixed to the desk's front panel, about knee-high, was a political bumper strip touting Jerry Brown for Governor.

Buck fit himself into a wooden armchair that could have been *Merc* property since before old Cory Flynn, Buck's ongoing morgue tenant, was born. Buck was glad to see the bumper strip, though. It might come in handy as an icebreaker for politics later on. Pointing to the outer office, he said, "Guess your deadline went OK?"

"Yeah...normal...for a change." Crandall forced a laugh.

"Where's tomorrow's *Merc* right now?"

"Grass Valley...at the printer's. That's who was on the phone. The staff take turns going down with the paste-ups late on Wednesday afternoons. Sharon Murdock's doing this one. She'll wait however long it takes for the press run, then bring the local copies back tonight or in the morning. Subscription copies the printer mails directly. I take a turn going down once a month myself...or used to..." Crandall's voice trailed off.

"Grass Valley and Nevada City are nice towns," Buck nodded. "You can catch a movie while you wait." There hadn't been a movie house in Downieville the last ten years, not since around the time Buck's father died.

"If you ever tail me, Sheriff, you'll find that's exactly what I do. The Del Oro Theater. Too bad it's all Disney and John Wayne."

"Beats what we have here." Besides, Buck thought, what's wrong with Disney or John Wayne? "But," he snorted, "why would I tail you?"

"Just a joke," Crandall said awkwardly. "Bad joke, I guess."

"Old one, too, in my line of work. But I am glad to see you doing better than the last time we talked, after your boy's funeral. Hope you don't mind my bringing it up."

"Hurts just as much whether people do or don't."

"No surprise there."

"Anyway, ah...Sheriff Thompson, Pat and I have both thanked you for how you broke the news and for helping with that gravesite, but those things mean more to us now than even a month ago. We'll never forget it, and we can never really repay."

"Appreciate the thought, but it's no more than my Daddy would've done. The only right thing. How's the Mrs. doing? Gettin' back on her feet?"

"Probably better than I am. She's home now with our other two."

Buck had been on the verge of saying that losing your only son was worse than what had happened to Buck's parents with Cal. Fortunately Jim Crandall's mention of "our other two" stopped him. Crandalls had a second boy, like Huey and Norma'd had Buck, but maybe theirs, retarded like he was, would be lucky enough not to realize he'd never measure up. "It'll take time," Buck said instead. "I saw how my parents were after losing my brother."

"People have told us a lot about Cal since we lost Toby. I never knew. Of course, Pat and I've seen Cal's grave now, too."

"Life plays rough," Buck nodded.

Crandall started to reply, but sat clenching and unclenching his right fist without getting the words out.

"At least," Buck continued, "*some* problems are small. If you keep callin' me Sheriff Thompson I gotta call you Mr. Crandall, and that don't sound as friendly as I'd like."

Crandall recovered his composure. "You're welcome to call me Jim. I'd prefer it."

"Means you'll call me Buck."

"Sure, in private. But in print or around town, I plan to stay with Sheriff Thompson. Journalistic ethics you might say."

Although Jim's face had gained color since Buck first arrived, he didn't look healthier. In fact, his eye sockets seemed deeper than before. "OK, Jim, I can live with that. And we're both supporting the same guy to be top dog." Buck pointed at the Jerry Brown bumper strip he'd noticed earlier. "My own office is non-partisan, but don't mean I can't vote in the Democrat primary."

The flicker of surprise on Jim's face said he'd gotten Buck's message. "Sharon and the other staff stuck it on as a joke," Jim shrugged. "They know I like him and thought I should own up."

"Zapped you good," Buck chuckled. "Takes sandblasting to get those off. A nice gal, that Sharon. I've known her family a lotta' years."

"Probably been around as long as the Thompsons."

"Longer. And building on how you put the *Sheriff* Thompson thing a minute ago, maybe I should say why I'm here. I'm hopin' to keep that title...officially...not with my friends...and I want the *Merc's* endorsement."

Jim dropped his eyes to the desktop. Raising them, he said, "Jerry Vargas has talked to me about that, as you probably know. He tell you what the answer was?"

"Far as it goes, yeah." Buck leaned back in the chair and stretched his legs up off the floor for a few seconds. His hat was on a corner of Jim's desk, and his nervous ear was itching, but he was damned if he was going to scratch it. There was nothing about this Crandall guy that should put Buck on the defensive. "You're not endorsing in any races...state, local, whatever."

"That's our decision, yes. I've told Ken Pritchard the same thing."

"Might be more honest than the Newfields' approach," Buck replied, "but it's not good for the *Merc*." Well, well, he noted, that caught the guy's interest.

"How do you mean?" Jim crooked his neck in Buck's direction.

"No matter how you cut it in this county, you'll never have people like you all the time. In fact, when cabin fever sets in these long winters, you can't have most of 'em like you most of the time. Was true even for my Daddy. If elections were in February, no incumbent'd ever win.

"But in the newspaper business, people don't need to like you. Long as they read what you print, who cares if they hate you and are only readin' to get steamed up. Newfields tried the plain vanilla angle and I bet circulation went down. Sure didn't increase. My advice is, take a stand and piss people off...pretty much every week. And don't just pick on one camp. Make sure everybody gets a turn being pissed."

Jim seemed intrigued. "I hadn't thought about it that way, but plain vanilla describes what I've been doing. We're strapped for revenue, and I couldn't see making enemies where I didn't need to."

"This paper's always been a tough go. Newfields didn't put it up for sale because they were making more money than they could stand."

"Yeah, come to find out," Jim grimaced.

"People around here are cranky. Be a shit disturber, they'll all want to read it, and when they do they'll talk about it, and the advertising'll take care of itself. What the merchants want is exposure...west county or Sierra Valley, doesn't matter."

"You could be right. A guy from a weekly paper in Mendocino spoke at a conference Pat and I went to last year and made the same argument."

Buck shrugged. "A look at people's gateposts tells you nearly everybody gets the *Sacramento Bee* or the *Reno Gazette* anyway. The

Merc can't compete covering Patty Hearst, Nixon and all that. Give people reason to read it on top of those city papers."

"Absolutely. Something Pat and I have known all along. Which is why we play up gold and high school sports so much. Our worst nightmare is that the *Gazette* will start a rural California edition and peel off the mountain counties."

"You're right to be worried," Buck acknowledged. "My point is, controversy sells."

"How about a cup of coffee? Still pretty fresh."

"Thanks, I could use one."

Jim got up and went into a hallway off the back of his office. Buck heard cups and glassware being moved about. "Cream or sugar?" Jim asked, still not visible.

"No, black'll do 'er."

"Same way I take mine." Jim returned and handed Buck a nearly full mug that said RAND on it. Whatever the hell RAND was, Jim had a matching mug of his own. But something about how Jim held his, and shielded it from Buck with his body, didn't seem natural. Jim sat down with the cup in front of him. Steam was coming from Buck's but not from Jim's.

Buck took a swallow. Not what he'd call fresh, exactly, but not the worst coffee he'd had. Not the worst this week, in fact. Jim took a pull from his cup too.

"But beyond controversy," Buck went on, "I honestly think the *Merc* should endorse me because I'm the best man for the job." He tried to gauge Jim's reaction.

"Hmm…can I…trust you?" Jim asked.

"As sheriff? You can trust me to be in the next four years the way I was the last four months."

"No, I mean can I tell you something? Strictly confidential?"

"Sure, if it needs to be."

"It does. Pat and I think you *are* the best man for the job and you've got our votes."

"Well, that much is good news. Why confidential?"

"We were openly supporting Pritchard until last month. People will think you bought us with your gravesite."

Buck shook his head. "The buryin' was never part of politics," he said. Well damn, looked like he'd outsmarted himself. It was more than politics, that Buck could swear to, but…OK…there was *some* politics. He took a drink of coffee to cover his discomfort and saw Jim immediately grab his own mug.

"Still," Jim countered, "you know people'll think it...and say it." Jim's manner was becoming more relaxed.

"Pardon my French, but you fart in this town, people'll say you crapped your pants. If you weren't bribed by evil old Buck, what brought you over?" Buck wasn't ready to give up on the *Merc* yet, even if he did have two more votes than he'd thought.

"Your coming to our house in person that night. I was suspicious then, too, but I checked and found out it's SOP. And how you worked with Hal Voorden and the Chilcutt family so those boys got a dose of tribal justice for that burglary in exchange for cheap bail. And the Darnell kid with his streaking. Word gets around. I have sources."

"Well, I am proud of those things, but they all add up to being Huey Thompson's son. You should'a known him."

"Wish I had. Marilyn Pezzola told me the Darnell kid was vintage Huey."

"Hell, listen to the news for ten minutes these days and college students someplace are running around with no clothes on. Young Russ Darnell is home from Sac State and just has to race down Main Street naked at midnight on Saint Pat's Day. No one even complained. We'd've laughed and done nothing if he hadn't run into my deputy on foot patrol and knocked him down rounding the corner past the Quartz Cafe. Had to book the kid and put a scare in him. What could I do?"

"Agree. But treating it as assault on an officer instead of indecent exposure, the charge was sure to be dropped. No DA could make that stick. " Jim laughed, took a pull on his mug, then laughed again.

"Which his hippie sister Edna never quite got," Buck smiled. "She cussed me out on the phone, called me a pig and said I'd made Russ a felon. Thank god the rest of the Darnells wised up and let it die on its own." In the middle of this, Buck had a memory flash of the camouflage-clad Edna singing that Beatles song at the Crandall boy's funeral.

"I considered *Officer Collides with Naked Man* as a banner headline," Jim said.

"Too bad you didn't run it. Would'a sold some papers. If I remember, all you had was a squib in the police blotter."

"The prudes had me gun-shy after the Ore House name thing blew up."

"Sounds like more vanilla creeping in."

Jim cleared his throat. "Let's say…let's say I wanted to endorse in the Sheriff's race."

"OK."

"That's a higher standard than who I vote for personally. Due diligence, journalists call it. Pritchard has been grilled pretty well at these candidate nights, so I know what I need to about him. But there's a couple of tough ones I'd have to ask you."

"Which are?"

"For one, what's the real story on Jared Smith? Why didn't your office make the arrest instead of the FBI?"

"Honest answer is I don't know. But notice how Pritchard never brings it up publicly…never…yet everyplace he goes the rumors start flying?"

"You're right, he doesn't bring it up. Oh…Buck, want more coffee?" Jim stood.

"Thanks. I'm fine."

"There's a little left. Think I'll finish it." Jim went into the back hall. Buck heard a splash in the sink, something being rinsed, a low gurgle of liquid, and a cupboard closing. Jim returned with his cup.

"I can't prove this," Buck went on, "so it's off the record." He looked at Jim, and Jim nodded assent. "The reason Pritchard doesn't bring it up, while his people keep stoking the rumors, is that he was behind it…you know, to embarrass me."

"That's what Om Gillette says. She had a letter from Jared recently."

"Look, it's one of two things, and both of 'em stink from my perspective. Somebody fingered Jared Smith to Pritchard for interstate flight, and he went to his Reno FBI contacts, who did him a campaign favor. My ex-wife has friends around here might've got wind of Jared's story, and they'd stab me in the back like that any chance they got.

"Other possibility is that Jared was a narc, and the Feds pulled him out that way to divert suspicion before other busts go down. Whatever it was, I'm Sheriff, I should'a been informed. You know I wrote the FBI and complained, don't you?"

"So I've heard."

"Well, I have contacts at their Sacramento office. They apologized out the gazoo and promised advance warning on anything else in the county no matter what. Also told me the request to bring Jared in had come from Reno...where Pritchard just happens to practice law...and had been handled by two agents who used to work over there."

"Why don't you go public with that?"

"Because I'm sworn to secrecy...and so are you. Off the record, remember. FBI internal information. All I can do is fight rumors with rumors."

Jim sipped from his coffee cup and rocked side to side in his chair. "You mentioned your ex-wife. The other question I have is harder. What are these stories I hear about you beating her...and your daughter...the older one?"

"Down in Eureka, you mean?"

"Supposedly charges were filed and you were drummed off the force because of it."

Buck looked square at Jim. "That's essentially true."

The diameter of Jim's eyeballs doubled. "Not what you told the hippies in Pike and Goodyear Bar, according to Om."

"Right."

"This off the record, too?" Jim wanted to know.

"No. I'll be straight and take my chances the *Merc* won't run it."

"Oh?"

"Yeah, whatever it takes to convince you I'm the best man for the job...not just good enough to vote for, good enough to endorse."

CHAPTER 16

Using the same small stone fly pattern as before, although in deer hair for better visibility, Greg had caught and released two more pan-sized rainbows by the time he reached the leftmost of the old bridge's wooden pilings. Then, grabbing on with one hand for support, he passed beneath the decking to continue upstream.

A pair of bats swooped through with him and out over the water, feeding on some of the same insects that had trout swirling in all the potholes he could see. He could also hear the occasional splashes of jumping fish, but the light had waned to the point that he never quite got one in view as it arched above the surface.

Since this was his first such excursion in many months, Greg made sure to pick his way, testing the depth with each footstep. The high flows of winter and spring always rearranged the bottom, so you couldn't count on anything being the same as it was. But ahead was a shale ledge with a riffle at its base, which looked hopeful. Two large, root-tentacled and waterlogged stumps had been lodged there in recent years but must have finally torn loose. The only things Greg had gotten from previous casts in that vicinity were flies snagged and lost or clumsy little drifts with no strikes. He'd give the unobscured riffle a few shots and call it a night.

Getting into the Downie as far as he could, he eased himself onto solid footing twenty or so feet downstream of his target. His first cast was short, into the last of the riffle and away from the ledge. The fly, in and out of view as it bobbed back toward him in the failing light, suddenly disappeared, but Greg knew the weight of his line had dragged it under, not a fish. He false-cast vigorously to dry any water the feathers might have absorbed and tried again.

This time he overshot but got a friendly bounce. The fly struck the blue-gray shale itself, a foot above the water, and tumbled into the riffle's far, upstream end, with enough play in his leader for it to float lazily in place. Wham! Greg saw the hind-section of a sizable trout in silhouette and felt his line tug even before hoisting the rod tip to set the hook. This was the biggest fish he'd had on near town by quite a bit, and it surprised him by not jumping or tail-standing across the surface, standard rainbow tricks for throwing a hook.

Instead it stayed deep, ratcheting line from Greg's reel across the channel upstream to the opposite bank, then turned to run toward Greg and downstream, violently creating slack that Greg, rod held as high as possible, rushed to take up before the fish could expel the hook and be gone. Next he had to bring the trout's head around and hope his leader would hold against the fish's weight and momentum amplified by the current. His rod bowed into an inverted U.

The leader held and Greg fought the fish in spurts, gaining four feet and losing three over and over until he could finally wade ashore and haul it behind him to net in the shallows. Wow! At least a sixteen-incher! Deep-bellied and weighing close to two pounds, it had resisted heroically for nearly five minutes. Greg also noted with surprise that it was a German brown, not a rainbow, which explained why it hadn't jumped. He could hardly see the speckled red and black markings on its glossy walnut flanks in the dusk, but the ruddy orange of its underbelly made identification easy.

He had never known they existed in the Downie, and the few other browns he'd caught in his life had been in lakes, fishing from a boat. He kept the trout below the surface, letting it recover its strength and reaching through the net to slide the hook from its jaw before guiding it into deeper water where he furled the net away from its body to free the tail fins. After hanging there uncertainly for a second, it darted off as though its escape had been self-engineered.

What a way to finish! Elated, Greg secured his net against his back, checked inside his vest for Ned's breakfast fish, tensioned the fly over the guard of his reel, and retreated to the bridge, where he clambered up to North Main almost across from Ian and Sandra's driveway. Their car was parked adjacent to the porch and lights were on in the house. They were his friends, of course, but he found himself hoping he'd pass by unnoticed.

* * *

Jim Crandall, fully primed, nodded for Buck to continue. How would Huey tell this story, Buck wondered? Praise the enemy for starters. Faint praise, that is. The cards were all dealt, so he'd better damn play them right.

"Just like his fat-cat uncle at the Feather/Yuba sawmill," Buck said, "Kenny Pritchard's a Republican, but that don't make him a bad man. I doubt he's being honest about the Jared Smith business, and I don't think he knows either the county or human nature as well as I do...but he's not a bad man. I'm not a bad man either, though I've done bad things. Goes back a few years, and I've changed. I used to drink then, as you know, and now I don't.

"But Luann, my ex, always drank too, and the truth is she liked being slapped around when she was feeling sexy. She'd start it, for the most part, and it was open-handed slaps and spanking. I don't remember once ever using my fists, but being drunk I couldn't swear I never did. Nothing to be proud of, that's just how it was.

"I straightened myself out real good when I first went into police work, and I'm a damn good cop. Luann and I were apart for a while. Anyway, we got back together and drifted into our old ways. She's a hellion if there ever was one. But things really got bad after 1964 when Huey died. I was a mess. Not just that he was my dad. He was the kind you couldn't imagine would die.

"This next part nobody's ever known except me, my old boss in Eureka and Curt Foley, who's dead himself. Curt supposedly had the records, or copies of 'em, but if he did, nobody has any idea where they are. One reason I'm answering you is I want it off my chest before those records surface, if they ever do. I figure if Pritchard had 'em, they would've surfaced already, and what I've come to think is Curt never really had 'em, or destroyed 'em after he found I could be trusted. See, he took a hell of a risk bringing ex-drunk Buck Thompson in as Undersheriff, and he might have thought he needed insurance so I'd get out of town quick if he did have to fire me."

Without moving his eyes from Buck, Jim drank the rest of what was in his cup.

"One night in early '67, when Cindy was 18, she came home from a date earlier than expected, and the little one, Ginny, was staying with a friend. Luann and I had gotten going, and Cindy walked right in the middle. I told her to mind her own business, but she got so fresh yelling at Luann to escape and call the authorities that I grabbed Cindy by the shoulders, shoved her down the hall to her room and threw her on the bed. With Luann screaming behind me, Cindy struggled the whole way. I was going to lock her in there or something. But I bruised and scratched her at the collarbone with my thumbs, accidentally tore her blouse and tore off one of her bra straps. When I slammed Cindy's door, Luann kept screaming and I went out in the backyard to get a hold of myself.

"Luann wrapped Cindy in a blanket, snuck her out the front and they drove to the station. I heard the car leave, but I didn't guess where they were going. Cindy was hysterical and Luann was obviously drunk, so the duty officer got them calmed down and said he was taking a report. Meanwhile, a patrolman called and got my side of the story. I was back in my head by then, and Luann had quite a rep in Eureka as a drinker and a troublemaker, so they didn't take her as serious as they did Cindy.

"Thing is, though, they never had Luann or Cindy sign the report, never dated it, and didn't use police forms, so it wasn't official. Just notes on plain paper. An officer I knew followed them home to make sure things were calm. I apologized to Cindy a hundred times, but she and Luann slept in Cindy's room and wouldn't come out. Next morning, Sunday, the chief had me into the station and said I could resign and he'd deep-six the notes or else I'd be suspended and they'd go with Cindy's complaint. Pretty easy decision. I handed him my badge.

"I'd also like to say I never had a drink after that, but it took another couple of days till I tossed a half-bottle of bourbon off a bridge over the ravine in north Eureka and ended the alcohol part of my life. They say drunks have to hit bottom, and I had. I was living in a motel by then and didn't go back to Luann. I moved to Sacramento, hooked up with AA, started driving truck again, and you know the rest. Cindy and Luann went nuts later when the Eureka force and the DA stonewalled them, but they'd been had. Only thing on the record was that an officer had *counseled* us regarding a family dispute.

"Anyway, it's all there...cronyism, police corruption, wife-beating, alcoholism, child abuse. You want to fry me, make that next week's front page."

"Exclusive interview with Buck Thompson," Jim said in a drained voice. "I can see it now."

So could Buck, and so could his stomach, which was in dire need of a Rolaid. "Do me one favor," he went on. Before you write that article, tell Mrs. Crandall the whole story and decide if you're still voting for me."

"I am," Jim said. "And if I know Pat, so is she. Pritchard's too much of a robot."

"Then you want me to win?"

"Yeah, guess so, but it amounts to almost a different question."

"That's what I'm trying to make you see. If you want me to win, I need you and the Mrs. *and* the *Merc*."

"Be realistic, Buck. I've already told everybody we're not endorsing. How do I get out of that? After tomorrow, there's only one more issue before the election. It's impossible to research all the races to a professional standard in that time." Jim finally seemed animated and engaged and something like what Buck remembered as his normal self.

Buck sighed. "I knew those things would be problems before I got here, and I'm not suggesting you endorse in all the races...or that you endorse only me. That *would* smell like a put-up deal. I've got a game plan, one you might want to think about."

"I'll listen, but the decision's mine, and I won't be making it now."

"Understood. However you come out, I'll read it in the paper. Here's my idea. We were talking about being controversial. OK, then pick the three hottest local races. Point out that you're not endorsing anywhere else, like you've said all along, but that fence-sitting won't do for Sheriff, Treasurer or the Sierra City Supervi..."

"Let's see," Jim interrupted. "That'd be you over Pritchard, Gina Peterson over Guy Farrell, and Will Jeffers over Rick Rodman. The straight west-county establishment ticket, leaving me with Loyalton pissed off and the newcomers pissed off. How does the *Merc* bounce back from that? Especially when Pritchard and Farrell win anyway. There won't be enough people who aren't pissed off to be worth attacking in the next issue."

"No, no, you got me wrong. Endorse Rodman for Supervisor over Will Jeffers. Newcomers'll love that and Rodman, hippie or not, can't be a bigger ass than Will. Gina can beat Farrell for Treasurer with the *Merc* behind her. You have to know she's the better candidate, and she's popular in Sierra Valley because of her husband.

"Bud Peterson's from an old Loyalton family, and they love him as head of Public Works because he spends most of the road budget over there. If Loyalton didn't want Gina in, they'd run somebody serious against her instead of leaving it to a dimwit ex-fertilizer peddler. Wasn't Gina's fault that the Supervisors sold a couple of the county's prize nuggets, but gold don't count as an issue except in the Yuba canyon. Endorsing Gina will piss more people off here and balance things in the east county for not endorsing Pritchard."

"You're saying," Jim laughed, "Thompson for Sheriff pisses Loyalton off and makes Downieville happy, Peterson for Treasurer pisses Downieville off and makes Loyalton happy, while Rodman for Supervisor pisses the natives off and makes the newcomers happy?"

"That's about the size of it. Plus selling a lot of papers and giving you time to do your *diligence* stuff 'cause there's only six of us." Anxious as he was over how vulnerable his revelations had made him, Buck almost broke a grin at what he'd just proposed.

"Oh," he went on, "one more thing. You'll've picked winners. Gina'll win by a bigger margin than me, but with the *Merc* I'll squeak past Pritchard. He don't know it yet, but I will. And Rodman'll take Jeffers. The old-timers will pee their pants over that one. The *Merc* could come off as the most influential rag this side of the *Washington Post*."

"I'd be lying if I said I wasn't interested," Jim replied, "but I'll have to think it over. And with or without the *Merc*, my gut says none of you three should count your chickens yet."

"Like you said before, it's your decision. Thanks for hearing me out."

"Lots of food for thought. Now I need to get home to Pat and the kids."

"Me, I got campaignin' to do." Buck rose from his chair and Jim quickly did the same. When they shook hands, the contrast between them in complexion, facial features, body type, hairstyle, clothing and posture made Buck wonder how they could even be the same species. But they were. He knew that now.

He continued the handshake until Jim withdrew first. Buck then leaned against the office doorjamb. "This is none of my business," he said, "so you can tell me to shut up, but you're not fooling anybody drinking vodka out of a coffee mug. I say vodka because that's what I did at breakfast on weekend mornings when I needed a hair-a'-the-dog more'n I could admit…to the girls or myself. Beer and bourbon were my regular poisons."

"It *is* none of your business," Jim answered, yet without showing affront. "I just didn't think I should be waving it in your face. You know…because you've quit."

"Sorry Jim, I don't buy a word of that one. Makes you the only person since I came back here who hasn't tried to test me."

"Yeah, OK." Jim was sheepish on the first word, defensive on the second.

"I'm not even askin' you to quit," Buck reasoned. "I can see you need the stuff, and after what you've been through, why not? Few weeks or months boozin' ain't the end of the world."

"Exactly what I tell Pat." Jim seemed to be willing his defensiveness away.

"Does sneak up on you, though. That's for certain. You decide to quit, call me, I'll help. Damn near impossible to go it alone. Better if you don't have to hit bottom first."

"Drew Ormond made the same offer. Part of his social work job he says."

"Might be easier with me since I'm not your friend. There's a small Downieville AA group but you're not gonn'a want that."

"Don't think so. Not in a town this size, and with the *Merc* supposedly a respectable institution."

"Crazy, isn't it? Everybody knows what everybody's up to, who's drinkin' what, and how much, but you come forward and try to deal with it at AA and there's all this shame laid on. Like you're less respectable for facing up to it. I love living here, but alcohol's a problem in all the mountain counties."

"I'll keep your offer in mind."

"Good. I'm real easy to reach. Night or day, I'll take the call or call you right back."

"OK." Jim began walking Buck through the darkened outer room toward the front door.

"Drew's been helping Ray Stark stay off the sauce," Buck added. "Part of Drew's job, like he says. I offered to help Ray myself, but he thought it'd be weird with my bein' Sheriff. Of course, Ray thinks your friend Drew is pretty weird too."

Jim chuckled. "Drew Ormond is weird...in all the right ways. But this talk of helping people reminds me of another question. What about the Eureka Chief? Would you cover for one of your deputies on the same facts?"

"No. Chief Morton's retired now, but he should've leaned on me more when Luann's and my troubles first surfaced. With my own staff, I'd intervene early, not fudge the story later. I appreciate like hell what he did, though, and I took it to heart."

"Maybe he knew you would."

"There was something else helped me. You got kids and a wife to live for, but maybe the most important thing is the memory of that dead boy. Better man you are, the more folks'll realize what the town missed by losing him. People here think like that.

"See, they all remember how Cal was so great...which he was. Better'n me in every department. But the more I achieve means Cal would've been that much better. I can't outshine him, can't compete, but the best honor I can do his memory…and Huey's…is to stand tall. Too bad it took me such a damn long time to figure that out."

They reached the outside door and Jim held it open. "Thanks, Buck," he said, voice suddenly thick. "I'm glad you came." Again shaking Jim's hand, Buck backed onto the deserted sidewalk as the noise of a slowly passing vehicle receded behind him.

After Jim, remaining inside, had re-closed the *Merc*'s door, Buck steeled himself for a walk across the street and an appearance at The Forks. He'd start by chewing some Rolaids from the display near the cash register. He could picture them in their shiny wrappers, and that session with Crandall had been one hell of a crapshoot.

Next week's paper would have Buck's destiny in it, one way or the other, and he couldn't predict which destiny it would be. If his old family and school friend Sharon Murdock wouldn't leak it to him in advance, he'd have to head for Grass Valley and grab the first damn copy off the press—assuming he didn't have some kind of coronary in the meantime.

CHAPTER 17

Cradling his fly rod against his arm, Greg clomped along the edge of the pavement in his waders with the sky slowly darkening into stars and most of the light now coming from neighboring houses and the glow of TV within. There wasn't a ditch along North Main in this part of town, but a superabundance of ululating crickets made up for the frog chorus he knew he'd have heard further out, near the cemetery.

He got no response after waving to old Charlie Koontz sitting on his porch. The guy didn't see him, didn't know him or whatever. People said Charlie used to be the champion hunter and stream fisherman of his time, including wet and dry flies in season, like Hal Voorden nowadays in Sierraville. They also said Charlie had been strong enough to lift a full oil drum off of a wagon, but Greg didn't figure that to be more than a tall tale.

At least he was safely past Sandra and Ian's place. And even if he had seen them, they probably wouldn't have mentioned legal issues, but the background tension he'd have felt didn't go with the joy of having just landed a big trout. While his role in the divorce proceeding had been settled, his discomfort continued over how hard it was to keep the issues in the two cases separate and how important both were.

He couldn't countenance Seth's losing all contact with Juan any more than he could Zack Brennan's railroading Seth out of town—which sure looked like what had happened. Seth hadn't broken the law or violated the state's ethical standards for credentialed teachers. Did that mean Greg himself would be next, or already gone, over stupid rumors about his coaching, except that Zack needed Greg's supporting testimony? Of course, Ian wouldn't be privy to those machinations. When Greg got the promised legal briefing on why Seth's claim of wrongful termination wasn't valid, a lot of reading between the lines would be necessary.

Molly, meanwhile, was so gung-ho about being Sandra and Karen's witness, that some of Greg's discomfort might have to do with the amount of time the three women were spending together and how ideological they were about it. FLA—the Feminese Liberation Army—they jokingly called themselves, which Molly had come up with.

She didn't think it was funny when Greg kept asking if she planned to change her name to Tania, like Patty Hearst had, and start carrying an Uzi, but he did feel, in a way, as though Molly had been kidnapped and persuaded to adopt a new persona. Then his wisecracks lost their humor for him too, after a shoot-out last week in LA had resulted in the fiery deaths of Patty's captors and possibly Patty herself. Still, he wondered if the fact that he hadn't been deposed in the divorce and wasn't really in the loop signaled that their real motive in recruiting him had been to neutralize his voice on behalf of Seth rather than any need for what he would say.

God, would the Seth Holmes crap ever end! Greg had idolized the guy, yet almost a year later the fallout still had him skulking past the house of two close friends. Ian and Sandra had arrived in town too late to have known Seth personally, and both were opposing him in court, so they had no conflict of interest as husband and wife. The situation wouldn't be burdening their marriage as it was Greg's and Molly's.

All this kept popping in his mind tonight because Zack Brennan had left a message at the school office that afternoon asking to meet with Greg next Monday in the company of Ian, with Seth's suit against the district as the announced topic. He assumed this was the briefing he'd requested, but it could well include an effort to force his hand. If Ian left the room, who knew what pressure Greg might face. Not that he hadn't gotten a bellyful of pressure from Seth and Molly already, but as Superintendent, Zack had major levers to pull.

At the edge of downtown, just before reaching the dark and empty community center, where the prom had been held, Greg veered left along the lane to the lumberyard. He smelled fresh-cut wood on the night air and saw the outline of the Travelall facing away from him, parked along the fence. Just beyond it, the Downie River gurgled invisibly among the rocks where Greg had made his first cast early in the evening. With all these crickets around, he thought, what sort of bait would they be? He'd never seen a fly tied to imitate one. Greg leaned his rod against the Travelall, opened the hatch and sat on the tailgate to remove his waders.

"Well, young fella', any luck?" came a man's voice.

Startled, Greg bumped his head on the angled metal hatch support. "Ouch."

"Didn't mean to scare ya'. Mel Cresta here."

Greg looked, and sitting on the steps of a mobile home stationed perpendicular to the Travelall sat a guy in a straw hat whose lined face was illuminated by the glowing coal of the pipe he was smoking. "Oh...Mr. Cresta. You did scare me. But I had a good night. Got seven, one of real nice size."

"That's what we like to hear. Let's see 'em." Mel flipped on a dim outside bulb near the trailer's door.

"Only kept a small one...for my son's breakfast. I put the others back."

Mel Cresta, using a walking stick, got up and came toward Greg. "Put 'em back? What are they, old friends?" He ran his hand up under the front of his hat and scratched his scalp. His glasses drooped down his nose, which he made no effort to correct.

"Could be," Greg laughed. "I might've caught some of them last year too." Greg pulled Ned's fish from his vest and proffered it at Mel. "This one's not much, but you know how kids are."

"I'd eat it," Mel said. "Not sure I recall your name, but you're a teacher, right?"

"Yeah...Greg Fulton." Greg put the fish away and stuck out his hand. "I know who you are, Mr. Cresta, but I get you mixed up with your brother sometimes."

"That's Nick, Mr. Fulton. He's out of town. I'm Mel." He and Greg shook, then Mel passed his fingers beneath his nose. "The one who smells like trout."

Greg laughed again. "Sorry about that."

"Don't be. I don't fish anymore myself 'cause of this gimpy leg, so a whiff is all I get."

"Well, believe it or not, I did catch seven."

"I'm convinced. Saw you catch and throw back a couple behind Starks' place during my walk tonight. Seen you do it before, too."

"That's how I know they'll be there next time."

"I understand. Not like it was years ago when we could catch and keep all we knew how and never miss 'em."

"Makes me jealous. Anyway, I caught a sixteen-incher on my last cast. Kind of amazing. A German brown. Never saw one in the Downie or knew they were around."

"One of Seth Holmes's babies all grown up." Mel scratched under his hat a second time.

"What do you mean?" This wasn't a context in which Greg would expect to hear Seth's name, but it seemed you couldn't get away from the guy.

"He and a bunch of the school kids planted browns up by Gold Bluff Mine, must've been in '68 or '69. Anyway, before his Peace Corps deal in South America. Holmes was friendly with somebody at the big hatchery in Sacramento and got a few hundred browns free. Kids hiked 'em upstream by yoke and bucket. Wildlife habitat project, they called it."

"I'll be darned." Greg had supported Seth's Democratic Party activities in 1972 and then his relief efforts for Nicaraguan earthquake victims, but earlier Seth must have been into grass-roots environmentalism as well.

"Plan was to have a native strain of browns in case the state was right about water quality going to hell. Browns handle impurities better. Far as I know, there's still plenty of rainbows, but now and again somebody'll catch a brown. They grow big, too."

"Gave me a rip-roaring fight."

147

"Too bad Holmes had to end up following his pecker down the highway. Wasn't the first to ever do it, but he's a real loss to the county. You know him?"

"We were good friends."

"Oh...yeah...I recall. And you're the one who coaches girls' basketball. Best keep a leash on your own pecker. Save you a lot of trouble. Where's Holmes now?"

"Chico. Trying to land a teaching job." Greg felt his cheeks and ears redden, but somehow this was a guy you couldn't be angry at.

"Nice enough town. He'll find a job, Holmes will, and in his spare time get elected mayor. They won't care if his girlfriend's of an age to be his daughter. Downieville's too small for that kind of thing."

Greg had stowed his fishing gear and was stepping into a pair of unlaced sneakers. He also wanted—strongly wanted—to change the subject, and not to anything about politics. "Hope you don't mind where I'm parked."

"Not a bit. I enjoy the company. Nobody fishes this stretch of river anymore, and most people aren't out and about of an evening the way they used to be."

"Seems a pretty tight-knit community to me."

"Oh, no. Nothing like years back. Nothing."

"Really? What's different?"

"The antenna tower on Oxford Ridge, mainly. The utility district ran TV cable into town, hooked everybody up as a public service, and all folks do now is stay home and watch. Hell, the movie theater closed down, the book clubs dried up overnight, the music groups fell apart, and the idea that you'd visit each other to play checkers or pinochle went out the window."

"A good bit of that still goes on among my friends."

"You newcomers are kind of throwbacks. And I don't mean *all* the social stuff is gone. There's some, just not twenty-five percent of what it was. Any dumb thing Tommy Smothers might say is supposed to be more important than what you'd hear from your neighbor just because Smothers is in front of a camera."

"The TV angle I'd never thought of," Greg said. "And you're right. Most newcomers I know were expecting more of the social stuff...an old-fashioned ideal of community that we weren't getting where we came from."

"Well, community's something you make. Doesn't just happen…and doesn't come free."

"There must have been plenty of other changes here, too."

Mel sucked on his pipe. "Big changes for me and my brother. We're retired and the yard has a new owner."

"Are either of you on speaking terms with Jerry Vargas these days? I hear he was pretty steamed when you sold to Feather/Yuba instead of him."

Greg saw Mel smile around his pipe stem. "He got over it, but he must've thought the Crestas were running a charity. Didn't want to pay near what the place was worth."

"I know Feather/Yuba's from Loyalton," Greg said, "but my friends were glad Jerry and his hardware store didn't get a monopoly on west-county building materials."

"So were a lot of ours. Didn't mind having Jerry not speak to me this winter anyway. Made a nice break. It was the Crandall boy's funeral got us back together. Our little tiff seemed silly after that."

"I know what you mean."

"Of course, no feud around here lasting less than two years really counts. You've always got your friends, your temporary enemies, your real enemies and your don't-give-a-hoots." Mel let out a puff of smoke.

Greg smiled in the dark but didn't know if Mel could see him.

"How's the water out there?" Mel continued. "Clean?"

"Yeah, real good."

"All the fuss the state makes about pollution," Mel said, "you'd never realize it was a lot worse when the mines were running. I'm talking arsenic leaching from the crushed ore. Sometimes you'd see rainbows like the one you kept that'd be deformed…big heads and skinny, curved bodies. I ate as many local fish as anybody, but I sometimes wonder if arsenic's not what's bothering Charlie Koontz and Norma Thompson."

"I've never officially met Charlie, but he doesn't seem too alert. Is Norma Buck's mother?"

"Right. And quite the gal in her day, I'll tell ya'. My brother and I count ourselves lucky to have most of our brain cells still firing."

"What the state worries about now is sewage," Greg said. "Because of all the septic tanks, I mean."

"Doesn't worry me a bit."

"No?"

"Well, it's not like it's from folks we don't know," Mel replied genially.

With a wave of his pipe, the old man returned to his perch on the steps while Greg began driving through town toward home. As he passed the almost completely dark *Merc* office, he saw Buck Thompson back out onto the sidewalk while talking to somebody inside. What was that about, Greg wondered? A late round of campaigning or a new police-blotter item for tomorrow's edition?

CHAPTER 18

June 6, two days after the election, school had taken an extra hour of recess, and the sidewalks were lined with people acting as if they had reason to celebrate. Some did, for that matter, but Buck would've had to be there regardless. Law-enforcement presence was always necessary at this kind of event, and technically he was still on duty.

Every spring there was a cattle drive through town from winter range in Yuba County to Butcher Meadow, above Sierra City. They moved around a thousand head, two or three abreast on Highway 49, and it'd evolved into a sort of low-budget Mardi Gras. But cow pies dotted everywhere didn't exactly set the stage for glory, so the next challenge for the winners was to make this look like a victory parade.

Nice of Jerry Vargas to offer his classic Stutz Bearcat for Marilyn Pezzola and two other top vote-getters to ride in, and damn nice of him to take time from his hardware business to drive the cranky old box of tin while his passengers sat waving in the back. Problem was, even though many of the cattle and the mounted cowboys who kept 'em in line still trailed behind, plenty were ahead and had left calling cards — perfumed ones, you'd have to say, or that was how the flies reacted.

Marilyn had won big as County Auditor. No surprise, she didn't have opposition, but she'd still pulled 86% of the ballots cast, better than anybody else by a mile. And Gina Peterson had held onto the Treasurer's job pretty respectably, posting a bigger margin than Buck had guessed, which meant the west county's anger over the gold sale had subsided to the point she'd gotten Downieville votes along with her Loyalton numbers. The cars of other successful candidates were strung out among the cows further back. The losers, for the most part, weren't around.

Gina was sure in the spirit, though, as was Marilyn, sitting next to her. They'd both been through this before so Buck was taking his cues from them. He couldn't match either of their smiles, and his uniform was pretty dull compared to Marilyn's apricot blazer, corsage and white silk blouse, but he'd finally gotten a good night's sleep and had on his best fitting pants. Typical of Marilyn, he thought, to have put herself in the middle, giving the more embattled Buck and Gina maximum chance to be seen by the crowd and to reach out and shake hands.

And cool breeze not withstanding, it was a beautiful day. Ahead among the cows, being escorted by two of the most Marlboro-Man cowboys, was the Clamper Band, cemetery director Phil Bosley and a handful of other duffers, who were blasting the brass off their horns doing *Sundown*, the new Gordon Lightfoot number that was so popular. Bosley always had a plucked rubber chicken draped over his bass drum and none of them could play worth a damn, but that was part of the fun. The elementary school girls in front of them twirling batons were probably too young to know the difference, music-wise, so weren't embarrassed by it.

Buck and the rest of the political contingent had joined the drive a quarter-mile earlier and were now rolling slowly past the gas station at Prospect Street toward the Quartz Cafe and the main part of town. A lot of kids had on their scout uniforms and were waving little American flags, while the high school Four-H-ers, wearing merit badges on their light green vests, acted as crowd monitors. The parking area by the Quartz was jammed with folks who'd walked over from the courthouse and the ranger station on early lunch breaks.

Buck also had a sheriff's car and a couple of deputies prominently stationed at the Quartz to protect against anybody getting too whooped up, though they'd never had trouble during past drives. Except for the road department crew cleaning up poop, and some stray balloons left dangling around, this part of the show would be over in forty-five minutes.

BELONGING

Marilyn's two younger daughters, the ones still at home, were dressed as nicely as she was and standing at the front of the crowd blowing kisses to their mom. Then Buck saw his own car, the Bronco, with a big bunch of balloons tied to the antenna and Sally and his mama leaning against it, waving at him like crazy. He removed his hat for a moment, using it to wave back. Buck hadn't seen mama dressed up and out like this in a year at least.

She looked great, and god bless Sally for making it happen. Buck couldn't guarantee Norma wouldn't get to rambling again one of these nights about how he'd never amount to anything, but she could see right now that he had and he did. You didn't get chauffeured around in Sally's pop's vintage car with Marilyn Pezzola unless you had something going for you.

It'd been a hell of a close one, eighty-eight votes, but the totals had only changed by one on the recount. Though Pritchard was undoubtedly pissed, he'd been graceful in calling to concede and offer congratulations. Carl Herndon, Pritchard's uncle at the Feather/Yuba mill, would just have to eat nails and stick to sawing logs. He might've bought out the Cresta's lumberyard, but that was all of Downieville he'd get.

The *Merc* endorsement had put Buck over the top, Pritchard admitted, and had really caught him by surprise. Buck could bet he and his uncle had called Crandall the minute the paper came out and reamed him up and down. It might have been fairer to warn Crandall about that, but there was no denying Buck's gamble had paid off. The *Merc* had endorsed him, Gina Peterson and Rick Rodman, exactly as Buck proposed, and hadn't run a breath of exposé on anything from Eureka. The endorsement, in fact, said Buck had shown "unusual personal and professional growth" over the years and was "fully prepared for the job." Well, he thought so too, and damn it felt good, not to mention the overdue pay raise.

Further along in the crowd were the two Cresta brothers flanked by Lonny Harris, drunk and with his butt hanging out of his jeans. There was a guy who needed some personal and professional growth of his own. Ray Stark was a few steps past Lonny, not drunk, and Drew Ormond had told Buck that Ray was doing pretty good these days. One of Buck's duties this afternoon was to be interviewed by young Billy Stark, who since the drowning had been selected to be co-editor of the new *High School Doings* column the *Merc* would be running. The other co-editor was from Loyalton, and the two schools would take alternate weeks. Good move on Crandall's part, Buck thought, or whoever it was came up with the idea.

And speaking of Jim Crandall, there he was standing with Greg Fulton, their wives and their kids just around the corner on Bridge Street, where the parade and highway turned to cross the Downie and head up-canyon. The two boys, Fultons' youngster and the one in the wheelchair, were sporting flags and the grownups were all waving. Buck waved back. "Good to see you, Greg…Jim," he called. "And ladies."

Buck couldn't hear their replies over the din of music, clopping hooves, mooing and yelling, but he saw their mouths move. The Fulton gal—Molly her name was—aloof, but still a cutie, figured to be the only vote he'd lost among the four. He'd noticed that the Pritchard sign had never come out of Fultons' yard after the Thompson one went up, or even after the *Merc* editorial, and something on her face just now told him why.

Marilyn Pezzola leaned over to Buck with a smiling admonishment. "After that *Merc* editorial you *should* be glad to see Jim Crandall. We all bet the gravesite business would make him prove his independence. It was a big risk being so generous. People are still grumbling about your motive…especially Pritchard's people. How did you ever bring that off?"

Chuckling to himself, he said, "Sorry…trade secret." Then he called into the press of onlookers, "Hey, Walt…Minnie! How ya' doin'!" followed by a tipping of his hat and some jerky waving—left, right, left—hoping it seemed to people like a natural rhythm.

Of course, the endorsements hadn't worked out for all concerned. Rick Rodman had given Will Jeffers a big scare in the Supervisor race, but Will, as incumbent, had prevailed by 19 votes, 178 to 159. Since that was the Sierra City seat, Will wasn't in the parade at this point, but they'd worked out a way to include him in the fold later. Officially everything was nonpartisan, but the Republican officeholders like Judge Sturdevant and District Attorney Bartlesman were in Teresa Powell's Cadillac, next car back, and Will certainly wouldn't fit in there.

After meeting with Crandall, Buck had gotten a pledge of confidentiality from Ernie Warrington, the part-time Search and Rescue chief, and let him know that Buck had lobbied the *Merc* to support Rodman. Since Ernie was also Rodman's unofficial campaign manager, and Rodman might have pulled off a win, Buck wanted to be sure he had good will in that direction. And when the *Merc* did endorse both Buck and Rodman, it was a plus with the newcomers to have Buck's name on the same ticket, so to speak, with one of their own.

What Buck had also done, and knew he shouldn't have, was to get a file on Rodman through the Sacramento FBI—they owed him a favor after Jared Smith—and let it sit on the corner of his desk during a meeting with Will Jeffers one afternoon. And darned if Buck hadn't been called out for a few minutes and had to leave Will in there alone with that file. All in all, Rodman's past had been pretty tame, but he'd been bartender at a gay bar in Oakland that was busted several times. While Rodman himself had never been charged with anything, the busts were a matter of record. Will wouldn't be any kind of politician, or worth much as Rodman's opponent, if he couldn't find a use for dirt.

To Rodman's credit, however, he'd taken the high road when it was leaked around Sierra City that he was a homo, saying he had no cause to discuss his private life or anybody else's in a campaign for Supervisor. Still, sexual perversion was probably what turned things Will's way. Buck had been on the phone congratulating him yesterday, and they'd found a little time to talk about the Sheriff's Department budget, their crummy radios and the need for a fourth drawer in the morgue.

Will had been real accommodating, too, and Buck figured that at least some of his problems with substandard facilities and equipment were about to be taken care of. Buck would've played up the *Merc* endorsement and had the same conversation with Rick Rodman if *he'd* come out on top. Last year, when Curt Foley was alive, Buck and Curt had lost a 3-2 Supervisors' vote regarding the morgue, plus another on the radios, and Will had been one of the three. Next time that wasn't going to happen.

But for now, the election was over. With any decent luck nobody'd ever get wind of Buck's meddling in the Supervisor campaign, and more important, Curt's file, if there was one, about Buck's Eureka days would never surface. Nor was Buck too worried that Crandall would come back and bite him. They'd had a deal, unspoken but understood: endorse me or destroy me. Crandall had freely chosen the former and Buck didn't see him welching on it. Still, if there was ever a hint of Buck's being Will Jeffers' source on the homo angle, he could see the *Merc* going for the jugular. But why would Will blab? He had as much, or more, to lose as Buck.

Actually, Buck hadn't heard a peep from Jim Crandall since their meeting—about drinking or anything else. No great surprise. The guy did look better, though, so if he wasn't laying off entirely, Buck would bet he'd cut back. And a little more time had passed, which was bound to help. Even so, it'd be years before anybody in that family would go more than half-a-day without thinking of their boy. The toughest would be spring, when the lilacs were in bloom, the light was at the same angle as that Sunday, and the river was making the same noise. Then the hurt would seem raw as new.

Marilyn had originally planned that they'd wait at a pullout once they got past town so the cows could gain some distance on them, straggle out to single file and share the road with other traffic. Then Jerry would zoom to Sierra City and they'd put Gina in her husband's Jeep with Will Jeffers in time to join everybody cruising through there. No doubt the Republicans would work something similar. They were all in politics, and parades were what you did when the opportunity came along.

But as they cleared the last few houses the plan changed, because Marilyn decided she'd rather turn around at the first wide spot to sneak home and have a bite with her girls. Buck begged off when Jerry offered to drop him and Gina for lunch at the Quartz and pick them up in twenty minutes. He said sitting under a tree along the river till the car came back suited him fine. This would also let Jerry garage the Stutz and switch to his Buick hardtop. He'd been muttering that the old roadster might not be reliable enough to handle the canyon on such a tight schedule.

Jeez, how long had it been since Buck sat under a tree? Since last fall, anyway, and a day not near as nice as this. The car was still inching along, but he could hardly wait to climb out. The river'd come down to a comfortable level, the water was clean like it'd been bottled at Butte Springs, the oaks were newly leafed out, and brodiaea was poking up its high-stemmed, bright blue flowers beneath the bunchy white blooms of overhanging ceanothus.

Hell, he'd barely had a night's sleep these past months until yesterday after the recount, when the handshakes and phone calls finally tailed off. Tomorrow and the rest of today he was going to take as easy as he could. Thank god last weekend had been quiet and he'd been able to focus on the election. The one before that, over

Memorial Day, had been a zoo. Sixteen thousand tourists had flooded in, according to the motel and campground tallies, and there'd been drunks and fights galore, plus a gunshot wound.

On top of that, there'd been a hiker stranded up on Gibraltar Peak with a seriously broken leg who'd had to be helicoptered out by medics from an air force base. Then a 4.6 earthquake had struck near Oroville Sunday night and shaken up Sierra County for real. Knocked over bookcases and scared holy piss out of people—tourists, locals, everybody. Earthquakes were supposed to be on the coast. Buck could never remember one here. The thing was, though, his staff had performed brilliantly.

Ernie Warrington's crew had been great with the rescue, Buck's deputies had helped calm people down after the quake, no drunks had been arrested that shouldn't have been, and vice versa. It was pretty obvious that the high price of gas was going to boost local tourism, not the other way around, meaning Jerry Vargas and Pete Lowry, over at the motel, were in better moods about their prospects than you could imagine. Should be a solid year for Jim Crandall and the *Merc* too. Jerry wasn't going to skimp on advertising, so no matter how pissed Feather/Yuba's Carl Herndon was about Pritchard's loss, he couldn't skimp either.

In fact, the way things had gone that holiday weekend, all the good front-page coverage and word-of-mouth his department had received might've been as much a key to Buck's win as the editorial. There was no way to tell. All Buck knew for certain was that he'd played every card he had, with a full share of luck in the mix.

Next weekend promised to be another quiet one, except that Buck would be with the Clampers in Poker Flat helping put old Cory Flynn into the ground. The snow had melted off the road and Buck's long-time resident corpse could finally go where it belonged. Not only was Buck looking forward to being the proprietor of a four-drawer morgue, he was looking forward to having all the drawers available for a change. And if he got most of his budget request through, he wouldn't be forced to dun the Clampers for the extra electricity Flynn had cost him.

About time for Buck to take care of himself, too. It was still premature to be asking Karen Holmes for a date, but some night next week, after he was more caught up on his sleep, Buck would get over to Nevada and find himself a piece of ass. Whoa, baby, it'd been much too long and they had some nice honeys at that Mustang

Ranch. He also remembered how funny Stan White thought it was when they were teenagers that ceanothus flowers smelled like sperm. Suddenly, as the Stutz convertible slowed to pull off the pavement, it lurched on its springs and redirected Buck's thoughts to the immediate.

Damn cows! Jerry was a ways beyond town, but the car was still surrounded by 'em. They shit all over, then walked in it. This would have been the right parade for that damned Farrell, if he'd beat Gina for Treasurer. A fertilizer salesman, the guy'd been, before he moved here. What a hoot—a fertilizer salesman! Buck startled himself by laughing out loud.

Marilyn looked at him quizzically. All these years she'd probably never seen him carry on like that. She was some gal herself. Gray had begun to salt up her bobbed black hair, and the line of her jaw wasn't quite as fine as it used to be, but if Sierra County had a queen she was it. Hugging her blazer around her shoulders in a swirl of breeze, she asked with genuine interest, "What's so funny?"

"Nothin' worth repeating," Buck answered. "Just happy, I guess."

CHAPTER 19

"Look," Molly said, holding Ned's hand while they watched the cattle drive and parade wend through town, "here comes Daddy's new best friend." She used the mocking undertone she'd adopted recently for anything that seemed macho, especially Buck Thompson.

"Is he one of the real cowboys?" Ned wanted to know.

"Mommy thinks so," Greg answered.

"No," Molly said. "Real cowboys are gentlemen."

"You don't give up, do you?" Jim Crandall put in, managing the wry smile that Greg had been seeing more frequently on him these last two weeks.

"You must know Jim and I voted for him," Pat said evenly.

"After the *Merc* editorial, of course," Molly answered. Greg worried she might get into the business of the donated gravesite, but she didn't. Molly's private opinion was that Jim and Pat had been bought, although she didn't blame them. "They were emotional putty all spring," she'd told Greg, which she blamed Buck for exploiting.

"He *was* the best guy for the job," Jim affirmed. "Of those two."

"How come the Segals, Karen Holmes, Edna Darnell and I don't think so?" Molly challenged. "Or Sandra and Ian?"

"Because you all like lawyers more than I do," Jim replied.

"Drew, Lynn Reynolds, Om and Greg agreed with us," Pat added. "So did Jeanne Potter."

"I know," Molly said. "And you won. Don't rub it in."

"Be fair," Jim countered. "I also endorsed Rick Rodman. Everybody lost there. But I'll tell you this...Buck will be sorry as hell if we find the *Merc* picked wrong." He and Pat exchanged looks.

"I'm with Molly," said Lisa, the Crandall's daughter, holding a small bunch of balloons. "I was too young to vote this time, but in four years I'll be against Buck Thompson for sure."

Greg and the blonde, teenage Lisa had walked down from school together to meet their families, and she'd told him the same thing. She didn't trust "that fat man...the one running for Sheriff...who came to our house after Toby drowned."

The car Buck was in moved closer, a flashy 1930s roadster that Jerry Vargas, wearing a boater hat like he was today, drove to celebrate the 4th of July and other events. Marilyn Pezzola, a very striking woman for her age, sat with Buck looking completely at ease, while the less-polished Gina Peterson also put up a good front. Buck...well, looked like Buck. Of course, he was surrounded by horses, cows and cow pies, so maybe his pinched expression was more authentic than Marilyn or Gina's smiles. Even so, all three made a point of waving to the crowd.

"Congratulations!" cried several voices together.

"Frank sees you from heaven, Marilyn, and he's proud!" called old Mrs. Lobdel.

"When Loyalton raises Thompsons, then they'll have a Sheriff!" someone yelled.

"I may barf," Molly whispered to Greg.

"Special for Buck? What about the Clamper Band?"

"Never mind. I'll applaud for Marilyn. *She* has class."

When they saw other kids doing it, Ned and Stevo waved the little flags they'd gotten from the American Legion booth, and also giggled uproariously at the goofy faces they were making for each other. The grown ups all waved as well. Marilyn Pezzola was occupied with Reverend White across the street, but Buck, who was closer to the Fultons and the Crandalls, waved back calling, "Good to see you, Greg, Jim…and ladies."

After Buck, Marilyn and Gina came an interval of plodding cattle followed by Teresa Powell's huge, be-finned old Cadillac with Teresa driving and the Judge, DA and Assessor waving out the open windows. Balloons were tied to the door handles and an obviously new bumper strip reading **Nixon, Even Now!** decorated the back.

"That'll be a collector's item," Pat joked, "and real soon. Impeachment hearings, he owes a quarter-million in back taxes, and somebody's printing Nixon bumper strips?"

"There's loyalty and there's crazy loyalty," Greg remarked.

"Well," Jim added, "we know who the Republicans are."

"I thought it was all non-partisan," Molly said.

"Sure, officially," Jim answered. "But take my word for it, those are the Republicans. The only officeholder who's registered independent is Earl Kenton, the Supervisor just re-elected from Alleghany."

"You're trying to tell me Buck Thompson's a Democrat?" Molly protested.

"Yes," Jim replied. "And Marilyn Pezzola, Jerry Vargas and Gina Peterson. I checked."

"Jerry Brown and Jerry Vargas in the same party," Molly laughed. "And Buck? I can't believe it." Cattle continued to stream by in the background.

"Come on, Molly," Jim cajoled. "The Kenny Pritchard you've made such a fuss over is Republican. You split your ticket." His resurrected smile made another appearance.

"At least I won on Campaign Finance and nominating Brown for Governor," Molly announced, without returning the smile. "Now he just has to beat one of Teresa Powell's hacks in November. Who won that primary? I forget."

"Read all about it in the *Merc*," Jim said. "We're late getting today's issue back from Grass Valley because of the cattle, but Sharon should be here any minute. Tag along to the office with me, Lisa. I'll walk you to school from there."

"OK, Daddy, but no more politics. Promise?" She looped the ribbon holding her balloons onto Stevo's chair.

"I promise...or not for the next half-hour." Jim gave Lisa a side-armed hug, kissed Pat and Stevo goodbye, then pulled Lisa away with him through the dispersing crowd. Greg, Ned and Molly remained with Pat and Stevo.

"Next fall *I'm* going to school," Ned Fulton proclaimed.

"What fun you'll have," Pat Crandall said, crouching to look at Ned's face and kiss his forehead. Greg saw her struggle not to let sadness take over. "OK, Stevo, time for us to go home. Do you want Ned to come and visit?"

"Yeff," said Stevo loudly.

Pat looked at Molly, who nodded her assent. "OK with you, Nedster?" Molly asked.

"Really OK," Ned replied. He eagerly lined up behind Stevo's chair. "I want to help drive, like Toby used to."

Molly walked to Pat and gave her a hug. "Sorry."

"No, it's all right. Helps keep the good memories alive." Pat, Stevo and Ned, balloons trailing in the air, headed across the bridge to Pearl Street. Wistfully, Greg watched them, and saw Molly drift a few steps in the same direction to gaze into the Downie and toward the Yuba through the bridge's green-painted superstructure. Rather than join her, he turned his attention to the thinning crowd.

Swarms of road crew guys and 4-H kids with brooms, shovels and carts started on street cleanup while the formerly high-stepping baton twirlers, their sequined skirts demurely below the knee, passed in a quiet two-by-two formation returning to elementary school. Jerry Vargas drove his shiny roadster back into town, transporting only himself and the two women. Some deputy had given Buck a lift to wherever he was headed next, Greg figured.

But now that the guy had won, Greg felt responsible, and he prayed that things worked out. Endless I-told-you-sos from Molly would only add to their continuing friction over Seth. Even after the *Merc* endorsement ran she had been adamant in refusing to take the Pritchard sign off their fence, and she'd threatened to deface the Thompson poster he had placed near it.

Next he saw Phil Bosley and the Clamper Band returning on the opposite sidewalk with their instruments under their arms, except for Bosley's bass drum and its dangling rubber chicken. Six well-padded, fiftyish men tromping along in high-topped black hillbilly hats, black bandannas, red shirts, and black suspenders who knew four songs and could barely play those. The band members didn't speak to Greg nor he to them.

But he couldn't help being reminded of his meeting last week with Zack Brennan, the Superintendent. Ian hadn't stayed the whole time but Downieville Principal Tom Mahaffy had. Although his two bosses had been open in answering questions about Seth's lawsuit, they'd gone on to relay citizen complaints that Greg was too much of a hippie to be a sound influence on his students.

When pressed, Principal Mahaffy had cited Phil Bosley and faculty member Coach N as being among the complainers. Greg now wished somebody would feed Bosley that fake chicken. In fact, he'd like to be there to watch.

The hugging at basketball games had come up, in addition to Greg's beard and his friendships with "people like Drew Ormond and Om Gillette." Everything had been polite and his bosses said they didn't necessarily agree with all the concerns. Greg still had their support, but they wanted him to know what was going around, since three school board members were up for re-election.

He'd already reviewed the meeting endlessly in his mind and couldn't sort out whether any of this constituted a threat that they would withdraw support if Greg testified for Seth, or whether he'd truly gotten nothing more than a heads-up. And it had to be a good sign that all three board members scored easy victories. But the complaints themselves infuriated Greg, and thinking about them made him stubborn. He wasn't good at resolving these kinds of conflicts, something he hadn't really known about himself, but lately they'd been coming one after another.

Greg was raised to believe that you didn't betray your friends and you didn't yield to Babbittry. Yet Molly had lobbied him to ignore both strictures, claiming "higher justice" in the matter of the divorce, and "pragmatism" regarding the school district. By his behavior, she said, Seth didn't deserve loyalty, and in the other suit, she perceived her family's livelihood to be at stake. She wasn't aware of Greg's real reasons for signing on with Karen in the divorce, but given that decision, she thought his testifying for the school district as Zack Brennan's witness was a no-brainer.

BELONGING

In terms of their impact on the Fultons, the county elections had been divisive, the Holmes divorce more so, and the school lawsuit threatened to be worse. Greg couldn't make up his mind between Zack and Seth for more than five minutes, and Molly was as scornful of his current indecision as she'd been earlier regarding Karen. He felt she wasn't trying to understand his concerns, and she seemed increasingly impatient when he brought them up. As a result, he'd stopped bringing them up, which led nowhere.

He desperately needed someone to talk to. It obviously couldn't be Molly, Jim had his own load to carry, Ian was compromised, and Henry Segal had already gotten an earful from Molly. Or so Greg assumed. She and Henry worked together, after all. But Greg *had* decided one thing: this weekend would be the end of wavering. By Monday he'd commit one way or the other if it killed him. Marty Allman, an old Berkeley friend of theirs, was coming this weekend to show his visiting nephew the Wild West, and Marty might be the ideal confidant.

He'd been to Downieville several times, but had a completely outside perspective. Besides, he was smart as a whip, a philosophy grad student at UC, raised in Greenwich Village, who, like his Harlem-bred nephew, was black. When the Fultons had lived downstairs from him while Greg was getting his teaching certificate, Marty and his Jewish girlfriend, Elaine, had been virtually Ned's alternate parents. She and Marty had since broken up and she'd moved to LA, but Marty's flat remained the Fultons' home base on their trips to the Bay Area, and Ned never missed a turn jabbering to Marty on the phone whenever the chance arose.

Molly, now returned from her lingering survey of what had been the drowning site, surprised Greg by taking his hand. "You look totally absorbed. Got time for a to-go sandwich from the Quartz Cafe with your wife?"

"Oh…think so. I'm due back in twenty-five minutes, but we can eat on the school lawn." They began following the plank sidewalk toward the west end of downtown. Crunching beneath their feet were coiled, yellow-brown, blossom remnants, separated from the overhanging locust branches by the spring breeze. These were black locusts, Seth had always insisted, common throughout the foothills and not, as local lore would have it, the Chinese Tree of Heaven.

"I'm so glad Marty's coming," Molly said. "It'll be great to see him, and maybe he can help you decide…well, you know what."

"I was thinking the same thing," Greg responded, looking directly at her.

She smiled. "They say that happens with married couples."

"Well, I do plan to talk with Marty. And I'm deciding by Monday, no matter what."

"If you can, good. And once you do, you'll feel a lot better. I'm going to back any decision you make...promise." She squeezed his hand to emphasize the concession just offered. "I'm glad the election is over. I don't know why I got so swept up in it. I'm really sorry. I hate arguing with you...about that...or Seth."

He was sure she meant everything she'd said, and felt huge relief at being free to go with his conscience. "I don't like arguing either." He drew Molly to him and kissed her forehead. "I love you. You have to know that."

"I do. And I love you." She snuggled for a moment against his chest. "I guess that's as amorous as we dare on the street. But next November," she went on brightly as they resumed walking, "there'll be nothing to argue about...at least politically."

"Unless you vote for another Republican." Greg couldn't resist a playful dig.

"No chance. And even if Jerry Brown loses, we'll finally be rid of Ronald Reagan."

"I'll never be rid of him. He signed both my college diplomas."

She poked Greg in the ribs. "Well, he won't be signing many more."

"Did Marty tell you anything about this nephew?" Greg hadn't been home for Marty's call regarding weekend plans.

"Not much. His name is Rashan, he turned thirteen last month and he's never been west of the Hudson. This California trip was his birthday present."

"Berkeley will seem like Downieville to him."

"Wonder what Downieville will seem like?" Molly laughed.

Ahead of them, going into the Quartz, Greg saw George Snell in his Deputy Sheriff's uniform and with him in a Forest Service shirt, Jeff Schoville, an older brother of the grave-digging Tommy. They were guys with whom Greg had played town-team basketball in the two years before he agreed to coach the girls. It had been fun and he missed it. More fun than college ball, in fact. Greg had mainly been a bench-sitter at SF State, on a team well below USF or Cal for talent, and he'd been too busy in grad school for anything but occasional pick-up games in the Berkeley parks.

And when he thought of it, not playing town-team pissed him off. He'd given up something he really enjoyed to put extra time and energy into coaching at school, and for what? Back-stabbing complaints and rumors about his personal life that were nobody's damn business. Not a sound influence? Bullshit! His team had gone undefeated. Wasn't that enough? Coach N, that out-of-shape hack, was jealous. No wonder Seth was so fed up with small-town small-mindedness he wanted to sue.

"I'm up for toasted cheese today," Molly said as they entered the busy restaurant. "What sounds good to you?"

CHAPTER 20

In a Chevy Nova borrowed from a fellow grad student, Marty Allman arrived that Friday night with his nephew Rashan. They'd driven the last hour in the dark, and by their journey's end Rashan barely seemed to know where he was or what he thought about anything. If Uncle Marty said Greg and Molly's spare room was a good place to sack out, that was enough, and within fifteen minutes, sacking out was what he did. Rashan had gotten off a plane only two days ago Marty reminded them, so was still a little jet-lagged.

After helping get Ned off to sleep as well, Marty stayed up with Greg and Molly talking, smoking some weed and listening to Marty's new Cal Tjader album before they all went to bed. On such limited exposure the Fultons had no sense of their teenage guest, anymore than he probably did of them. The only new thing they'd picked up was his surname. Gangly in a sweatshirt and jeans, "Rashan Briggs" was how he introduced himself. He wore an Afro, a style Marty had never favored, and displayed a facsimile of Marty's fine-boned face minus the goatee and glasses. But Marty's skin was almost the color of a French-roast coffee bean, while his sister's son was a cup of plain cocoa.

BELONGING

By morning, however, Rashan had peered from all the windows, seen the densely wooded ridges, the rivers, and the canyon, and had decided that going outside "really wouldn't be cool." He'd "brought books and magazines to read," he said.

Marty was amused. "Don't sweat it," he assured Greg while Rashan was taking a shower. The kid had never seen anything like this except in the movies, but he'd adjust; or he wouldn't. Showing the boy how big and how different the world outside Harlem was had been the main objective in having Rashan with him for a week. Besides, Marty said, he was supposed to be "the eccentric uncle," so he had something to live up to. For that, "Downieville was ideal."

Ned hung around until he got Rashan to read to him, then badgered the older boy to come into the backyard and throw a stick for Jojo. No dice. Ned and Jojo went by themselves.

After lunch, Rashan spotted Greg's chessboard and persuaded Uncle Marty to take him on. Several matches followed, and Greg recognized that Rashan was a competent player. Not that he won, but he held his own, and Marty usually beat Greg. In fact, Marty had enjoyed some spirited matches with Henry Segal, a very good player, during a previous visit. Rashan also kept up a patter to the effect that everything in New York was bigger, better and more expensive than anything he'd seen in California. By this point Greg was growing impatient, and from Molly's frequent eyeball-rolling, so was she.

Finally, Rashan asked, "Well, what you do here...you know... for fun."

"Outdoor stuff, mostly," Greg answered. "Swimming, fishing, hiking, skiing."

"Swimming? You got a pool?"

"No, mountain lakes or...or...the river." Greg suddenly had difficulty saying the word. Callow as he was, Rashan was already older than Toby would ever be.

"They cold?" Rashan wanted to know.

"Too cold now, but great in July and August," Greg answered.

"I forget how to swim anyway," Ned put in.

Rashan nodded. "What else you do?"

"Tennis." Greg could have mentioned basketball, too, but Marty had said Rashan didn't like it.

"You got playgrounds?"

"A playground...with two courts," Greg replied.

"Where? Out in the woods?"

"No, at the school. Want to try it? We have extra rackets."

"OK, cool. Hey, Uncle Marty, like on TV. Arthur Ashe, man! Arthur Ashe!"

Though Greg would usually walk, Rashan wanted to drive, so everyone got in the Travelall for the three-block trip. Molly and Ned planned to use the swing set, Greg and Rashan would play tennis, while Marty, notoriously poor with hand-eye coordination, shagged balls. Rashan stared wide-eyed out the car window like an archetypic yokel in Manhattan. Downieville's citizens stared back—all with curiosity, some with vague unease, but none, that Greg could tell, with hostility. In an unintended census through the driver's window, he saw Superintendent Brennan, Sally Vargas, Grant Trabert, Scott Millard, Sharon Murdock, Brenda Lowry, Lou Bishop, Gina Peterson, Nick Cresta and Lynn Reynolds, as well as tourists and other locals whose names he didn't know.

Marty had drawn similar attention on previous visits and had thought it was funny. This time he made no comment, but Greg could tell he enjoyed the spectacle as well as his young charge's reaction. It hadn't occurred to Greg, however, that Rashan, after his enthusiasm for the idea, would have never played tennis before. Marty quietly imparted this knowledge at a courtside bench, along with the prediction that the boy "wouldn't in a million years admit he hadn't played."

Greg would have to teach or coach as though he was reminding him of forgotten skills, not introducing new ones. Initially, Rashan did a lot of whiffing, and in the next stage Marty had considerable shagging to do, but eventually the balls stayed in or around the lines and Rashan managed to rally fitfully as long as Greg hit him bunnies. The kid could obviously learn, but it would be a big stretch to say he was a natural.

Inevitably, they attracted onlookers, including Mel Cresta in his cardigan sweater and Panama hat. When Greg played Henry Segal, who was also fairly good, it wasn't unusual to have people like Mel stop and watch. In this case tennis was only part of the attraction, yet happily, that nuance didn't seem to affect anything.

"Arthur Ashe! Arthur Ashe!" Rashan cried after any halfway decent shot, whether he or Greg hit it. Soon Greg let himself relax into the scene. Then Molly came to hit a few with Rashan while Marty, Ned and Greg horsed around and shagged balls. They played about an hour and finished by sitting on the bench, pleasantly sweaty, watching the sun track west toward City of Six Ridge.

"Uncle Marty," Rashan said after catching his breath, "this like that movie we went to. People act like they never seen one black person in their life."

"What movie?" Greg asked.

Marty laughed. "*Blazing Saddles*, the new Mel Brooks. A riot. We saw it Thursday in Berkeley."

"I just read a review," Molly said. "Supposed to be great."

"Got this wild nig..." Rashan caught himself, "spade, I mean... sheriff in a cowboy town. Craziest thing I ever saw."

"Exactly why I took you," Marty smiled. "Preparation for Sierra County." Marty grandly spread his arms to frame the jumble of buildings between the church steeple on the far left and the courthouse roof away to his right.

"I want to see that movie, too," Ned said.

"So do I," Molly seconded.

"Doesn't sound as if it'll show in Grass Valley," Greg said.

"Doubtful," Marty agreed. "See it with me your next time down. An absolute classic. It'll play a long time in the Bay Area, and I'm going again for sure."

"Why's this town even here?" Rashan wanted to know.

"Gold," Molly said.

"No way."

"Really," Molly insisted. "Millions and millions of dollars came out of these hills and rivers. People still find it."

"That true, Uncle Marty?"

"Yes."

"Tomorrow morning we can take you to an old mine near Sierra City," Greg said.

"Any gold left?"

"Probably, but don't get your hopes up."

"Listen, this tennis way easier than hoops. I find a little gold, OK, but you see the prizes they give on TV for a brotha' like Arthur Ashe? That's for me."

Greg had strong doubts Rashan would be turning pro in this lifetime, but why quibble? With tennis having successfully demystified the world outside the Fultons' living room, things were poised to go well. Saturday night became a home-cooked dinner, a walk along the river, more chess, and repeat installments of Cal Tjader.

Rashan kept requesting George Clinton and the Funkadelics instead, but it got to be a joke, because he quickly realized that neither Marty nor the Fultons had any idea what he was talking about.

Sunday morning they went to the Kentucky Mine, a picturesque relic of slag-heaps, collapsing structures, and caved-in tunnels above Sierra City, then to an outdoor lunch in a meadow near Volcano Lake, up a four-wheel-drive road in the heart of the Buttes. On the way, Greg saw a patch of what looked like wild onions lining a mostly dry swale and wondered if they were edible and when they should be picked. There were supposedly old-timers who ate mushrooms from the oak forests below Goodyear Bar, a far riskier proposition, but Greg wasn't going to bring home anything he wasn't sure of. Maybe Mel Cresta would know.

Rashan banged rocks everywhere along the meadow's edge looking for gold until Molly alerted him about rattlesnakes. After that, he decided that sitting on the hood of the Travelall to appreciate the view was "way more cool" than "getting scratched up" by brush. As to why there was still snow on the towering basalt spires only a short distance away even though it was summer, Rashan declared it didn't make sense, "because everybody knows heat rises."

"Thanks," Marty said to Greg while they were taking turns riding Ned around on their shoulders by the shore of the lake. "Rashan's having the time of his life."

"Hope so. You sure?"

"Absolutely. He's told me over and over he should have listened when I wanted him to bring his camera. He was saving all his film for the Golden Gate."

"Sounds sincere," Greg laughed.

"Molly says you want to talk to me."

"Yeah, Marty, I do. Think we could get an hour alone before you go?"

"Don't see why not."

"Good. I'm wrestling with something kind of heavy."

It was mid-afternoon when they got back to town and Molly suggested that she and Ned walk over to Crandalls. Rashan was invited, but declined, and Greg figured he'd hole up in his room, since Marty had made clear that he and Greg had private business. But no, Rashan amazed them all by wanting to walk around on his own. "I handle 125th Street, I can handle this place," he said. "Gonn'a make like I'm Cleavon Little."

Greg was puzzled until Marty clarified. "The star of *Blazing Saddles*," he said. Then, with a rumbling laugh, he told Rashan, "Just don't go punching out any horses."

Rashan swung a fist in slow motion into the palm of his other hand and flashed a hundred-watt grin. "Relax. Nothin' to worry about."

Marty laughed again. "More *Blazing Saddles*," he said to Greg. "You got to see it."

Molly and Ned left, and minutes later so did Rashan. Marty stood with Greg at the kitchen window, both holding freshly poured glasses of jug red, and watched Rashan, a Mets cap pulled over his Afro, stroll in his rubber-legged way across the Yuba bridge into downtown. A sheriff's car, inbound for the courthouse, approached, slowed to a crawl, then continued over the span. Greg looked at Marty and shrugged. Rashan no longer seemed to mind being stared at, and Greg had grown comfortable that nothing worse would happen.

"So fill me in," Marty said, sitting at the table. "What's this heavy thing?" He removed his eyeglasses and stroked his goatee as he always did to facilitate good conversation.

* * *

Jesus, Buck thought, bringing his cruiser back to its normal in-town speed, a strong tourist season was one thing, but did they have to be black? And possible juvenile delinquents? Where were that boy's mom and pop? Hope he wasn't here on his own from Marysville or Sacramento. Oh well, could be worse. At least he didn't look like some Black Panther or other revolutionary.

After the Patty Hearst shoot-out last month maybe those bastards would realize what they were up against, although Patty, confirming that she and her Tania persona were alive, had shown up Friday on a widely broadcast audiotape pledging "SLA Forever" and saying she'd gone permanently underground. While she probably meant Canada or New York, Buck knew he could count on Thelma Zerloff's spotting her again in Sierra City anytime now.

But still strange, seeing that black kid on the bridge, because Friday Buck'd had a racial incident, if you could call it that, in his own office, and it had even been tied in with the Hearst mess. This

German tourist had shown up: a beefy guy, sunburned, in Bermuda shorts, T-shirt, and a cowboy hat, who spoke next to no English.

He'd been polite and friendly and kept pointing at himself, saying what sounded like "Ya, poll-it-zer," or pointing to his hat and at Buck, saying "Ya, Chon Vayne." He'd also been interested in the bulletin board's *Wanted* fliers, and was especially looking for somebody he called "Schvartz."

When they figured out for sure what language it was, one of the deputies coming off duty said that the woman lawyer, Sandra Torkin, spoke some German and offered to go to her office behind Johnson's Mercantile and see if she would help. A couple of minutes later she'd shown up, not looking in the best of moods, and by damn she could translate.

In Buck's mind Germans were the ones who'd killed Cal, which was as far as he'd ever carried things. This guy, it turned out, was a police officer on vacation from Stuttgart. He loved cowboy movies, had been passing through Sierra Valley on the way to Reno, had seen campaign posters left over from the election, and had decided on the spur of the moment to drive to Downieville because he couldn't pass up meeting a real Sheriff.

His wife even knew some English he said, but she was so exasperated at him over all the extra driving she'd refused to get out of the car. Smiling like an idiot, he repeatedly pumped Buck's hand and had Buck put on his official uniform hat while Sandra popped the flash on the guy's camera taking four or five pictures. Finally he got into a discussion with her about the *Wanted* fliers and this Schwartz he was looking for. If Buck had any extras the German was angling to take them as souvenirs.

Well *schwarz*, Buck learned, pronounced schvartz, was German for black and what the German had been saying was *schwarzer*, which was German, more-or-less, for nigger. Sandra hadn't actually said the word, but she'd made clear when Buck began to catch on that it was in bad taste. And she was right. Buck had served with some mighty fine black men in the Army and at the police academy, and he didn't think of himself as racist, not compared to plenty of folks around here, and he didn't mind sleeping with black women either, at those places over in Nevada.

Anyway, the situation had seemed so ridiculous, that this vacationing cop in his Bermuda shorts and western hat had driven all the way here to get *Wanted* fliers of blacks, Buck had busted out laughing. He hadn't meant anything by it, and he'd worried at first that the German would know Buck was laughing at him and take offense. But no, the German cracked up too, while Sandra stared daggers at both of them.

Buck had already given the guy an extra election poster, but now he wanted to get rid of him, so he pulled out a stack of duplicate fliers and put them on the counter for the German to pick from. Sandra started to leave, but the guy grabbed her arm and babbled some more. *"Der schwarzer!"* he demanded. *"Der schwarzer Patty Hearster."*

Sandra glared at Buck, tight-lipped. "What he really wants is Patty Hearst's Negro," she said.

"Huh?" Buck responded.

"You know, Donald DeFreeze...Field Marshall Cinque of the SLA. It'll be a big deal with his friends in Germany."

"Jeez," Buck said. "Well, I had one. If it's there he can take it. DeFreeze is dead."

Sandra spoke to the German coldly, pulled away and stopped at the door. "I told him," she said to Buck, "that he could take what he found, but there wouldn't be many blacks because you used them for target practice."

Then she left, and Buck had been stewing about it ever since. Whether she believed him or not, he'd have to try telling her his side of the *Wanted* flier story. It was pretty obvious that Sandra and her husband had voted for Pritchard, but Buck didn't want to be further on the outs with the west county's leading defense lawyer. For things to go right, everybody in law enforcement had to get along, no matter how they voted, and the misunderstanding he'd created would already be circulating among the newcomers. Shit. All because of some damn German. Buck had been laughing more lately, which should be good, but now it had gotten him in trouble.

Ambling across the road at the turn to the courthouse was Greg Fulton's black Lab. A sweet old pooch. Never bothered folks. Somebody must have accidentally let it out of the yard. Buck wondered if Zack Brennan, the Superintendent, had held his meeting with Fulton yet. Buck had stopped by the district office and given Zack a word to the wise on what people like Phil Bosley and Tony Nordstrom were saying about Fulton's *lifestyle* — that's the word they used these days — and choice of friends. Zack told Buck that he'd already heard more than he wanted on the basketball hugging, so Buck had focused on other issues.

Not to be too negative, Buck had also related how Fulton had been a real brick in identifying the Crandall boy's body and in helping dig the grave. Those things counted and showed the guy had potential. Zack had been noncommittal, but said he'd get with Fulton to share Bucks' concerns, keeping Buck's name out of it, of course. Finding teachers as effective and as motivated as Greg Fulton in a small, rural district wasn't that easy, which Zack had wanted to be sure Buck realized. Zack's other big worry was the Seth Holmes lawsuit, and he didn't want to do anything to push Fulton onto Holmes's side. Buck knew the ins and outs there, and had been one of the voices arguing for Holmes to receive his walking papers, so he'd listened sympathetically and let Zack talk.

Hey, wow, what an eyeful! Through Buck's windshield the hawthorn tree outside the road department had maxed out its blossoms since Buck had driven by this morning—cascades of pink, more of a watermelon pink than he'd remembered other years. And parked beneath its branches was Bud Peterson's Jeep, the one they'd used in the parade Thursday. Bud and Gina were probably both at their desks doing Sunday catch-up work, which the taxpayers never considered when they bitched about county salaries.

Buck was damn glad Gina had another term coming. She was the kind of bright young gal you needed to keep around, and nobody could fault her for effort. In fact, it made Buck feel good that Marilyn Pezzola and later Buck had hatched a way for Gina to win. Gina herself had all but given up. It also made him feel good that they didn't need Seth Holmes running the Democratic Committee to get people registered or bring out the vote. Marilyn had done a top job. Buck gave the guy credit for showing how it was done back in '72, but that horny fool wasn't the only one who could do it.

Right now Buck was headed home to join Sally and Norma for Sunday dinner after attending the Cory Flynn funeral in Poker Flat. Colorful, but sad too. Flynn's cabin, the last decent building over there, had been damaged by snow and there was nobody to fix it up. The Forest Service was getting real antsy about dwellings on mining claims, so when the original owner died, and there weren't heirs, new occupants couldn't take over. Donny Remo, his night dispatcher, had volunteered to keep an eye on the entire proceedings from a sheriff's four-by-four, and he'd ferried his boss a round trip on the last rocky, mile-long grade from where Buck had parked above the townsite.

Digging the hole had been a bitch of a job, people said. One goddamn boulder after another. A bunch of guys, including Lonny Harris and Ray Stark, had helped, and while Ray might have had a beer or two, he'd worked his ass off and stayed sober. Then, when the time came, the Clamper Band had bleated out their version of *Amazing Grace*, which was so lame old Flynn would have loved it.

CHAPTER 21

Marty Allman drained the last of his wine and slid the glass toward Greg, with a finger leveled low against it to show he wanted only a little more. "Don't forget, I'll be driving soon. But quite a story. Is this Janet Carr some great looker?"

"Seth thinks so, but she wasn't the best you'd see, even around here. Or compared to his wife, in my opinion. Funny you'd hit on that." They were still seated at Greg's kitchen table.

"Well, if she's a stone babe, he might be the victim...in a sense. Otherwise, it's...true love, let's say...or he's the victimizer."

"Either way, that's the basic background. What do I do? You know...between Seth and my boss?" Greg's glass was empty, too. He poured himself most of another and gave Marty the amount he'd indicated.

"Why ask me?" Marty joked. "The only time I met Seth was at a party you had more than a year ago. I liked him, but the other actors and the situation I don't know at all."

"It's a question of ethics. You're a philosopher."

Marty laughed. "I'm glad to help talk it through, as long as we both remember what John Maynard Keynes said."

"I thought he did economics."

"And a bit of philosophy. Anyway, the quote goes, 'Economists predict the stock market because people expect them to, not because they can.'"

"I'm not sure Wall Street and ethics belong in the same breath."

"Just as wild and woolly, believe me. Hardly anybody's made ethical schemes the thrust of their work since Spinoza. Think back to your Phil I class. How do you derive a should from a could?"

"I recall the problem but not what my prof said."

"That's because the problem is more memorable than anything the prof could have said. A Brit named Stuart Hampshire still does so-called moral philosophy. Also John Rawls. But Quine and Carnap and the people I'm reading for my dissertation don't address it...and don't believe it can be addressed."

"Come on, Marty."

"OK, but there's no magic bullet. All we can do is refine the question. Let's go to first cause. Why do ethics matter? Why not flip a coin?"

"They matter to me."

"But why? Are you trying to please God, increase your own happiness or contribute to the community? Those are the accepted bases for moral action."

"Forget God. I assume there is one beyond the universe, in some abstract, cosmic way, but it's inconceivable he/she gives a shit."

"Then I can't dodge by referring you to the parson beneath that slender, white steeple we see out your window."

Greg smiled. "The other two though, yeah. Some of each...increase my own happiness and contribute to the community."

"Long term happiness or short term?"

"Long term. Short term I'd fold and do what Molly wants, or find a way to duck the whole thing. But long term, if I do what's right, I'll be happier."

"Why?"

"Golden Rule, I guess. I want to live in a world where people give the same weight to their decisions about me that I'm giving this one about Seth."

"OK, we're getting someplace. What about community? How do you define it? Family? Friends? This town? The county? Or the state, the nation, your race, mankind?"

"Family and friends for sure. Maybe just one friend...Seth. And the town. There's the conflict."

"So it's about loyalty?"

"Yes. And about standing up to the system." Greg drank some wine.

"The system's not always wrong, and the individual's not always right."

"I know that."

"And the most ethical choice isn't necessarily the one that forces the chooser to bear the greatest personal cost."

"I know that, too. What are you saying?"

"That loyalty is a highly mutable good. If Seth truly got shafted, the presumption is you should stick up for him...unless...the degree to which he got shafted is outweighed by the damage he did to the community. Let's try Thomas Hobbes, who wrote, 'If either the rational requirement *or* the respect for custom breaks down...expect catastrophe.'"

"Well, Seth got catastrophe. He wasn't thinking rationally and he violated local norms in a big way."

"Right, but you're who I had in mind. Satisfy yourself on the rational level that you know what happened, then hold it up against local custom and see where you stand."

"I'm clear on what happened. Seth did something he knew was wrong...in terms of his marriage, and his responsibilities as a father...but that he couldn't keep himself from doing. Then he was so overwrought and tortured with guilt, he let himself be railroaded out of town."

"Did this Superintendent guy...Zack Brennan...lie to him?"

"No."

"Threaten him?"

"No. He said Seth hadn't technically broken any district rules, but that Janet's parents had complained to the Teacher Licensing Commission in Sacramento on grounds of moral turpitude."

"And?"

"I don't know, but Zack agreed it was a toss up if the Commission would investigate. Janet wasn't a minor and wasn't Seth's student at the time. But I could tell Zack wanted Seth gone."

"In his shoes, wouldn't you?"

"I suppose...to make life easier. It's just that he didn't tell Seth about the seventy-two hour waiting period...and neither did I."

"So you forgot, and had to look it up later to really be sure. But not your responsibility. Couldn't you assume that if you'd heard about it somewhere along the line, Seth would have too? He's older and more experienced by what? Ten years?"

"Almost that. But what if the school board president is lying and Zack didn't tell any of them either?"

"Something you can't know. It's up to Zack and the board members to make their own moral choices. And up to Seth's lawyer to home in on that point. Same with Seth's claim that Zack is interfering with Seth's getting another job."

"Zack denies it. I asked."

"Do you believe him?"

"I think so. I want to. Look, Seth was a star. His evaluations were through the roof. Zack had no reason to torpedo his career. He says he's handling Seth's references personally because that's SOP if there's legal action pending.

"Zack's main rationale...at the time, and during my meeting with him the other day...was that this was just too small a town, so something had to give. Think about Berkeley High. If a teacher did what Seth did and shacked up with a former student in El Cerrito, who would even know?"

"True. And if Zack has been bad-mouthing Seth over a supposedly voluntary resignation, Seth's lawyer ought to be able to find witnesses who'll say so. Either way, you won't be testifying on that. Where you come in is the meeting, and whatever side you're on, the opposition will cross-examine the hell out of you."

"I know," Greg said glumly. He tried to envision Seth's life with Janet in Chico. He and Molly had been invited there more than once, and Greg would have gone if she'd been open to it. Maybe all this would be easier if he'd seen them together in such different surroundings. Or maybe — oh, who could know? Memories of his one-on-one with Seth at the restaurant replayed in Greg's brain.

"Why did Seth attend that face off with Zack?" Marty went on. "He must have realized he'd be risking job consequences. Why did he take you with him instead of a lawyer? Why didn't he...or you...balk when Zack's own observer was a no-show and you had to do double duty?"

Now a new set of memories began to play. "I...I keyed on Seth and he pushed to go ahead. I think...I've asked myself this a hundred times...but I think subconsciously he wanted to be punished."

"So, did he get shafted?"

"Yes, in the sense that he was emotionally fragile, he didn't have a full grasp of his rights, and lost his job solely because of the size town he was living in."

"OK, Seth got shafted. But mildly shafted, not extremely shafted, is what I hear."

"I could buy that."

"Would he still be suing if he'd gotten another job by now?"

"Probably...fairness and justice count big in his book." Greg took another drink. "Spring is the main teacher hiring season. For all I know he has a position lined up in September. We've been out of touch since that dinner with him I sneaked past Molly. Something I'd promised her not to do."

"When you announce your decision, come clean on that too. Better if you'd told her up front, but not such a big lapse, really, given the weight of all the rest. She'll get over it."

"Easy for you to say. She's fierce about honesty between spouses. It won't go down well even if I side with Zack. Way worse if I side with Seth, but I'm trying not to let that bias me. And here's the kicker...in terms of deciding this, seeing him...and lying about it...was of no benefit. "

"Except you had to see him to know that. But benefit? Ha! Utilitarianism! So let's revisit those community interests, such as the benefit of avoiding the troubling moral example...to the kids and other teachers...of having Seth and Janet in plain view all the time. Or, of avoiding the additional pain to Seth's wife...ex-wife...and Janet's family. Or, on the plus side, that Seth would be more available to his son if he were here, or that Downieville might benefit if his being around ultimately made people less censorious."

"This community always benefited from the energy Seth brought to causes and activities. That's the real loss, along with his teaching. But less censorious? Fat chance! I didn't tell you yet how the assholes are on *my* case."

"If the guy's as good as you say, he'll get another job and some less censorious community will benefit...from the teaching and the civic-mindedness, both. His social utility's lost to Downieville, but not lost overall. Now what's this about getting on *your* case?"

"Something else I hope won't color my judgment, but it does piss me off. Royally." Greg recapped the hugging controversy, the stupid griping about Greg's beard and the rumors about his hippie friends and how he must be a dope-smoker himself.

Marty stretched in his chair, clearly having the best time since he and Rashan had arrived. "Worse yet," he added, "all that stuff's true, and you have black people...no, black men...staying at your house. Dangerous shit. The beard thing isn't new, by the way. You've complained about it before."

"Plus all the fucking double-speak! The Sheriff, a former alcoholic, buys beer for the town drunk; the local Lion's Clubbers...not to mention the numbskull Clampers...get blotto at their meetings; guys go around in public with their asses half out of their pants; and you need a scorecard to know who's screwing who else's wife or husband. 'You're a teacher, you're a teacher,' my boss says. Bullshit! I'm a human being, not a living example."

"I don't smoke weed around Rashan," Marty countered, "and not just because my sister would freak. It would overshadow more important things I want him to get from me. He's too young to sort out the distinctions.

"The *higher standard* argument is key to what makes teaching...or being in the clergy...true professions. The job includes embodying what people support but know they often don't live up to. With older students like mine there's less of that, but even at UC, if I started hugging them, or doing weed in my office, or supplying it to anyone, and there were complaints, you bet I'd be hauled into the Dean's Office, lose my TA slot, and maybe get kicked out of the doctoral program."

"You should get kicked out," Greg agreed. "I don't do anything like that. My beard and my friends are none of their damned business. And I hug my players during games the same way my high school coach hugged me. Did that make him a homo? As for using dope, it's a hundred percent private. I never smoke around Ned or my students. Never. One or two weekends a month, or sometimes when Molly and I want a little more sexual bang. I'll be goddamned if this town gets to tell me what to do."

"So stick to your guns and let them bitch. Just be discreet. You say you have tenure. They can't run you out unless you invite it." Marty had been distracted by their discussion, but now swallowed the remaining wine in his glass.

"Where does that leave me with Seth?"

"I don't know. You have to choose. But there're limits and tradeoffs to everything. You know it, and Seth knew it. Like you say, at Berkeley High, a married teacher could carry on with a nineteen-year-old former student and nobody'd notice, or probably care. Here you're visible, so you have to walk more of the walk. But

Berkeley teachers don't get to go trout fishing on school nights or have impromptu picnics in the middle of a Sierra Club calendar."

CHAPTER 22

Molly came back into the living room. It was after 8 p.m. and Ned was asleep in bed with Jojo. "No luck reaching Marty yet," she said. "Guess they're stuck in traffic."

"Or out for pizza. It could've just been teenage funk. We don't really know there's a problem." Looking up from his copy of *Psychology Today*, Greg was trying without success to reassure her, but couldn't shake his own apprehensions.

Rashan hadn't seemed at all normal when he returned from his walk. He'd been anxious to leave and had shown nothing like the excitement Greg would have predicted from his having purchased a sealed test tube of Yuba River water with sprinkles of gold and white quartz sand in the bottom—a popular local souvenir—that earlier in the day would have had him hopping around waving it in everyone's face. Instead, he was withdrawn, and all he had wanted was the Fultons' confirmation that the gold was real, which Greg and Molly both gave.

Their concern had been amplified by Rashan's refusal to admit that anything was wrong and by his notable churlishness when Marty pressed him for an explanation. Greg could see that Marty was troubled as well. He had peremptorily gathered up their luggage, loaded the car, and said good-bye while Rashan sat waiting in the passenger seat.

"Sorry," Marty told them, "no idea what's up. Might just be homesick. After we're on the road a while he'll probably talk." Marty and Greg hugged, then vigorously shook hands.

"We'll call you later tonight," Molly said, embracing Marty when he separated from Greg.

Marty had then picked up Ned to exchange rounds of loud face smooching, but Rashan didn't stir from the car, and through his rolled down window offered the three Fultons only a single dispirited handshake each. "Good luck with your decision," were Marty's final words to Greg while backing out of the driveway.

"Can Rashan come to see us again?" Ned had asked as soon as Marty left.

"We hope so," Molly answered, having kept Ned in her arms since taking him from Marty. "But he lives very far away, in New York."

"Is there an old York?" Ned was in query mode.

"Yes," Greg said.

"Which is farther?"

"The old one," Molly told him. They had then headed into the house. "Well," Molly continued, "Ned and I enjoyed our visit with Pat and Stevo. They're all doing better these days. Lisa was off hiking with Jim." She lowered Ned to the floor and he wandered away down the hall. "Did Marty help you sort things out?"

"Indeed he did," Greg answered.

"And?"

"I'm following his advice. I've made a tentative decision, which I'm living with for a few hours to see if it feels right." And it had, Greg thought, until Rashan's sulky return began raising old doubts that set Greg struggling again.

"But you're not telling?"

"No. As Marty recommended, I didn't even tell him. You'll know tomorrow at the latest."

"Good. Then maybe we'll feel like we're actually living. Ever since Toby, it's more as though our lives were just happening to us."

"You're right. But I'm afraid we can guess what happened to Rashan."

"Yes," Molly had replied, "one of our charming fellow citizens called him a word beginning with N that I refuse to say."

"And I don't want to hear," Greg stolidly agreed.

They'd eaten a quiet dinner, watched TV, and gotten Ned tucked in, constantly checking to determine when they could call Berkeley. At the earliest feasible time, Molly had gone to the phone while Greg tried to relax. He was too restless for a book, so had picked up a magazine.

After her first attempt at calling produced nothing, Molly rejoined him, putting her favorite *Brandenburg Concerto* on the stereo and opening the volume of Anaïs Nin's *Diary* she'd been pecking away at. No sooner had she removed the bookmark, however, than the telephone rang. Greg leaned forward to respond but Molly jumped to her feet.

"I'll get it," she insisted, and was there on the second ring. "Hello. Oh, Sandra, hi. No, we're fine. I thought it might be our friend Marty from Berkeley. We've been nervous that something weird happened while he was here."

Molly proceeded to tell Sandra about Rashan's sudden mood change and got an earful in reply. "Your buddy Buck Thompson," she said disgustedly after hanging up. "It could've had something to do with the Sheriff's Office."

"What could?" Greg wasn't tracking, and the last thing he wanted was a resurgence of Molly's irascibility about the election.

"Rashan, of course! Sandra went to the courthouse Friday to translate for some German tourist, who turned out to be a cop from Stuttgart trying to get *Wanted* fliers showing *schwarzers* as mementos for his friends. *Schwarzer* in German is like nigger. The guy already had one of Buck's election posters, and when Sandra said what else the guy wanted, Buck and the German started yukking it up like they were at a KKK convention. She got so furious she walked out."

"Oh, twelve times shit," Greg responded, putting his hands on top of his head. The image of the sheriff's car on the bridge flashed into his consciousness. Nothing had happened then. Marty and Greg had seen it pull away. But who was to say the driver hadn't circled back later looking for sport?

Why had he voted for goddamned Buck Thompson, Greg wondered. Since he was only Acting Sheriff, the Supervisors could have sworn in Ken Pritchard by now, and let Pritchard start proving that with him running things racist crap wouldn't be condoned. Goddamn it! Or would Pritchard be just as bad? Why should Seth Holmes or anybody be sacrificed to the standards of this redneck sideshow?

The doorbell rang, and as though he could see through walls Greg knew it would be Buck. A Sunday night, not two full months later — the perfect capper to Molly's suspicions. His esophagus knotted and his mind filled with Toby lying in that ghastly drawer. "Your turn," Molly said pointedly, "whoever it is."

"Sure, I'll go." Greg got up, certain that she was remembering Buck's grim previous visit as well.

Six long steps to leave the living room, six more past the telephone table and bookcases to the base of the stairs, then three more to the door. As the bell rang a second time, Greg flipped on the porch light and grabbed the door handle. It was Ray Stark.

"Mr. Fulton," he said awkwardly. "Hate to bother you, but it's kind of important. Not about Billy, either. You been the best teacher that boy's ever had. If my little girl grows up to play basketball for you, I'll be real proud. "

Greg was moved, almost exhilarated at what he'd just heard, but still felt whipsawed by feelings left from the drowning and by confusion about Ray's reasons for being there. "Thanks," he finally managed. "Glad to know it. Come on in."

"I'm too sweated up. Only be a minute. Your Mrs. and your doctor friend been real nice to us at the clinic, too."

"OK, I'll come out. Call me Greg, by the way." He stepped onto the porch. It was a sweet-smelling, late spring mountain night, just turning dark, with the river pulsing in the background like a slow, sustained release of breath.

Ray stuck out his hand and they shook. "Excuse my corny outfit," he said. "The tourists like it, and I just got off work."

Ray was wearing coveralls tucked into lace-up boots, a long-sleeved undershirt, a bandanna and a misshapen Clamper hat — in other words a younger, clean-shaven Gabby Hayes. And a sober Gabby Hayes, apparently.

"So what's up?" Greg had finally adjusted to the fact that Ray wasn't Buck.

Ray cleared his throat. "Scott Millard was runnin' our booth while I been over in Poker Flat most of the weekend...you know, helpin' on the Cory Flynn funeral. Hell of a deal cuttin' big windfall trees off the road, hauling the casket in, and getting the hole dug. Boulders like you wouldn't believe." Ray paused and sought Greg's eyes. "I done my full share, you should know. We got him in the ground about three this afternoon."

"Oh, right, I remember, the old guy Buck had in storage all these months. There was a little squib in this week's *Merc*." Now Greg was more confused. Why would Ray come to tell him this? Residual guilt from the fiasco at the Downieville cemetery?

"Anyway, my first customer when I got back was a black kid. I didn't know 'cause I'd been away, but I heard later he was your house guest."

Greg's mouth went dry. Oh, shit, here it came. "Yeah, he was." Bigger and taller than Ray, Greg straightened his stance and squared his shoulders to remind him of that.

"Well, I'm real sorry about what happened. See, after he bought a little tube of gold dust, the kid turned around and bumped into Lonny Harris...or Lonny bumped him. Kid says, 'Beg your pardon,' real nice, but Lonny...you know Lonny...he's been diggin' in Poker Flat all day same as me, but he must'a drunk a case of beer.

"I brought him back into town. He's walkin' around all right, but he's mean. Lonny gets in the kid's face and shouts 'What's your name, boy! What you doin' here? Listen up! I said what's your name?' Kid is scared to crap, but he finally answers...think I heard this right...'Cleavon Little,' hardly gettin' the words out. 'Cleavon!' Lonny yells. 'What kind of nigger name is that?'

"Deputy Snell come right over to break it up. I grabbed Lonny's arm and we got him away from the kid. I called Lonny on it, too. Told him that kid was my customer, and if he didn't care, I did. Lonny'd'a swung at me, prob'ly, if the law hadn't been close by. Snell led Lonny off, but I don't know if they booked him or just drove him home."

"I'll be damned," Greg said, dumbfounded. "Thanks Ray. No kidding, thanks." Cleavon Little, Greg was thinking. Rashan could just as well have used Arthur Ashe. Lonny would never know. "Then what?" Greg asked.

"I wanted to apologize, but the kid slipped away...psst, like that." Ray snapped his fingers. "I got busy with another tourist, and didn't see him again. Wasn't till half-hour ago Mel Cresta said he was stayin' with you."

"Not anymore. He drove back to the East Bay with his uncle."

"Oh, too bad. Know how to reach him?"

"Sure. Why?"

Ray reached into the chest pocket of his coveralls and pulled out a crumpled five-dollar bill. "I sold Cleavon that gold for $15, the tourist price, but for locals we charge $10. If he's your guest, he's local. Fair is fair. Think you can get this to him?" Ray handed the bill to Greg. "And let him know I'm sorry about Lonny too."

"Absolutely. I'll phone tonight and send the money tomorrow." Greg had been about to reverse his tentative decision to testify for Zack Brennan, but he suddenly felt it lock in. And OK, maybe it *was* self-serving. That's what Seth would say when Greg told him, which Marty had already anticipated by noting that the easiest road wasn't always the least ethical.

If you didn't have God, what did you have? Yourself, your family, and your community. He was eager to go inside and talk to Molly. There was Ray's almost unbelievable news to announce, plus his own decision and his admission about secretly meeting Seth as he had. If the former two helped her forgive the latter, fine. If not, they'd find another way work it out.

But first they had to call Berkeley and have Marty put Rashan on. Greg again shook Ray's hand and the river noise somehow seemed louder and more engulfing. "Be proud of yourself, too, not only of your kids." Greg said. "That's something special you did."

"Nothin' special," Ray answered, backing away into the darkness. "In this county, Greg, we look out for each other."

EPILOGUE

In January 1979 Buck Thompson, having run unopposed, was sworn in for his second full term as County Sheriff. Rudy Johns, a bright young Native American officer from Sierra Valley, continued as the appointed Undersheriff. Buck's mother Norma died in 1977, not long after which he and Sally Vargas were married at a Reno wedding chapel.

Also around the time Norma died, the Fultons moved from Downieville to Nevada City where Greg became a teacher and freshman boys' basketball coach at the 2,500-student Nevada Union High School. Motivational hugging remains part of his standard coaching repertoire. Molly Fulton, pregnant with the couple's second child, works as a technical writer for a Grass Valley electronics firm. Greg gets up to Sierra County fairly regularly during fishing season, and enjoys spending time on the backcountry stretches of Wild Plum Creek with local Paiute leader Hal Voorden.

Seth Holmes returned to full-time teaching at Durham High, south of Chico, in fall 1974 and immediately dropped his lawsuit against Sierra Consolidated School District. He has since served as Vice Mayor of Chico and hopes to become Mayor. He and his wife, the former Janet Carr, have a three-year-old son Leland, who is the apple of his grandfather's eye. Gina Peterson and Marilyn Pezzola were each handily reelected to office along with Buck and constitute what he refers to as the "good angels" of Sierra County politics. Loyalton resident Ken Pritchard continues to practice law in Reno.

Dr. Henry Segal moved to Oregon in 1978 with his wife Meg and their daughter Paige so he could join a thriving medical practice there after Downieville's NIH funds ran out. Maureen Brady, a nurse-practitioner from San Jose, took over Henry's duties at the clinic. Ian Dudley and Sandra Torkin, now divorced, have moved to British Columbia and Massachusetts, respectively. The hippie threesome of Om Gillette, Edna Darnell and Lynn Reynolds remain in Goodyear Bar, with Lisa Crandall as Om's roommate. Lisa attends the Grass Valley extension campus of Sierra Community College part time, and is dating former streaker Russ Darnell, Edna's brother, who works for the county assessor's office.

Jim Crandall separated from Pat in 1976 and moved to Santa Fe, where he heads the public information office at Los Alamos National Lab. When Karen Holmes and her son Juan left Sierra City for Santa Fe soon afterward, various Downieville rumors and suspicions seemed confirmed. After divorcing Jim, Pat Crandall tried for several years to make a go of the *Mountain Mercury* on her own, finally selling to the company that also publishes the Grass Valley *Union*. Pat and Stevo returned to Santa Barbara to be near her mother and stepfather. Drew Ormond has just accepted a job at a mental health center in Montana and is ready to move.

Lonny Harris left for Alaska in 1975, where he has been working in the commercial salmon fleet ever since. A largely sober Ray Stark still does carpentry in the west county and runs his gold booth with Scott Millard outside the Quartz Cafe as a summer sideline. His son Billy is attending the University of Nevada on a journalism scholarship. Ernie Warrington was elected County Supervisor from Sierra City in 1978 upon the retirement of Will Jeffers for medical reasons. Rick Rodman served as Ernie's campaign manager. The Ore House has blossomed into a solidly successful business, jointly run by the openly gay Rick and his new lover, Saul Wexler.

Marty Allman received his Ph.D. in analytic philosophy from UC Berkeley in 1975 and currently teaches in a tenure-track position at University of Louisville. His nephew Rashan has become a competent club tennis player and something of a wunderkind at NYU film school, where he runs with a group of students revolving around Spike Lee, a brash, ambitious would-be director.

Jeanne Potter moved from Pike City in 1976 to train as a paralegal in Sacramento. Upon graduating she found work there at a downtown law firm. Satya gradually evolved from Pike hippie to an outlaw biker, and was recently convicted of selling cocaine to an undercover agent in Yuba County. Jeanne persuaded a lawyer at her firm to represent him pro bono, but the case ended in a plea bargain with Satya spending significant jail time. No one locally has laid eyes on Jared Smith since his departure with the FBI.

Also on the list of the departed is Nick Cresta, whose travels from Sierra County became permanent after he met, married and moved to Hawaii with a sweet young thing of sixty-five. His older brother Mel remained a philosopher and proponent of tolerance until the week before Buck's reelection, when he joined in death another town legend, Charlie Koontz, and many of their friends along the crushed granite paths at the base of Oxford Ridge. Greg Fulton and Phil Bosley both served as pallbearers at Mel's funeral.

Toby Crandall's gradually weathering headstone lies adjacent to the Thompson plots and is visited frequently by his sister Lisa. If she has flowers to leave, she puts a few at Norma Thompson's stone as well. Buck and Sally return the favor when they visit Norma. Lisa occasionally sees Buck's daughter Ginny at the cemetery, on Ginny's days off from waitressing at Lake Tahoe, and the two have struck up a bit of an acquaintance.

Somehow, Toby's death forged all these disparate people into a community. It may not function that way in the usual, day-to-day sense, yet it is one nonetheless.

Glossary of Newcomers

Marty Allman - 29, UC grad student and long-time friend of Greg and Molly Fulton

Rashan Briggs - 13, nephew of Marty Allman, and a visitor to Sierra County from Harlem

Colin Crandall - 64, retired magazine editor from Chicago, father of Jim

Lisa Crandall - 15, sister of Toby and Stevo, daughter of Jim and Pat

Jim Crandall - 41, husband of Pat, and *Mountain Mercury* co-publisher

Pat Crandall - 37, wife of Jim, and *Mountain Mercury* co-publisher

Stevo Crandall - 8, cerebral-palsy-afflicted brother of Toby and Lisa

Toby Crandall - 12, brother of Lisa and Stevo

Ian Dudley - 29, lawyer, County Counsel and Sandra Torkin's husband

Guy Farrell - 61, retired fertilizer salesman, and a candidate for County Treasurer

Greg Fulton - 33, teacher and girls basketball coach at Downieville High School

Molly Fulton - 32, wife of Greg, and receptionist at Downieville's medical clinic

Ned Fulton - 4, son of Greg and Molly

Om Gillette - age unknown, hippie queen of Goodyear Bar, and girl-friend of Jared Smith

Juan Holmes - 6, adopted Nicaraguan son of Karen and Seth

Karen Holmes - 39, Seth's estranged wife, waitress at Ore House Pizza

Seth Holmes - 42, Greg's former mentor, lives in Chico with Janet Carr

Drew Ormond - 45, county social worker, quasi-hippie and founder of the newcomer group

Jeanne Potter - 26, hippie resident of Pike City, single mother of two

Lynn Reynolds - 27, hippie neighbor of Om Gillette and Drew Ormond

Rick Rodman - 35, owner of Ore House Pizza, and a write-in candidate for County Supervisor

Satya - age unknown, yurt dweller, gold miner and hippie kingpin of Pike City

Henry Segal - 31, physician, clinic director, Molly Fulton's boss, and husband of Meg

Meg Segal - 27, Henry's pregnant wife

Jared Smith - age unknown, hippie boyfriend of Om Gillette, and re-cently busted by FBI

Sandra Torkin - 28, lawyer, Public Defender and wife of Ian Dudley

Glossary of Natives

Sam Beals - 51, Dispatcher, Sierra County Sheriff's Department

Lou Bishop - 14, high school student and river accident survivor

Phil Bosley - 56, President of Downieville Cemetery Board, drummer with E. Clampus Vitus band, and member of Elect HBT Committee

Zack Brennan - 54, Superintendent of the Sierra Consolidated School District

Janet Carr - 20, daughter of Leland, living in Chico with Seth Holmes

Leland Carr - 55, small-scale mining entrepreneur and father of Janet

The Chilcutts - two 20-something Paiute brothers recently busted for grand theft

Shep Conrad - 51, proprietor of Hi-Grade Market, and County Treasurer Gina Peterson's uncle

Francine Cooper - 63, Historical Society matriarch and maker of famous cheesecake

Mel Cresta - 74, town philosopher, former owner of lumberyard with brother, Nick

Nick Cresta - 71, frequent traveler, former owner of lumberyard with brother, Mel

Edna Darnell - 27, Goodyear Bar hippie, friend of Om Gillette and Lynn Reynolds

Russ Darnell - 19, Edna's brother, busted for streaking while home from college

Cory Flynn - gold miner, dead at 92 and awaiting burial in his hometown, Poker Flat

Curt Foley - former Sheriff, protégé of Huey Thompson, and patron of Buck, dead at age 52 in a plane crash

Jesse Foster – 42, Luann Thompson's oldest friend, an enemy of Buck

Beth Freeman – 68, Pike City wife of Virgil Freeman. Also a second cousin to Norma Thompson, Buck's Mother

Lonny Harris - 28, logger, snowplow driver, sometime troublemaker

Carl Herndon - 60, President of Feather/Yuba Industries in Loyalton, and the uncle of Sheriff candidate Ken Pritchard

Will Jeffers - 62, incumbent County Supervisor facing write-in candidate Rick Rodman

Charlie Koontz - 77, retired gold miner and pack train driver, father of Marilyn Pezzola

Pete Lowry - 48, proprietor of Gold Pan Motel, member of Elect HBT Committee

BELONGING

(Glossary of Natives – Continued)

Tom Mahaffy - 48, Principal of Downieville Schools, and Greg Fulton's immediate boss

Scott Millard - 27, part-time Forest Service employee, gold miner, gold vendor and volunteer gravedigger

Sharon Murdock - 35, mainstay of the *Mountain Mercury* office staff

Coach N (Nevoceisewizcj) – 49, long-time teacher and boys basketball coach at Downievill High School

Tony Nordstrom - 47, Tricia's father, owner Sierra Pines Resort, member of Elect HBT Committee

Tricia Nordstrom - 18, high school basketball star and sometime singer in the church choir

Bud Peterson - 40, head of County Road Department and husband of Gina

Gina (nee Conrad) Peterson - 36, County Treasurer, in reelection battle vs. newcomer Guy Farrell

Frank Pezzola - husband of Marilyn, killed fourteen years ago at age 30 in a car wreck

Marilyn (nee Koontz) Pezzola - 42, County Clerk/Auditor, unopposed for reelection

Teresa Powell - 60, heiress to Bush Creek Mine fortune and Downieville grand dame

Ken (Kenny) Pritchard - 38, lawyer, resident of Loyalton, and candidate for County Sheriff

Tommy Schoville - 30, Forest Service employee and volunteer gravedigger

Billy Stark - 15, high school student and river accident survivor, son of Ray and Janice

Janice Stark - 34, wife of Ray and mother of Billy

Ray Stark - 35, part-time carpenter and gold vendor, volunteer gravedigger, heavy drinker, father of Billy and husband of Janice

Buck (Harold B.) Thompson - 43, Acting Sheriff, black sheep son of the late Huey Thompson, and a candidate for election

Cal Thompson - son of Huey, brother of Buck, killed in WWII at age 19

Cindy Thompson - 25, daughter of Buck and Luann, now lives in Santa Rosa

Ginny Thompson - 16, daughter of Buck and Luann, spends summers with Buck but lives mainly with Luann in Eureka

(Glossary of Natives – Continued)

Huey (Hewell) Thompson – died, age 67, in 1964 during his eleventh four-year term as Sierra County Sheriff

Luann Thompson - 42, ex-wife of Buck, remarried and living in Eureka

Norma Thompson - 75, ailing widow of Huey, mother of Cal and Buck

Barbara Trabert - 56, church choir director whose husband Grant sings in the choir

Jerry Vargas - 59, proprietor of Downieville Hardware, father of Sally, and chair of Elect HBT Committee.

Sally Vargas - 34, daughter of Jerry, hired housekeeper/companion for Norma Thompson

Hal Voorden - 63, Sierraville Paiute leader and school district maintenance supervisor with great skills as an outdoorsman

Ernie Warrington - 26, Downieville High grad, Stanford civil engineer, County Search and Rescue coordinator, volunteer gravedigger and financial backer of Ore House Pizza; married to Diane Warrington, nee Powell

Stan White - 44, son of Reverend White, overseas oil rig operator, Buck Thompson's closest high school friend

Thelma Zerloff - 69, Sierra City widow with a vivid imagination and too much free time

Printed in the United States
221343BV00001B/49/A